WATERMELON RED

By Leigh Armstrong

Cover design by Philip Andrews Photography

Editing by Terri Shelton

Printed in the United States of America

First Print August 2020

ISBN: 978-1-7326939-2-0 Paperback

CONTENTS

PROLOGUE

My eyes try several times to focus on the lights above me. Sirens repeat over and over in an attempt to clear the road. There are two EMT's working to stabilize me, so why don't I feel any pain? One of them reaches over me to grab a bag from a holder, then pauses looking down at my sheet.

"I thought we had patched all the stab wounds."

His partner lifts the sheet.

"My god, what did he do to her?"

We enter the hospital, and I am taken down a hall, around a sharp corner, then into a triage room. My EMT's pull me over to a bed, helped by three nurses. I glance at the blood-soaked sheets as the gurney is wheeled out of the room. I want to thank them, but they are so incredibly busy. There's an organized frenzy going on, as orders are being put into place. A new face appears to my right, and my eyes begin to slowly blink again.

"I'm Doctor Spanga, can you tell me your name?"

I try hard, but this feeling of sleep comes over me, so I barely whisper, "Amelia."

"Good. Amelia do you know what happened to you?"

As the words come out of his mouth, my eyes flutter, my heartbeat slows down.

"Her pressure is dropping. Get her to the OR--STAT. She's bleeding internally, call the lab."

As they wheel me out into the hall, I can hear alarms going off, as other medical personnel run into the next room. Some-one else is in distress. I try and stay awake; I need to know if it's Chase.

"Is that the other victim?" Doctor Spanga asks.

"No, it's her attacker. His heart just stopped."

CHAPTER 1

Amelia

It doesn't matter how many times I dress for work in clean clothes, when I return home, I'm wearing my day. Smeared paint, food, and runny noses decorate my khaki pants and shirt. Not to mention the chunky mulch, small rocks, and Band-aids in my pockets. I happily live the life of a toddler teacher every day, and at night I attend classes for my Master's in Education in hopes of being an elementary school teacher someday. It's what my grandmother, my mom, and my two aunts and three cousins have already achieved. I have one semester left, then I am on to a student teacher position. But for now, I teach, cuddle, and play eight hours a day, five days a week with the most adorable ten kids you could ever meet.

I'm a 25-year-old woman who dreams of one day having children of my own and a partner who will enjoy a simple easy life right here in Virginia. I live beside my grandparents in a cozy cottage with my three-year old yellow lab, Poppy. My house is comfortable, filled with distressed furniture from flea market finds and my prize possession, a white claw foot tub my grandfather helped me install. He is a former contractor who loves to help me with projects around the house when he doesn't have a scheduled fishing date with his buddies on Wednesday and Saturday mornings. My grandmother, on the other hand, turned to baking after her retirement, supplying local restaurants with her home-baked desserts. I like to think I've acquired some of her talent, creating similar delights of my own. My grandparents have been in love since elementary school and are still going strong, giving hope to those of us who struggle with finding the right one.

My parents fell in love during a debate in college, and they married two years after graduation, then had me five years later. My mom tends to sway my father in making decisions for the family; for instance, her leaving an established teaching position and him giving up his real estate business to do mission work around the world last year. It was a sudden move after my attack, leaving me confused especially when I needed them more than ever before.

Almost daily, I think of that day and everything leading up to it. Chase and I dated in college. It didn't take long before I was taken by him, I even felt he could be the one. He made me feel safe and above all I trusted him. But when he lost his ability to play baseball because of an accident his senior year, his world spiraled out of control. I was his girlfriend and even though I noticed some subtle changes, I didn't know about the drugs. He was kind, playful, and affectionate when we were together. He was always holding my hand, brushing his fingers against my neck, or sitting where our bodies always touched. But the night he attacked me, I sank into a dark world I didn't recognize. I was stabbed seven times by my boyfriend, and he didn't even know it was me.

I work every day to rebuild what he took from me but only with the support of my grandparents, friends, and the open arms of my tight-knit community. So, today after work, I'm meeting my friends, Jordan, Lily, and Sophia to buy a dress for an upcoming country music concert. Jordan has a big surprise for us and has requested we all buy brightly-colored dresses to mark her special event. I like to experiment with bright colors, but I tend to fall back on the lighter side of the pallet when it comes to clothes, so I'm not sure how well this will go, but I've promised to try.

Jordan landed a dream job in advertising right out of college. She's ambitious, fiercely independent, and comes from a family of five, being the only girl. She's beautiful, confident, and loves to travel. She's not dating anyone right now but seems to gravitate to the tattooed-covered muscle guys. Sophia is also single, lives near her parents on their dairy farm in one of those tiny houses she built with her father at age seventeen. She is down to earth, easy going and athletic. She's a sweet person who tends to hide her cute little body under baggy clothes. She's been trying to land a teaching position at a prestigious private school in the city for over a year now, which is her dream job. Lily is dating Zach and has been since sixth grade. She's classy, feisty, and has a head for numbers, which landed her a position with Fife & Barnes auditing accounts all over the state. Tall like Jordan, she is comfortable in her skin. They say I'm strong, courageous, but sometimes when I think back on this past year, I don't always feel the same.

*

I pull up to the mall and immediately see Jordan and Sophia standing outside of Sophia's car. One of them is dressed in jeans and a t-shirt, the other in a tight-fitted dress, holding a monogrammed cup. I park my car next to Lily's where she is sitting inside, hands waving all around expressing her frustration to her boyfriend. Their fights are comical, never harsh, just simple. There are times I think he does it to see her get fired up, and she falls for it every time.

Jordan leans on my open door.

"Hey mamma, what's up with the work attire?"

"Please don't call me mamma, I teach children; I don't have any. Besides we are trying on clothes, and then I'm going home to a hot bath and a glass of wine, while I listen to the music of the country singer we will see in concert tomorrow night.

She smiles. "Girl get out of the car. You like your tub too much. Clearly, I need to find you the perfect little dress for tomorrow so you can catch the eye of a living, breathing guy. In fact, let it be known that all of you need to get on board and get in the mood to find a killer dress. I have a great space for us, and I'm not taking you bitches unless you bring your A game. It's my birthday wish, and we know I get whatever *I* want for my birthday."

I roll my eyes at her. "How many drinks have you had so far?"

"This is my second double, and don't judge. I work hard all week; this is my time to enjoy a beverage if I want. Besides my car is a phone call away."

I start to laugh at her, slinging my backpack over my shoulder, then I tap on Lily's window.

"Come on Lily. Tell Zach you will yell at him some more later."

She rolls her eyes at me then shakes her head before the next words come out of her mouth to him. I walk over to Sophia who is leaning against her car, also amused at Jordan's speech.

"Hey Amelia, how are all the little children?"

"Good. Do you have any news today?"

"I begin at Smithson Private School in the fall!" She's now jumping around pulling me with her.

"That's wonderful. I'm so happy for you."

"Thank you for all your support and the many bottles of wine to calm my nerves during this long wait."

"I'm here anytime you need me."

Lily finally joins us.

"Zach is having a boy's night out tomorrow night, and I think they might be going to a gentleman's club. I don't want him to, so that is what we were arguing about."

Jordan rolls her eyes. "What's wrong with him going there? You act like he's never been."

Lily's face drops, surprised by her comment. "Jordan, do

you know something?"

Jordan looks at me and Sophia then back to Lily.

"What? All the boys have gone to Spencer D's, or to those other places in the city at least once since they turned 21. Heck, I've even been there."

I touch Lily's arm. "Don't worry it will be fine."

Lily looks over at Jordan. "Tell me everything. I need to know what you saw and what the girls look like."

*

Inside the mall we hit up the food court, eating pizza and enjoying ice cream at Papa J's. When Lily finally feels better about Zach going with the guys, we are ready to buy dresses for the concert. We try on several before deciding on bright-colored mini dresses--just as Jordan requested.

At 9:30, I arrive home, lock up, fill the tub, and turn on the music of Beau Reston, the headliner for tomorrow night. Pinning up my hair, I look over to see my new dress hanging on the door. What got into me that I agreed with Jordan to purchase a vibrant, red mini dress? I discard my robe climbing into the tub then lean back with a long sigh, as Poppy settles beside me. Her chin rests on the edge of the tub, and her eyes are on me as we begin our nightly talk.

"Auntie Jordan always tries to push me out of my comfort zone, doesn't she? She knows I don't like the attention on me, yet she still tries. Maybe she knows what I need now more than I do. She paid for the tickets, so I guess I need to find my confidence and go through with this." Poppy makes a little grumbling noise as I take another sip of wine agreeing with her.

CHAPTER 2

Amelia

After a shower, a shot or two of tequila, and multiple freak outs, I stand in front of my mirror wanting to back out. Then my front door springs open.

I yell out to Lily, "I'm in the bedroom."

She comes in wearing a blue strapless dress, the color of ripe blueberries and says, "Wow!"

"It's not me at all. I feel like I'm begging for attention. What was Jordan thinking?"

"That is the brightest red I've ever seen you wear, but you are rocking it. Don't you feel strong and powerful?"

I twist while watching the fabric move across my body. I push up my boobs squeezing them together.

"Be honest, do I look okay?"

"You look amazing. Come on, doesn't it feel good to get out of your everyday plain teacher clothes and dress in this daring little number? I mean seriously, look at your legs. I know you don't like being upfront, but this cute little toned body needs attention from someone special. Put yourself out there, embrace this new look, and who knows what might happen tonight."

"It does *fit* me. Okay, tonight I want to have an open mind so I'm going to drink and enjoy the heck out of this concert."

Lily runs up and puts her arms around me. "That's my girl, but first let me cut off the tag."

*

The concert venue is amazing with a huge stage and big screen TV's adorning each side. Jordan chose a bright yellow dress for herself. Sophia is beautiful in a green dress that compliments her skin tone and eye color. She's following behind Jordan carrying something in her hands, as Jordan carries four beers, handing one to each of us.

Jordan clears her throat. "We look fabulous! Our first concert of the summer, and I have a big surprise."

She grabs the envelope out of Sophia's hands giving her the bottle of beer, then pulls out lanyards with ID's attached. Passing them out to each of us, we all look at them, then back at her. I'm the first to speak.

"Are these All Access Backstage passes?"

Jordan is about to bust out of her dress with excitement.

"Yes! There was a promo at work, and I won! Who better to share this experience tonight than with my best girl friends? Therefore, I wanted you all to look your best because you might just get to meet all the entertainers and be right up front in their faces, close enough to touch them and see them sweat. What do you think?"

We all look at each other, then scream, catching odd looks from those around us. We hug her, telling her we love her. Suddenly, we are approached by a guy wearing snug fitting jeans, sporting a cowboy hat and credentials around his neck.

"Excuse me ladies. I am the representative for Spotters Boots. Which one of you is Jordan?"

She raises her hand. "Oh, that's me. Are you Tim?"

"Yes. I will be your guide throughout the night. Now let's start with everyone's name."

We introduce ourselves and when done, he escorts us backstage for free beverages. We are among other excited winners who get the VIP treatment tonight. Tim is thorough, giving us the schedule for the night with details on the meet-and-greet after the concert with Beau Reston and XOXO. He turns us loose for a while to grab food or drinks, while he helps another guide.

"Jordan, this is amazing. Thank you so much," I say.

"Well, all of you have birthday's coming up, so this is my gift to you. We have spectacular spots next to the stage, food and drinks, and we get to meet Beau Reston later, in the flesh." She reaches out her hands to us and we join in our little ritual of celebration. "The four of us deserve a great night, I love you all so much."

We are huddled in a circle when Tim comes back eyeing us curiously. Jordan and Lily reach out to pull him into our group hug. He is one of us for tonight, so he needs to get used to us.

*

After a couple beers, I make my way to the bathroom. There is a scurry of commotion down the hall, but I can't see for all the people. I enter to do my business and then head out again to join my friends, when I stop and adjust the strap on my shoe. I'm careful not to bend over to show my underwear in this tiny dress, so I pick up my foot and tend to my shoe as the crowd moves past me. I hug the door frame trying not to fall, when I spot Lily trying to get my attention, pointing towards the mass of people pinning me to the door. When all is clear, I move over to her.

"What were you pointing at?"

"You missed Beau. He came in to say a quick hello, then he was ushered away to prepare for the concert. He's so cute."

"Well, I guess I will see him later, besides he's probably over all this meet and greet stuff anyway."

"Who knows, a lucky lady could be his game changer tonight."

"We are here to have fun, maybe catch the eye of a cute guy in the crowd. I don't think a love connection with the handsome headliner will happen tonight. I read he's been linked to a few women this past year including, Maura of XOXO."

"Is this you keeping an open mind tonight? Love can happen anywhere, Amelia."

"Just being real."

She hooks her arm in mine, and soon we catch up with the others.

CHAPTER 3

Beau

Tonight is one of many concerts on a full schedule that the record label set up for me to promote my album that dropped two weeks ago. The radio spots, phone interviews, and parties have kept me incredibly busy. It's what I always dreamed about, but some days I get a feeling that "something's missing".

When I was young, singing along with my grandpa Walker out on the porch or in the barn, was all I ever wanted to do. Writing songs came naturally to me around the time when I was nine and fell for a girl at school. I wrote her a song for Valentine's Day. She didn't feel the same about me, but with my broken heart, I began to write. Writing songs helped me get through many disappointments with girls. As the years passed, my writing improved to more grown-up topics, but still, my writing hasn't brought me any closer to personal happiness. I often wonder if I will ever find a woman who can put up with my hectic life, but I'm hopeful.

I'm a North Carolina native from a family of peanut farmers. At the age of fourteen, I was discovered at a school talent show. My father said I could go out and sing my songs, but I was not dropping out of school or sacrificing going to college. No, his boy needed to be grounded first, a sensation later. So, it's what I did, and I am forever thankful for both my parents in their support of my dream and their endless guidance. My older sister is married with two kids and owns a children's clothing boutique in our hometown. My younger brother just graduated high school and is looking forward to attending college in the fall.

When my first CD came to the house, my mother became emotional. The cover was taken in one of our green fields in the spring with me leaning against an old fence line on our property. I wore cowboy boots, jeans, and a worn-out tan shirt I always wore while working on the farm. My thick brown hair and the way I stood, mixed with the stoic look on my face, reminded her of her dad. My grandpa passed away my second year of college, leaving a large hole in the heart of our family. He would have enjoyed every crazy minute of my musical journey and probably would have been right along beside me. Instead, his guitar travels to each concert as a little reminder he's always with me.

*

Tonight's performance in Virginia includes a new group to country music, XOXO. They are an all-girl band who is making a move up the charts quickly. Maura is the band member I was linked to a while back, but we're only friends. Media blew it up quickly, which is why I am so vigilant about posting social media myself. If it comes from me first, I feel I can help squash the rumors before it gets messy.

*

There is a meet-and-greet after the show, so nights like these go longer than usual. As I'm ushered down the hall by my manager Jason, and security, we are surrounded by reporters. Then, I catch a glimpse of a woman standing outside the bathroom who seems to be fixing her shoe. I try and look around everyone to see her better, but we're walking fast-bunched in this small hall. She's wearing a red dress that reminds me of the color of a ripe watermelon from my uncle's farm in the middle of summer. As I'm walking by her, she straightens her dress letting the hem brush against her legs. Her head is turned, and all I see is her light brown hair in a knot at the back of her neck. Then, I spot the All Access Pass.

When I arrive at my dressing room to prepare for the concert, I see her walk away, meeting up with another girl in a bright blue dress at the end of the hall. I catch one more quick glance, and enter the dressing room as the door shuts. I move over to Jason who is looking at something on his phone.

"Tell me you saw her."

"Who?"

"The girl back by the bathroom."

"*What* are you talking about?"

He is looking at his phone again not listening to me. I reach over taking it out of his hands. Now he's paying attention.

"She was standing by the bathroom fixing her shoe. She was wearing a red dress. She has light brown hair. Come on, those legs. What, are you dead?"

"No, just busy. I'm managing a singer, setting up meet and greets, working on promotions, you know, *managing*."

I grab his shirt. "I need you to find her. I want to meet her. Come on how hard is it to find a girl in a red dress in this crowd?"

He looks down at my hand on his shirt. I remove it, smoothing the fabric, feeling kind of guilty/embarrassed for over-reacting.

"She really caught your eye."

"That she did. But I guess it's not important to you to find my future wife."

He puts his hand over his heart. "That hurts. I love you like a brother and would do whatever you need me to do; you know that. Have I not proven my devotion to you?"

"You have and I apologize." We both laugh. He is like a brother, and we've gotten closer since he signed on with me six years ago.

"Thank you. I will keep my eyes open for your future wife out in the sea of fans. I remember the days when your mere presence drew the ladies to you. What's going on? Where is that guy?"

"Dude, really? My reputation is hyped up by what people write about me. I don't possess any supernatural powers to draw women to me."

"Yeah, you're right. Your ability to write, produce, sing an original song, and look like a god, probably doesn't help your game. But lately you do seem off. What's up?"

"I'm right here."

"No, you're not."

"Don't start. I've done everything the label has wanted me to do. I've kept up my end of this contract, and I am grateful they took a chance on me, knowing what could happen."

"But?"

"But I want more."

"Personally?"

"Yes. We've poured ourselves into this job, and now we just have each other. Sorry to say man, but you are not my type."

Jason smiles. "You are not my idea of a good time either. I agree. Maybe finding a special woman to go through all of this with you would be nice."

"So you will find the girl in the red dress?"

He hesitates briefly. "Of course I will. How is your throat?"

"It's okay. I tried the honey-warm-water concoction and didn't talk for a full three hours today. I worked on writing two songs to give my throat a break. I won't let it take control again."

"Cut yourself some slack, Beau, you've worked steady for years and will continue to work hard, which is why we keep trying new remedies on your throat. I'm going to check things out. I'll be back soon."

"Thanks."

Jason leaves me in the room by myself, so I can rest my vocal cords, which is our normal routine before a performance. XOXO is performing while I sit and think about my voice. Being diagnosed with vocal cord damage about four years ago has led to many changes. The night I was to sing in Waco, Texas, my voice decided to not work. After spending time at the doctor's office and disappointing thousands of fans, I received an unfavorable diagnosis. Many singers have dealt with this, but you never know how bad it can get or how it will affect your career until it's too late. *So, I started thinking, what if this was my last performance, my fall?* If I couldn't sing, would I be happy to just write songs selling them to others without performing?

CHAPTER 4

Amelia

We met some of our friends from high school while making it back to our seats. They made it clear they were jealous of our All Access Passes, begging us to slip them up front, but we were taking no chances. Being able to meet one of country music's most eligible bachelors and the all-girl group XOXO could possibly be a once in a lifetime chance. But, I couldn't help thinking what I would say to them.

We are standing out in the crowd because of our brightly colored dresses. But I know this is exactly what Jordan wants, and she is getting lots of attention in hers. Lily is taking pictures and sending them to Zach, who was released to go out with his boys tonight. Sophia's attention is on Tim, our guide.

I used to believe in love at first sight and the so-called butterflies-in-your stomach-feeling, at least I did before the attack. I had boyfriends before I met Chase that year, but none quite like him. I was a funny girl, easy going and one who would take risk to a certain degree. I wanted to help everyone, stepping in and speaking up for the underdog. I attended parties and even drank, but I never lost control or risked my plans for the future. I dreamed and scribbled my life out on paper--married after grad school, a house in the town I grew up in, and our first child three years later. I thought Chase could be the one to bring my scribbles to life as we both wanted similar things, but now I'm overly cautious. It's been hard to trust, to relax around people, but I said I would try, so as I drink another beer waiting for the main attraction, I pull out my phone to post my first story of the night.

*

The music gets louder, as lights begin to flash and the announcer lets us know that Beau is about to take the stage. Tim checks with us to see if we need anything then excuses himself. Sophia grabs my arm, pinching it rather hard.

"Amelia, Tim is so cute and funny."

"So, you like him?"

She plucks my arm with her finger, "Yes."

"Good, because I think he's into you."

Just then the drums begin a solo intro and Jordan throws her hands in the air screaming loudly. Sophia, Lily, and I begin to yell, clap and jump up and down when Beau finally makes an appearance. People rush the stage, pushing us along with them, but I slip out of the crowd to the left. I try to catch a glimpse of him, as security begins to back everyone up. Once security has done their job, I can now take my place next to my friends. Beau finishes his first song and is speaking to the audience, when I finally *see* him. I'm staring at this guy, not able to turn away. He's wearing blue jeans, sneakers and a white t-shirt with a ball cap on his head. He's holding his guitar snug next to his body and in a flash, I picture myself wrapped in those arms. He turns looking in our direction. Was he looking at me? I turn away momentarily to see if there was someone behind me, but when I look back, I feel his eyes on me again. He's lips are so close to the mic. I turn my beer up taking a long swallow. The next song is fast, and he rushes back to the bass guitarist, and they play together. Soon he's back over to my side. I feel the hair stand up on my arms, and my cheeks feel warm. What did I just experience? I smile an awkward smile, then turn up my beer again. He moves across the stage to the other side, and I feel he turns to look our way a few times during the song. Tim comes over, leaning down to speak to me.

"Amelia, do you know Beau?"

"No, it's the first time I've seen him in concert. He's *really* good."

As the next three songs are played, Beau walks to our side of the stage a few more times, and each time I feel he is looking right into my soul. A know it's a crazy thought, but I feel it. Each song is a story and he holds the audience's attention with each word. His song, "Slow Fall" begins to play. It's about a guy who must live without his girlfriend because a drug overdose takes her away. At the end of the video, Beau is in a field standing alone, running his fingers through his hair crying, then he hits the ground on his knees. I connected with that song and what he might be feeling, and I can't turn away from him. Jordan bumps into me.

"What do you think, better in person?"

"Yes, definitely," I respond, coming back to reality.

"I bet his drummer is good in bed. He's making my head spin; I mean look at him." She puts her arm around me growling in my ear.

*

Beau takes a break off stage. A person who appears to be a stage crew member, announces that they need four ladies to volunteer to come on the stage for Beau to sing a new song to, a serenade. Four stools are placed in the middle of the stage. That's when the guy speaking introduces himself as Jason, Beau's manager. He looks out over the crowd and chooses Lily, two other females, and then he picks me.

"Me? No, no, no I can't go up on stage. Not me."

Lily stops and comes back to grab my hand, pulling me along the front of the stage over to the steps. As Jordan screams out after us, I'm trying to break Lily's grip, but she is very persistent that I go with her.

I grab her arm at the top of the steps when she mouths, "Oh my god, look." I turn to see thousands of people. I panic, and my heart begins to race and I can feel blood racing through my body. I just might faint. We are escorted over to our stools, and Jason asks us for our names. He tells us to stay seated. I realize that Beau is going to sing parts of the new song to each of us. I look down at Jordan and Sophia who were freaking out holding their phones ready to snap pictures of this whole crazy scene. I'm trying to plot my departure when the lights dim, the loud background music stops, and all I can hear is a guitar. The crowd is silenced almost instantaneously. Beau begins to sing behind us, and I feel my body react immediately. His voice causes my skin to tingle. He walks towards us stopping at the first girl, never looking away from her. It was intimate, sweet. Then his eyes land on me. I hold my hands in my lap squeezing them, what's wrong with me? He takes her hand then leaves a kiss on it, moving to the next girl.

She seems to also enjoy the personal attention because she slides her arm around his waist and leans into him. He reaches down with such carefulness and takes her hand, leaving a kiss just like the first girl. Then he moves to Lily.

She is impervious to his charm, not affected by the smell of him or those blue eyes. It is already affecting me, and he hasn't even made it to me yet. I repeat in my head, *He's just a man singing a song, you will not see him again. Breathe, smile and don't fall off the stool.* He smiles at her then kisses her hand, moving to me.

He moves around to stand beside me, and I teeter slightly on the stool. His hand steadies me at the small of my back easily, without anyone noticing, but I do. I can feel each one of his fingers through my dress on my skin. He stands beside me, perfectly executing the rest of the song. He holds out his hand waiting for me to take it, I smile and comply. We walk over closer to the edge of the stage. I can't look away from him. Why can't I look away from him?

The song ends and we stand staring at each other, when

the audience breaks the moment with their loud cheers. Beau squeezes my hand placing it to his lips, he smiles, then turns to the crowd getting them to quiet down, never letting go of my hand. I feel his thumb brush across my palm, then I'm released from his grasp. He thanks us all for being a part of the new song and asks the crowd to give us a hand. They are all riled up, yelling and cheering as Jason returns to escort us off the stage. The band begins another song as I look back once again at him all the while thinking, *What the heck just happened*?

Sophia reaches us first as we make our way back down into the crowd.

"You guys are so lucky."

"He's so handsome. Did either of you get a picture of me with him so I can send it to Zach," Lily inquires.

Jordan holds up her phone to show her she did. "Sending it to you now. Amelia, what about you?"

"He's…" I look up at him and I feel my cheeks flush again. "I need a beer or a shot. That was…"

Jordan smiles. "Well looks like the lust bug has hit our girl. I can't wait to see what happens at the meet-and-greet."

If I'm reacting this way now, what am I going to do later in close quarters? "Drinks, I say, we need drinks."

CHAPTER 5

Beau

The concert is done, and for the next hour the crew and band hobnob with those who hold All Access Passes. My head isn't in it tonight because I want to see the girl in the red dress, who I find out from Jason is named Amelia. He came through for me tonight, bringing her up on stage, but now it's up to me. Her blue eyes, the soft rosy tint on her cheeks, and that nervous smile. I tried to be cool about it because she seems shy, but I could tell she was also looking at me and only me.

Jason enters the room.

"How you feeling? Do you need any pain medication before we start?"

"You sure have turned into my mother lately," I reply, a bit irritated.

"Well she made me promise to take care of you. Those vocal cords are very important to your career; let's not take any chances. I'm sorry the label set up this meet-and-greet. What's it like, the sixth one? You probably need to go to the hotel and rest."

"She will be at the event, right?"

"Who?"

"Man, come on."

"Oh yeah, Amelia."

"She's wearing a pass, so I hope I get to talk to her, but what if she doesn't want to talk to me? What if I'm not her type;

maybe I should shower."

He comes over sniffing my shirt. "You do reek."

"What, really?"

"You've never been this interested in a fan before let alone this nervous. What's up with this girl?"

I sit in a chair with my legs supporting my elbows leaning my chin on my fist. "First she caught my eye with the mini red dress, then her legs, and then her hair."

"So, it's a physical curiosity?"

"Maybe at first, but then it turned into a need to see her face, to hear her voice or to hold her hand. On stage I was able to experience that, but my physical attraction to her compels me to dive deeper wanting to know more about who she is. I want to know little details about her life, her favorite dessert or song. My heart is racing in anticipation of seeing her; this has to mean something."

"Song writers. Ok, pull yourself together and let's see what is drawing you to her. Have you ever been this excited and scared all at the same time about meeting a perfect stranger?"

"No."

"Is this going to be a long night?"

I shrug my shoulders while smiling–hoping it will be.

*

I enjoy meeting the fans and hearing why they like my music, but continuing to have small talk with the fans tonight will be hard because I just want to meet *her*. Jason enters the room and I can hear the noise on the other side of the door.

"It's a good crowd tonight. Let's go meet the future Mrs. Reston."

There are a lot of people standing in the hall, cameras start to flash, and people are calling out my name. I have two security personnel along with Jason to walk me down the hall. I go inside a room for the first fifteen minutes, then the guys in the band join me. We've all been friends since elementary school except for Wade, my drummer whom I met four years ago, and we all agreed from the beginning to do fan events together.

I thank everyone for coming and begin making my way around the room, as my eyes wander, looking for Amelia. Twenty minutes into the rotation I see them, four women wearing brightly colored dresses. I approach them cautiously not wanting to say the wrong thing. Why am I so nervous?

"Ladies, thank you for coming tonight. I hope you enjoyed the concert."

The yellow dress walks over to me first holding out her hand.

"Hi, I'm Jordan. This is Sophia and you've already met Lily and Amelia."

I reach out my hand to each of them trying not to let my eyes linger too long on Amelia, but it's an epic fail. Sophia has a kind smile, Jordan seems to be in charge, and Lily wants to send a picture of us to her boyfriend. Amelia's dark blue eyes have long lashes that hit her cheeks when she blinks, and my eyes fall to her lips which are a sweet red. Is this only a physical attraction?

I'm standing in front of her as she blurts out, "I enjoyed your concert."

"Thank you. Favorite song?"

"Slow Fall, but the new song tonight, that was really sweet."

She's a little nervous but is smiling. She has dimples perfectly placed on each check, which is cute as hell. Jason clears his throat bringing me back to my responsibilities and his cue for me to move along.

"Please excuse me, but I have to speak with the others who are here. I hope you all stay until the end." I step away, then turn back to Amelia. "I'd like to talk to you some more. Can you and your friends hang out a little longer, and I will come back after I have mingled with my fans?"

She looks at them, and they shake their heads yes to what I'm asking. A powerful nudge of encouragement from Jordan has Amelia grabbing her side. She frowns at her friend then turns her attention to me.

"Can you give us a minute?"

Now I'm smiling and wondering how I turned into a junior high school boy, waiting for a girl I'm crushing on to say yes to the dance.

"Of course, just catch up with me."

CHAPTER 6

Amelia

"He just invited us to stay longer, I can't believe it. Why?"

Lily hooks her arm around mine.

"Amelia, he's interested in you. What do you want to do?"

Jordan pokes me again. "He's a beautiful man, what's stopping you?"

"I don't know what to think, I mean is he serious?" I look over at him speaking with others, and he smiles over at us.

Sophia grabs my hand. "Don't think, just do."

Tim comes over to us, handing out bags of band goodies.

"Amelia, he's a nice down-to-earth kind of guy. He treats everyone with respect, and he doesn't have women in and out of his bus like the tabloids say. I've never seen him do this before, so he must be seriously interested in you."

"But what will we talk about?"

"He's a normal guy who happens to be really famous," says Tim. Jordan hits him in the arm with her fist as he reaches for the spot with his other hand. "Ouch."

"Thanks for making her even more nervous, Tim."

"You know what I mean," he says.

"I might just throw up." As I try to regulate my breathing, Lily gives me water.

"You owe him nothing, so what do you have to lose?" says Lily.

They're all waiting for my answer.

"I guess if you guys are good with it."

They all practically say the answer at the same time, "YES!"

That was an attention grabber for everyone including Beau. He looks at us and smiles. I nod as he does to me, a silent acceptance that we would stay. I wanted to keep an open mind about meeting someone tonight, but who knew it would be the guy who was the headliner of the concert.

*

About 25 minutes later, the four of us are sitting in the room waiting for Beau to return. When he does, the whole band follows him, along with XOXO, Jason and other crew members. Jordan spots the drummer immediately and leaves us without a word. Sophia goes to Tim, and Lily stands next to me waiting for Beau.

"You're nervous, aren't you?"

"Yes. I don't know what to say to him. I mean he's a big deal."

She places her hands on my shoulders looking me square in the eye.

"You are a big deal, a beautiful, warm and loving young woman. He is lucky you said yes. Your doubt right now is fear. Just listen to him. If he comes across arrogant, we leave, if he looks at you wrong, we leave. Simple as that. Oh, here he comes."

I turn around to see; he is now wearing khaki shorts and a fresh pullover t-shirt. The sight of him evokes a nervous giggle, which escapes me, and Lily squeezes my arm.

"You will be fine. I'm going to meet XOXO."

She walks away leaving me alone, just as he approaches.

"I'm glad you guys stayed," he says.

"Thank you for asking us."

"Would you like to get a drink, maybe some water?"

"Sure."

His hand rests on my lower back as he guides me towards the temporary bar in the room. Music plays in the background as the room gets more and more crowded.

I need to say something. "Is it like this after every concert?"

"If we are not too exhausted, yes. Besides we get a two day break before heading to our next event, so, just a warning--there might be more drinking and blowing off steam tonight."

"Where is your next stop?"

"Nashville. Have you been?"

"Once, when I was fifteen, my parents took me on a road trip and that was one of the stops. I hear it's quite the tourist destination with lots of bachelor and bachelorette parties and famous people just walking in and out of the bars."

"It has definitely gotten bigger over the years, but they accept entertainers like old friends. Do you live here in town?"

"I do."

"What's your line of work?"

"Nothing as glamorous as this. I'm a toddler teacher by day at the community center in town, and I'm finishing my Master's in education at night."

"How much longer do you have before you graduate?"

"A semester. There are a lot of teachers in my family. Does anyone else sing in your family or did you get all the talent?"

"My grandfather. He was a country/bluegrass singer as well as a song writer. He was the person who got me interested. He would play with his band of brothers. They *were* actually his brothers with one brother-in-law. They were farmers by day, singers on the weekends."

"He seems like a cool grandpa."

"Yeah, he was."

"I'm sorry; he passed?"

"Yes, my second year of college."

"Grandparents can love us like no other. I'm sure he would be proud of your accomplishments."

"That he would."

"Do you write most of your songs?"

"I do. Writing songs started when I was nine and it was my first love, singing is a close second."

He looks over at Jordan standing close to his drummer.

"Does she like drummers or does she like Wade?"

"She finds him attractive."

"Most women do. He's a good guy."

"I thought most women fall for the singer."

"Wade gets a lot of attention everywhere we go. He is tall, covered in tattoos, and can come across as being a bit moody. Do you like drummers?"

"He's not my type."

"What is your type?"

"It's not a type, really, more like a feeling, or a reaction I get. There's longevity in relationships throughout my family but not yet for me. My parents have been married for 31 years. My grandparents met in high school and are still together."

"Do they live near you?"

"My grandparents live next door to me, and my parents

live 45 minutes away."

"Tell me about teaching toddlers, because it seems scary."

"It's not. I love kids and I have been around kids since I was in high school. They are different every day, funny, and curious. They love unconditionally. I have a classroom of ten beautiful children who for eight hours a day make me smile. You can't have a bad day around them because they find the fun in everything."

My attention momentarily turns as someone walks by with a plateful of food, sparking my interest. Beau notices.

"Amelia, are you hungry?"

"A little."

"Come with me." He grabs my hand guiding me out the room, without us being noticed, then into his dressing room where there is a table of food.

I look it over. "You didn't eat any of this?"

"No, I don't like to perform on a full stomach. Afterwards I usually like to eat. Help yourself."

My eyes roam over mini cupcakes, cookies, and ham biscuits along with other delicious choices.

"Do you request food, like are you one of those demanding stars?"

"No. I don't. I ask for bottled water, hot tea, and soup."

I look at him with concern, which he notices.

"I damaged my vocal cords a while back, so I look for things that soothe my throat before a concert. Sounds lame, huh?"

"No, not at all. I do remember a headline or two about your throat issues." I grab a ham biscuit. "Can I get you something?"

He reaches for a cupcake.

"I did eat one of these earlier."

I watch as he pops the mini cupcake into his mouth, and I take a vanilla one topped with white icing.

"How do you handle all the press, the excited fans, and being on the road so much?"

"I don't think anyone enjoys losing their privacy, but I love what I do. I enjoy interacting with the audience and watching them sing my songs. As for the schedule, it's just part of the job."

I see him eyeing the scar on my arm.

"Bike accident. I was learning how to ride a two-wheel bike, crossed a ditch, and fell off. I cut it on a piece of broken glass."

"That must have hurt."

"It did. Six stitches later I was back on my bike tackling the same ditch."

"Fearless. Is that a tattoo on your ankle?"

So, he's looking at my ankles? I smile. "Birthmark." I pick up my leg. "See it looks like a flower petal."

He bends down to look at it. "It does." A bit uneasy, I move to another question.

"What was your inspiration for the song, 'Damaged'?"

"I was 16 and in love with a cheerleader. She dumped me for a quarter back."

"Is she the inspiration for 'Heart of Stone'?

"Yes. You told me about Nashville, where else have you traveled?"

"I'm a true hometown girl who takes a yearly trip with my friends to the beach, and sometimes the mountains. I don't travel much; I study and fix up my house."

"I have a cabin, which is a work in progress in North Carolina." I can see him thinking. "Name three things you like to do at the end of a hectic day."

"Play with my dog, Poppy, take a long hot bath, and drink a glass of red wine. What do you do before going to sleep at night?"

"I like to write. My thoughts, song lyrics, or things I want to do in the future. It's like a bucket list, you know like some people who want to jump out of an airplane."

"I like writing thoughts or goals too, but the airplane thing seems scary."

"Or a less traumatic bucket list item might be going to Niagara Falls or thinking about the things I like about someone I just met."

I wonder if I will be the person he writes about tonight. "What's the worst part of what you do?"

"False reports about me. I know the truth about what I do, but when the wrong information is printed where my family can see it, I don't like it. That's why I try and handle my own social media posts before things get out of hand."

"How often do you get home?"

"Every chance I get. I have a sister with two kids and a younger brother. My family owns a peanut farm in North Carolina. I have a lot of aunts, uncles, and cousins who live near there. It's the best place to clear my head, recharge."

There is a knock on the door. When it opens Jason comes inside looking around. We smile back at him.

"Beau it's two in the morning. I hate to break this up, but we need to get back to the hotel and go over a few things."

I was apprehensive about staying to meet with him, but now I don't want to leave.

Beau speaks up. "Give me a minute or two and we will be out." He gives his manager a look that sends him out the door.

"I should go, I didn't know it was that late. I'm sure it's been a long day for you."

"Amelia, I want to see you again."

"When are you coming back to Virginia?"

"I'm here for the next two days. Will you have lunch with me tomorrow?"

My inner hopeless romantic wakes up, seizing the opportunity to see him again. She is jumping up and down and just did a back flip while screaming, "Heck yeah!" *Don't think, just do* plays in my brain.

"Sure. Can you come to my house for lunch? I mean is that allowed?"

He smiles. "What time, and can I bring something?"

"May I have your phone?"

He doesn't even hesitate and hands it to me. "How about 11:30 and I'm putting in my address, phone number, and what you can bring." I hand it back to him. "Don't look at it until I'm gone."

"Ok. May I have your phone?"

I hand mine over to him. When he's done, he hands it back to me. Don't look at it until *you're* gone."

I walk to the door with him and see Jason standing in the hall. I see my friends and Tim further up the hall. I grin at Beau, but careful not to give away our secret lunch date tomorrow.

"This was nice. I would never have guessed this morning that I'd be sitting with someone so famous having such a normal conversation and scheduling a secret lunch date."

His smile is charming and his eyes never look away from me, warming my cheeks. I reach for his hand to shake it, and we both hold on because neither of us wants this to end. I look down at our hands and see a scar on his thumb.

"What about this scar?"

"Fishing hook, when I was five."

"That must have hurt."

"It did."

I let go of his hand. "Nice to meet you, Mr. Reston."

"Wait, what is *your* last name?"

"Mathews."

"I've enjoyed talking to you, Amelia Mathews. I'll see you tomorrow."

I get halfway down the hall and turn to see Jason disappear into the room, but Beau remains standing where I left him. I give him a little wave goodbye. He throws up his hand to wave back and Jason reappears. I reach my friends. They are all smiling and begin to throw questions at me.

On the drive home I learn that Jordan kissed the drummer, Sophia and Tim planned to have dinner Sunday night, and Lily said she found a new interest in XOXO since meeting them. I told them what Beau and I talked about but said nothing about our planned lunch date. If he is real, the same guy I just spent time talking to, then I hope he keeps our lunch date so we can learn more about each other. If not, no one needs to know about it.

CHAPTER 7

Beau

I look at my phone as soon as Jason leaves me alone in the hotel room. Amelia gave me her address, her phone number, and what I could bring for lunch. All she said was, "You." I sit back against the headboard thinking about her, noting in my head every freckle, the shape of her face, and the soothing sound of her voice. Reaching for my journal, I begin to put down words to describe our first meeting, all the while hoping tomorrow comes quickly so I can see her again.

*

The next morning, Jason knocks early, about 8:30 a.m., turning on lights and opening the curtains. He does this often after a concert. He picks up the phone calling room service and orders up breakfast for the two of us. I make my way into the bathroom and slip into a shirt. He is now sitting on the sofa looking over some papers, and I sit down in a chair opposite of him, downing a bottle of water.

"You are prompt this morning."

"Good morning to you. How is your throat this morning?"

"Fine. What's with the sour face?"

He leans back.

"Have you seen any social media posts this morning?"

"Nope, I just woke up."

Jason looks at his phone. "Your introduction to the new song was a hit. You are coming across sweet, romantic, and sexy.

You have had several marriage proposals, which is the usual."

"Then what's the issue?"

"The label wants to know if the girl last night is serious."

"Why?"

"The label heard you invited a concert-goer backstage."

"I'm not allowed to speak to women now?"

"You can."

"Does my contract say I can't speak to *certain* women?"

"No."

"Then what's the problem?"

He throws the papers back on the table and smiles.

"Look, I want you to find someone, be in a relationship, and have little Reston babies running up and down the aisle of the bus. Getting involved with a woman right now, they feel, is not a good time because you are on tour. I don't agree with them, I'm just the messenger."

"It's bullshit. They can't tell me how to manage my personal life. I will call them today if I need to, and get that sentiment across to them."

"Not needed. As your manager, I will correspond on your behalf. They don't want you to lose out on accomplishing everything you've aspired to achieve because of rash decisions."

"Rash? I'm interested in this woman. She sparks an energy inside of me I've not had in a long time, and I want to see more of her while I'm in town. They don't get a say in my personal life until it affects my performance and obligation to them."

There is a knock on the door. Jason stands and says, "I'll get it."

A cart is pushed into the room. He signs the ticket, closing the door behind him.

"I'm always thinking of my obligations to them, to my fans, and to everyone. I respect how fast you can be on top one day in this business and out the door the next."

Jason sits a plate in front of me.

"We knew things would change when they got burned by Rex Davis and Derrick Hanes. They should know you better by now, but I just needed you to know what they are thinking especially with social media breaking things before we do. I will handle the concerns of the label. Now, tell me how you really feel because I saw how you looked at Amelia last night."

"I've thought of noone else since meeting her last night, so I made plans to have lunch with her today."

"Where?"

"Her house."

"Really? When were you going to tell me?"

"I wasn't until just now."

"This isn't going to end with just lunch is it?"

"I hope not. Now I will need transportation and maybe a disguise."

He rubs his eyes like I just threw sand at him.

"I will help you get to her, but promise me not to fall in love right now."

"I can't promise that."

Jason leans back on the sofa.

"I figured that."

CHAPTER 8

Amelia

I can't believe that Beau is coming here to my house for lunch today. My alarm went off at 6:00 this morning allowing me to sleep very little last night, but I want to thoroughly clean the house and go shopping. I spent time on all his social media sights last night, which gave me insight on what he likes to eat and what he enjoys doing. What I found was a busy schedule of events and little time to relax, so I'm giving him a glimpse into my normal, laidback Sunday afternoon. I realize that this could make or break him wanting to see me again.

At the store I chose pork chops, green beans, and twice baked potatoes. Dessert was an easy choice, a family recipe of banana pudding with homemade whipped cream. Checking my phone, I see that Lily called so I call her back. She picks up on the first ring.

"How are you feeling today, Mrs. Reston?"

"You did not just say that."

"Come on Amelia, this guy was eating you up with his eyes last night. How long do you think it will be before he calls you?"

I didn't want to lie to her, but technically he has not called only texted, so not a lie.

"He meets a lot of women, so I doubt if I'm still on his radar."

"Stop saying that. Why can't you be someone he wants to know more about? Give him a shot and just enjoy yourself. Look, Zach came home this morning and is still asleep, so

I wasn't able to talk to him about his experience last night. Would you be okay if we skip the movie today?"

I forgot about the movie. "Sure, maybe next week."

"Thanks Amelia. Love you."

"Love you too."

I will have to buy a few bottles of wine to smooth this over with my friends. I am keeping today's 'date' with Beau all to myself, but the reaction I had to him last night is one I can't sweep under the rug.

I sit down on a bar stool in my kitchen looking over the groceries I just bought. Poppy comes over laying her head on my leg, and I put my hands on both sides of her face. "I'm taking a leap of faith with this guy, Poppy." I kiss the top of her head and she trots away to find a toy. I stand, determined to give this my all, and begin to prepare for my lunch date.

*

My shower did nothing to relax me, but I'm dressed and ready. I chose white shorts and a pale pink bohemian style blouse putting my hair in a messy knot. He is about to see the real me without makeup or shoes. I guess rip off the Band-Aid before getting too invested.

I walk into the kitchen checking on the pudding that's cooling on the counter, when I hear a vehicle in my driveway. Making my way to the front of the house, I see an old red truck. A man gets out wearing jeans and a pullover grey t-shirt with a cap on his head, and he is wearing sunglasses. Beau?

I open my door, not wanting him to stand out on the porch too long for the neighbors to see. His smile is as genuine as last night, but it drops off his face as he enters looking at the everyday me. This may not be good, maybe I dressed down too much. The door shuts behind him as Poppy comes to greet him. He takes off his hat, running his fingers through his hair.

"May I?"

"Sure. She's very friendly."

He kneels to her level, rubbing his hand over her back. She is loving the attention when she drops to the floor exposing her belly.

"She likes me." He stands up.

"Hi."

"Hi. Did you have any problems finding the place?"

"None. You look great."

I'm noticing the light blue specks in his eyes. "Thank you. I wanted you to experience the real me and just hoping you don't flee."

Does she have any idea how gorgeous she is?

"You told me to bring me, so I did, but also I brought wine. Can I help you with anything? I'm pretty handy in the kitchen."

"I would love your help. We're actually putting together one of your favorite desserts and mine."

"Banana pudding?"

"How did you guess?"

"I can smell the cooked pudding."

"Keen nose." We enter the kitchen. "Can I get you a drink? Maybe some wine?"

"Do you have beer?"

"I do. It's from a brewery here in town."

*

We share the layering process for the banana pudding, and he has me laughing at stories from his childhood. While I prep pork chops for the oven, he washes the potatoes. When everything is ready, we sit at the island enjoying our food, and begin sharing even more information about each other. He thinks I am a saint for working with children, and I'm learning how un-affected he is by his fame.

After loading the dishwasher, we take our dessert to the living room. I'm sitting on my sofa next to a well-known singer/songwriter eating banana pudding. I still can't believe it, but it feels good. We have brushed against each other for the past two hours, and I feel the hair standing up on my arm, like an electric surge through my body, intense and hot.

"Amelia, what are you thinking about?"

"Honestly?" *Don't tell him about the surge.*

"Of course."

"I can't get over how normal you are."

"Is that good?" he asks.

"Yes. I mean you are the only famous person who has ever been in my house before, and you make me feel relaxed. Are you always this easy going?"

"Usually. I've never been favorable to the frenzy that goes along with my job. The person sitting with you is the same person who is on stage. If not, my parents would let me know right away."

"Do they attend your concerts?"

"Yes. They've also been to a few awards shows over the years."

"Well they seem supportive. My girlfriends, the ones you met last night, are like my sisters. They have strong opinions about things also, but I know they are there for me when I need them. Is it easy to trust people in your kind of business?"

"I trust until they give me a reason not to trust. Jason keeps me on track, but lately he is like having my mom on the tour."

I smile at his comment. "What about perks; there have to be a ton of those."

"I get to do what I love every day. But there are other perks like giving back and helping in many communities, *and* meeting people like you."

"Very smooth."

"Just speaking the truth."

There it goes again--the heat on my cheeks. "Would you like to watch a movie while we eat dessert?"

"Um, can we just talk?"

He just wants to talk, who is this guy?

"That works."

For the next three hours we stretch out on the sofa getting to know each other. His mouth is distracting me as I keep staring at his lips. He's funny and animated with his stories and politeness, always asking if I need anything. He excuses himself to use the bathroom, and I flop back onto the sofa with my hands on the sides of my head wondering what is happening. What is this wonderful feeling? I want to touch him, and three beers in, I even want to kiss the mouth I've been staring at. I get up in search of water, repeating in my head to get a grip and slow down my thoughts. Bottles in hand, I find my way back into the living room to see him standing in front of the fireplace looking at a picture of my parents.

"You have your mother's eyes," he says.

Just then my phone vibrates somewhere on the sofa. He walks over pulling it out from between the cushions. He hands it to me, when I notice who it is.

"It's my grandmother."

He turns the bottle up to his mouth as I try and listen to her, but I'm pulled by some force to just look at him as I respond to her.

"I'm glad you had fun. Yes, it's been a while since I've seen them. Of course, I will. Pork Chops, and you? That sounds delicious.

Then she asks the question. A friend. Yes. I will, thank you. Okay, I will see you after work tomorrow. I love you too. Good night."

"Sorry about that."

"No problem."

I move closer to him breathing in whatever he is wearing or showered in, and his scent fills my brain with euphoria once again. He's leaning against the mantle with his left shoulder. I begin to explain my family when he picks up a picture just past my head. Did he do that on purpose? I hope so. He looks down at my mouth as I tell him about the picture making me very aware of how close we are. Poppy's whining alerts me she needs to go outside.

"That's my mom and dad on their wedding day." Poppy is pacing with enthusiasm. "Excuse me, I'll be right back." When I return he's sitting on the sofa. "Poppy is all good, she's enjoying a snack." I sit on the other end.

"Amelia would you like to have dinner with me?"

"Sure, what are you thinking?"

"May I cook for you?"

"I won't say no to that offer. What do you need?"

"Eggs, cheese and bacon. My breakfast specialty is an omelet, which is also good for dinner. I thought we could watch that movie and maybe in a couple of hours, I can fix us dinner."

He wants to stay and cook us dinner? I grab the remote. "Let's pick a movie."

CHAPTER 9

Beau

My arm has fallen asleep, but if I move, I'll wake her up. She fell asleep about 30 minutes ago, and I do not want to disturb her. She is peaceful and smells like fresh-baked cookies. Jason texted the schedule for tomorrow and we are leaving at five in the morning with an extra stop, which means I need to leave, but how? I've just met a remarkable woman and leaving her behind for many weeks is not at the top of my list.

She stirs then realizes she was leaning on me. She sits up, then groggily says, "I must have been tired." She touches my shirt. "Just making sure I didn't drool on you."

"I wouldn't care if you did." I tuck a piece of hair behind her ear. "Are you hungry?"

"That's right you offered to cook dinner."

She stands holding out her hand to me and we walk to the kitchen where we find Poppy eagerly ringing the bell at the back door. Amelia loosens her grip on my hand, but I hold on making her turn to me. I watch her lips part to say something then what happens next isn't me, but her and I'm grateful. She kisses me, a move that clearly surprises her, but one we both want. Just as I imagined while she was sleeping, her lips are as soft as I expected. My right-hand rests on her cheek and neck as my left hand guides her closer to me. The kiss is what a first kiss should be, sweet and tender, one that burns a permanent spot in your brain. Poppy whines loudly and hits the bell again. I back Amelia up so I can reach the door to let the dog out. I close it, pinning Amelia between me and the door continuing our kiss.

We only part when Poppy begins to bark to get back inside. I don't know about Amelia, but I've never kissed anyone like that before. I peer down at her stepping back so we can both catch our breath.

"I'm not going to forget that." I walk to the fridge.

"Nor will I," she says.

She walks to the cabinet pulling out bowls, and I pull out a stool for her.

"Please sit."

"I don't mind helping."

"I know."

She sits watching me work my culinary skills on nearly perfect omelets, and like we've been all day, we're never without something to say. As much as I want to ignore my phone, it has gone off three times. We both know it's time for me to go, but neither of us want this date to end. On the fourth call I answer. It's Jason and I give him a short response that satisfies him enough to get off the phone. We clean up and I say goodbye to Poppy. Amelia walks me to the door, handing me a container.

"I would like to see you again."

"I'd like that, but I know the tour will keep you busy."

I am holding the container of leftover pudding with one hand while lacing my fingers around hers bringing our hands up to my chest leaning in to kiss her again.

"This was a great first date."

She smiles. "I agree. I'm glad you asked me to lunch and thank you for fixing dinner."

"I can cook other foods, so maybe I will cook at my cabin for you someday."

"I'm going to hold you to that."

I kiss her, then kiss her again, knowing I need to leave.

"Goodnight, Amelia."

"Goodnight, Beau."

*

I pull out of the driveway already missing her. I wave, knowing it will be a while before I see her again, unless I come up with a plan. My phone vibrates as I see Jason's picture. I choose not to answer him because I want to give myself a few more minutes to think about the best date I've ever had.

As I walk into my hotel room, I text Jason that I've returned. He texts back, *See you in 15 minutes*. Fifteen minutes or so go by, and I hear him knock, then let him inside.

"Well, how did it go?"

"You really want to know?"

"I think I do."

"It was better than any date before. She made lunch, and we made the best banana pudding I ever put into my mouth. We had so much to talk about, and she kissed me, then I kissed her, and it was amazing."

"I get it. You like her."

"No, I like her a lot."

"Where did you leave it?"

"I told her I would call."

"Well that is one way to keep in touch."

"Yes, but it's not what I want."

"I know. Baby steps lover boy."

CHAPTER 10

Amelia

I arrive at work, before coffee, no breakfast, and I realize the only thing giving me energy today is thinking of my date with Beau. Last night after he left, I reminisced about our time together and a lot about the kiss. When I realized it was 2:30 in the morning, I went to bed falling asleep with thoughts of hoping to see him again, but the reality is it might be a long time.

Today I'm in the classroom with a summertime employee, Angela. We begin to change the kids into their swimsuits, when she asks me how the concert was and if I met anyone. She goes into how meeting a guy at a concert would be the ultimate fantasy. She describes how their eyes would meet, while he sings a song only for her. They go out after the concert and she quits her job to join him on the road. If she only knew Beau was at my house yesterday.

"Come on Amelia, you are still young, did you hook up or not?"

"Angela please, little ones repeat the words they hear. We don't need a parent coming in to complain."

"Sorry, did you at least talk to someone, anyone?"

I notice a smelly diaper on one of the kids and go around looking for the one who needs a change, hoping to avoid her question.

"I wonder who is messy?" But it doesn't stop her, she continues.

"The last guy I met at a concert was a lighting guy who

graduated from my high school three years before me."

"How did it go?"

"His wife didn't like me much."

My mouth drops open. "Oh my."

When I'm done with sanitizing the mats, and washing my hands, I begin to sing the pick-up-your-toys song when two of the kids begin to fight over a toy, one grabs on to my leg in need of some love, and a few of them pull out the blocks instead of cleaning them up. I really wished I hadn't missed coffee this morning!

The first week after meeting Beau...

On Monday I received three texts in the morning from Beau and had a phone conversation with him over lunch. He was busy in the evening, but if it wasn't too late, he was going to call. Unfortunately, I fell asleep in front of the TV with a half-eaten bowl of ice cream resting on my belly. I had forgotten to take my phone off silent from being at work that day and missed his call.

Tuesday morning, I sent him an apology and went to work before getting a text back. I had to work through lunch and was unable to check my phone. When I got off at 3:00 he had sent me a picture of a pool in the hotel and a "wish you were here." The next text came about 5:30, but I was at the gym and then headed off for a light protein-packed dinner with my cousin. Our next chance to talk was through FaceTime about 1:00 a.m., when he was back in his hotel room. He played me a sample of a song he says was inspired by me. We didn't stop talking until 2:00 in the morning.

Wednesday, I dealt with a stomach bug sweeping through my classroom. I learned most of the kids were not coming to school, so I spent time creating projects with an ocean theme for the next few weeks. I busied myself putting up new artwork, along with disinfecting the room. I went to lunch about 12:30

but was unable reach Beau. He called me while I had Poppy at the dog park before his concert and then again about 12:30 after the concert. His voice sounded hoarse, so I talked him into having tea with me, and I told him about my friends, while he just rested his voice. We hung up about 1:15.

Today is Thursday and before I left home this morning, Beau had sent a video of himself trying out the new song with Adam, one of his guitar players. I couldn't stop smiling. I can't believe he wrote a song about me! I have three sweet little toddlers all to myself today, all of them girls who enjoy baby dolls and dress up. I turn the radio on to our acceptable station and hear Beau's voice. It's an upbeat song and the four of us dance, while all pretending to be a princess, a doctor, and a cat. I'm a superhero and wear a great patched cape my grandmother made last year for the classroom.

As lunch approaches, I want to fly into the office and grab my phone and see if I have any texts, but my replacement was a no-show with the stomach bug. I eat leftover lunch pizza and find out I have to stay until 2:30 when someone can take my place. The kids are asleep, which gives me time to think about Beau. I miss him, but how can I miss him this soon? I lean my head against the wall. Why am I even thinking about it? He has so many women paraded in front of him at every concert, a social media account that has numerous devoted fans, and he's on TV! I stand up. Who am I kidding? I've got things in my life he knows nothing about, and maybe he doesn't even want to know. Trying to distract myself, I begin to sort out blocks, but my mind still goes straight back to him. I sit at the table after checking on my sleeping students. I rub my hands together looking at my fingers remembering the way his hands felt against my skin or the way his blue eyes resemble the Caribbean waters I've seen in pictures. A whimper is heard, as I see little Lana's head move, and I realize it's time to get back to work. Maybe I'm moving too fast or not thinking clearly. He's hexed me in some wonderful way leaving me confused but also intrigued.

After leaving the Center, I wait until I get into my car before checking my phone. I flip through all the texts he has sent. The last one says, *"Worried, please text back."* He is probably on the bus, so I call him. He picks up immediately, but he wants to FaceTime. In a panic I move my mirror to check my face. No makeup, my hair needs some attention, but I don't let it stop me from seeing him.

His face appears and thoughts of my disheveled appearance diminishes.

"Amelia, are you okay?"

"I'm fine. Stomach bug going through my room and no staff, so I couldn't get to my phone until now. Sorry if I look a mess."

He smiles resting a hand on his cheek. "No, you look good."

"Where are you right now?"

"In the bus." He stands. "Let me give you a tour and if I appear unsteady, it's the drivers fault."

"Wait, no one can see me, right?"

He moves the phone as four guys wave and say hello. I bury my face in my hands, mortified.

"Hi, everybody."

He proceeds to show me where he sleeps, the cabinet full of snack foods, and the fridge. I even get to see the shower. We end the tour with him lying on his bunk. I hear a muffled voice, then he gets up to open the door. I hear him say "yes, give me five minutes." Then he comes back to the bed.

"We are stopping to eat. Will you be home later?"

"I will. Rest your voice so we can talk later."

He places his hand over his heart. "You care about me."

"Bye Beau."

"Bye Amelia."

CHAPTER 11

Beau

By the time we get back on the bus, it's about 10:00 p.m., and I hope Amelia is still awake. I text her first to see if this is a good time. She responds requesting to FaceTime. As she comes into view my mouth becomes suddenly dry, and I try to stay cool, but she's in a tub full of bubbles.

"Beau, hold on Poppy is barking too loud for me to have this conversation."

The water starts to move causing bubbles to fall over the sides, and I see dog paws on the tub as she falls backwards.

"Amelia!"

She wipes off her face sputtering. "Please tell me you saw none of that."

"I saw it all. Good save Mathews. What's up with Poppy?"

"She wanted to play with her new ball, in fact she has wanted to play with it all night. So, I threw it to her, and it went under a cabinet and she couldn't reach it."

"Hence the barking?"

"Yep and she startled me by throwing the ball in the tub."

"The splashing?"

"Yes. Hold on while I give her a bone to keep her busy."

She turns the phone so I can see only a wall, then returns to get back in the tub turning the phone back around.

"How was dinner?"

"Good. We played a game of hoops outside the restaurant at a park right next door, and I had banana pudding, which, by the way, was not as good as ours."

"Ours *was* pretty delicious. Tell me about your next stop."

"This next venue is big, with a slew of well-known singers who have been in the business for years and some newly-discovered performers. I've been practicing a lot."

"Why, Mr. Reston, are you nervous?"

I lay back on my bed with my hand behind my head.

"I just want to do well."

"I've been spending some time recently fan-stalking you, and I have to say talent is not something you need to worry about--or confidence. You are a natural."

"Thank you. What times are you working tomorrow?"

"In at 6:30, but I get to leave at 12."

"Plans for the weekend?"

"Not really, we might go and listen to music at Zena's. Just another low-key weekend."

"Low key sounds nice."

"Give me a few minutes to get out?"

"Sure."

She sets the phone on a stool next to the tub. I can't see her, but I see her arm reach for the towel as drops of water hit the screen. When she turns back to the phone, I see she's wrapped in a blue towel. She wrings out her hair, combing through it with her fingers. She turns back to the phone.

"Oh no you are covered in water."

She wipes it off then puts the phone on the shelf next to her then reaches for a robe hanging on the back of the door. I know because I saw it when I was there. I keep talking as she brushes her teeth and applies lotion to her face. When done, she picks up the phone and walks into her bedroom, falling across the bed.

"Amelia are you concerned about people finding out about us? If you are, I understand. I haven't heard you saying anything about what your friends and family think of us talking."

"Because I haven't told them. I wanted this time for us to get to know each other."

She smiles, making me want to jump through the phone and kiss her.

"This life isn't for everyone, but I would like to try it with you."

"Promise me if you lose interest in me that you will be up front and open with me first. I don't want to hear about you ending things through social media."

"I would never do that to you." I raise my hand. "I promise."

"Thank you. I want to try. I just might need some guidance."

"That I can give."

"Now, I need to get some sleep, and so do you."

"Goodnight, Amelia."

She places her fingers to her lips then places them on the phone.

"Goodnight Beau."

The phone lands on my bed, and I have an idea. I begin to research flights. My next step is getting Jason on board. When I have everything worked out, I call him back in to talk.

"Hey, have a seat, I need a huge favor."

"I don't like how this is going, so should I just say no, now?"

"Really?"

"What's up?"

"I want Amelia at the concert this weekend; in fact, I want her with me the whole weekend."

"I'm listening."

"I want to fly to Virginia tomorrow and pick her up."

His face just drops as the worry creeps over it. He stands pacing from one side of the room to the other, just a tiny path.

"How?"

"I have it all worked out; I just need the okay from you. I won't miss anything and then the next two weeks I will be the model client for the label. I will be here for whatever you need me to do."

"You like her that much?"

"Yes."

"Tell me what you see in her that you haven't seen before."

"She's straight with me, holding nothing back. For example, tonight she was taking a bath and brushing her teeth. She's different than most of the girls I meet. They are only interested in what comes along with being associated with me, what party can they attend and even meeting other singers through me. Amelia seems interested in getting to know who I am, not all the notoriety."

"Does she know you are coming?"

"No. Will you be a part of my future or not?"

He shakes his head for a few seconds, then grins.

"Tell me about your plan."

I look down at my phone and pull up his number, then, I send him the flight information. His phone buzzes. His eyes look at the screen.

"I'm going with you?"

"Yeah. You need a break."

He leaves the room shaking his head.

"This might be difficult to pull off with both of us going, but I will make it work."

"I appreciate it."

CHAPTER 12

Beau

The flight to Virginia gave Jason and I time to purchase a few hundred dollars in gift cards for classroom materials and coffee gift cards for the teachers at Amelia's center. It would be around lunch time when we arrived, so I called the local pizza chain to have a dozen pizzas delivered for lunch. I sit in the passenger seat of our rented car tapping my fingers on my knees until Jason calls me out.

"I've never seen this side of you before."

"She might turn down my offer or think I'm insane. Is this a little over the top?"

"Yes."

I reach over hitting him in the arm. "Thanks for the encouragement."

He pulls into the parking lot then turns off the car. The Center before us is covered in brick and decorated with a blow-up surfer at the front door with a sign that states, "Catch a wave into summer fun". There are pinwheels across the grass and a bright blue bus sits to the right of us. I look around finding Amelia's car and with everything in hand, I get out making my way to the glass front door and push the buzzer. A woman responds, "How can I help you?"

"I'm here to see Amelia Mathews. My name is Beau Reston."

What happens next even startles me. Two faces pop up in front of the door, and I hear squealing as the younger one runs away, around the corner out of sight. The older lady remaining speaks.

"Excuse me sir, we will need your ID. Can you hold it up in front of the camera, please?"

I take out my wallet and show my ID to her, then to the camera. She smiles and the door releases allowing her to step outside with me.

"Please come inside. My name is Mrs. Steele; I'm the director. We can never be too careful with security."

"I understand and I apologize for the unannounced visit, but I'm here to surprise Amelia."

Two ladies come around the corner in a haste bumping into each other as I step inside. Mrs. Steele looks at the one who had fled the office minutes before.

"Maggie who is taking over Amelia's class?"

"Miss Carol."

"Mr. Reston if you will follow me, I can show you to her room."

"Well before you do that, I have some gifts for the Center."

"Gifts?"

"She told me about the Center and how hard everyone works here. She also said you rely on donations, so I have gift cards for books or toys in the classrooms and gift cards for the teachers for coffee or treats. Do I give them to you?"

She's stunned and doesn't respond. I clear my throat and she blinks coming back with a response.

"Um, you have to forgive me Mr. Reston, we don't usually get famous people in our Center in addition to someone who's so generous. I think I'm a little star struck."

"Thank you. I am flattered." The buzzer sounds again. The pizzas have arrived.

"Did you?"

"I did. Sometimes I cause a disturbance and who doesn't love pizza. May I?"

She makes a motion for me to open the door. "Please and thank you."

One of the girls escorts the pizza delivery guy to the kitchen.

I'm taken to Amelia's room by Mrs. Steele, who keeps looking back at me as we pass into an even longer hall, where I see doors opening and people peeking out. She opens the door to Amelia's room, and we find her sitting on the floor with kids all around her. She is dressed like a fish and is reading them a book. She looks up briefly to acknowledge us when it hits her it's me. She's no longer animated playing the part of a fish in fact she has frozen. I did it, I've surprised her, but is it a good one? Mrs. Steele walks over encouraging her to stand up. She does but stumbles over a little one standing next to her making a miraculous recovery. She pulls off the costume balling it up in her arms blowing at a piece of hair hanging in her eyes.

"Amelia, you didn't tell us you know Beau Reston."

The kids wrap their little arms around my legs babbling words I don't understand. They are strong for their size and persistent, as a few of them even take my hands trying to pull me over to a play kitchen set. I look at Amelia to gauge what she's thinking, then she smiles teasing me with her indelible dimples.

Mrs. Steele moves even closer to her.

"Why didn't you tell us?"

She looks at me grinning. "We just met."

"Amelia, he's in our building, he donated gift cards for classroom items, gift cards for the teachers, and bought us all pizza for lunch. What's happening here?"

I look at them, but neither are offering to help me in my time of need. One child pushes another child, then one grabs a toy accidently hitting another friend, and then they all start to cry. Everything was under control until I came in, so I did what I do best. I begin to sing. They start to look up at me as the crying subsides. Some are clapping while others move their feet dancing. I find a tambourine and begin to use it in the song, and when I finish, they're all generous with their squeals. The lunch cart comes inside the room and like magic, they make their way to the table, losing interest in me. Amelia and the other teacher begin to put them in chairs and wipe off their hands. I start another song as their plates are prepared, and just like that the room becomes quiet. Peace is restored. The other teacher comes over with a piece of construction paper.

"Mr. Reston that was amazing, could you autograph this for me, I'm Angela."

"Of course."

The door opens as a woman with red hair comes in holding a bag.

"So, it's true, you are really here." She holds out her hand. "It's my pleasure to meet you Mr. Reston, I'm Ms. Carol. Do you know your songs tell such wonderful stories?"

"Thank you. Each one is a story of an experience in my life."

She looks past me to Amelia. "Well she's a good girl and very special to us, so I'm sure what you write in the future will be favorable about her."

"You have my word."

"She needs to fess up when she knows a good-looking country music singer."

"This was all a surprise; she didn't know I was coming."

"Well, if she doesn't love this surprise visit, I can give you my number."

I reach out shaking her hand. "I will keep that in mind."

Amelia begins to tell Carol a few things about the kids as Angela stands near the table watching as they eat. Mrs. Steele has yet to leave the room, but when Amelia walks over to me, Mrs. Steele makes her way to the door and waits for us.

"Amelia, did I mess up?"

She reaches over taking my hand. "No. I'm surprised, but more than that, I'm really happy to see you." She looks to her kids. "Okay little fish, use your fins to say goodbye to Mr. Reston."

They begin to flap their arms, which I guess are their fins. I wave back at them the same way while making fish lips, as I follow Amelia out the door. When we step into the hall everyone's door is open, looking towards us. Amelia stops suddenly causing me to bump up against her and she turns to me.

"Are you in a rush?"

"No."

"Would you like to meet the teachers?"

"Of course."

"Let's zip in and out. Then you can explain all of this."

We did just that. I met all the teachers and saw the Center. It did need some attention, so I make a mental note to speak to Jason later about some options. I text him that I am almost ready, when the staff asks me if they can take some pictures. They thank me for the donations and invite me to come back anytime. Amelia and I walk outside, and I drape my arm around her shoulders, making our way to her car.

"How can you be here right now? You have a huge concert in Nashville."

I point to a black car in the parking lot. "Jason is waiting for us in that car to take us all to the airport."

"Waiting for us? What's going on?"

"I want you to come back with me to Nashville. I bought a ticket for you. We can spend time together tonight and go to a few parties. Tomorrow there is breakfast, then we can have time together before the concert. What do you say? Will you be my date?"

"Your label is okay with all of this? What if I distract you from your responsibilities?"

"The label knows I'm bringing a *plus one*, the plane ticket was paid for by me, and Jason is cool with all of this. He wants what I want, and I want you." I rub my hands up and down her arms sliding them down to hold her hands in mine. "What do you say?"

"I'm not sure if I have appropriate clothes for the parties, and I need someone to watch Poppy."

"Can we ask your grandparents or one of your friends?"

"I can try."

I lean in kissing her. "Thank you."

She looks past me to Jason in the car. "I can't leave my car here all weekend so, do you want to ride with me?"

"Of course." I run over to Jason then come back to her car taking my place in the passenger seat.

She is smiling as I buckle my seat belt. "When you decide to do something, you go big."

"You have no idea."

"Oh no, what else is planned that's going to shock me."

"It's all going to be good I promise. Do you trust me?"

"Definitely."

CHAPTER 13

Amelia

I can't believe that Beau was at my job today and gave all those donations along with lunch to the whole staff. What is this, how could this be happening to me? I'm taking a big leap of faith with him, and the truth is I want to. My grandma asked me to text her while I was gone and tell her where I would be, and send the occasional picture. She didn't seem worried at all about me leaving with Beau. When Grandpa came to the back door to pick up Poppy, he had a goofy look on his face, which made me giggle. I introduced him to Beau and Jason, then I left them to talk while I packed.

Now what did Beau say I needed? Casual for breakfast, an outfit for a party, and then something casual for the concert. I'll have my own room, but I pack a couple cute options just in case we spend hours talking together in one of our rooms. Looking over my packed bag, I feel that pang in my stomach. The one I've gotten many times before. He's different, I have nothing to fear from Beau. This week talking to him, texting and following him on social media, has made me feel good, better than I have in a long time. Laying my hand over the scars on my body makes me realize how soon I will have to tell him about the attack. I breathe in and out, slowing my racing thoughts and my heart. I want this with every fiber in my body; I want this with Beau.

I grab the bag and go down the hall to the living room, where I see all three talking. Beau reaches for my bag, and Grandpa kisses my cheek whispering, "You're in good hands; I can sense he's a good boy." I'm living in some dream world because my protective grandfather just gave his okay for me to leave the state after only spending a few minutes talking with Beau. I kiss my sweet dog goodbye and leave behind my quiet life, entering one that scares me a little, but one that also excites me. Beau winks at me as I walk past him. A small gesture, that wink, but one that calms me.

On the plane we talk about the scheduled events and what I should expect. Prior to our flight, inside the airport, I called the girls to let them know where I was going. Lily was excited, Sophia was in class, and Jordan called me a name I will never say out loud. They were all happy and not one of them seemed concerned, just happy for me.

Arriving at the hotel in Nashville, we enter through a back entrance allowing us to keep our existence a mystery for now. Beau walks me to my room, opens the door, and follows me inside. He looks around when I ask, "Is something wrong?"

"No, just making sure everything is okay. My room is across the hall. You can order anything you want from room service. We have about three hours before the first party. Do you need anything?"

"No, I will get a glass of wine sent up, maybe a bottle."

He moves over wrapping me up in a solid hug, forcing me to exhale and lean my body against him.

"Don't be nervous. I'll be with you through it all. There will be pictures and questions like, are you Beau's new girl? Who are you, where did you two gorgeous people meet?" He grins.

"I'm okay with pictures, but we have only known each other a week. What are people going to say when they find out I'm not famous, that I'm a toddler teacher."

"You are a beautiful, strong and intelligent woman who caught my eye at a concert, and in one week you have turned my world upside down in the best way ever."

"How many people are going to believe that?"

"I'm not concerned about anyone but you. I've never experienced anything like this before Amelia, and I'm hoping you feel the same."

"I feel we've found something, and I hope that this is not short term."

"So, you like me?"

"Yes, I do."

"Where we go from here is up to us."

"I just don't want to embarrass you or myself."

"That would never happen, just be the woman I see in front of me." He kisses me then walks towards the door. "Oh, by the way, how is your right hook?" He blows me a kiss shutting the door behind him.

I hope he's not serious, but if it comes to blows for my man...Wait did I just say, *my man*. I giggle, nervously falling onto the bed. I think I'm in a relationship with Beau Reston. Rolling over I grab the phone ordering up a much needed bottle of wine.

Time passes quickly and with the grooming I had to do along with the glasses of wine, I am finally done. I stand wearing a cobalt blue pleated halter style swing dress with black ankle strap heels. Not a lot of time left to curl or straighten my hair, so I opt for loose hair with a little product to keep the waves separate. What was I doing all this time? I glance at the mirror and hear a knock on the door. Opening the door, my eyes take in every inch of him and he does the same to me. He's wearing dark grey slacks and a white long sleeve shirt and jacket.

"Please come inside. You clean up nice."

He takes my hand. "Blue might be my new favorite color."

"Oh, but *red* brought us together."

He steps close and kisses me, as his fingers touch my arms and goosebumps pop up giving away how he affects me. Another knock at the door brings Jason into the room dressed in blue slacks and a white shirt, carrying his jacket, as he looks at both of us looking at each other kind of ignoring him.

"Are you both ready for what might happen tonight."

Beau responds, while squeezing my hand, "Yes."

"Pictures, people asking you questions about how you met, and asking Amelia information about herself. Look, I'm not trying to put a damper on your new relationship, but what you say tonight could change her life."

Beau turns facing me. "Still okay?" He looks deep into my soul reassuring my inner escape artist not to wig out. *I can do this, and he will help me.* I nod and smile. He turns back to Jason. "The lady is ready."

"Well let's get this new budding relationship in the news."

*

We climb into a car that takes us over to the first party. It is a small event space, and inside are reporters from magazines, TV, and radio; they are set up all over. Beau is to meet individually with each to promote his current album and tour, as well as the charity that brought everyone here tonight. This left me to stand and wait at times on the sideline. His eyes stay on me, his smile and a wink keep me relaxed. We show no affection other than hand holding, so right now no one knows anything other than that I'm his date for the evening.

As the fourth interview ends, he makes his way through the crowd, grabbing my hand as we sneak off to a table over by the wall and snag two glasses of wine.

"You look so comfortable in all of your interviews."

"It gets easier the more I do. I know it's not much fun just waiting."

"Actually, I've enjoyed watching how things work."

He turns my face to him with just a finger. A quick peck on the lips then a deeper more intimate kiss. First one in public tonight and one that obviously is seen by someone as a flash brings us out of our moment. We stop but keep looking at each other.

"They might be on to us," he says.

"Then you should kiss me again."

He does, but this time we are stopped by a hand on each of our backs. Jason notices the media beginning to gather around us. He has us turn to him with a slight gesture of his hands.

"You could have warned me."

Beau smiles at me. "An impulse kiss, it's unpredictable when it happens."

Jason clears his throat looking at me, and I shrug my shoulders then sheepishly grin.

"Well, Mr. Impulse, your next interviewer is ready for you."

Beau sits down at KVW radio's booth with the interviewer Mitch Stephens, a local Nashville radio host. He seems to be in his 40's, a six-foot-tall hulk of a guy. He positions his earpiece, gets out his notes, and waits for the cue. He leans in talking to Beau, then looks towards the crowd of photographers. A signal is given when he begins his interview.

He welcomes Beau, they speak about the tour, and then he asks the question.

"Who did you bring with you tonight?"

"Amelia Mathews is accompanying me this evening."

Mitch leans back in his chair looking over at me. I'm stuck, feet planted firmly to the floor unable to move when I hear him say, "Well let's bring her over."

This is my moment to trust him. I begin my walk over to them and I'm greeted by both men.

"Mitch I would like you to meet Amelia. We've been dating

for a short time, but she was gracious enough to join me this weekend."

"Nice to meet you Mitch."

"Nice to meet you Amelia. Please take a seat."

Beau pulls out the stool for me to sit and he takes the one next to mine, draping his arm over the back of my chair. Mitch begins.

"Amelia I'm going to be honest with you, there might be some fans listening today that will be upset tonight knowing Beau here has a date. How long have you two known each other?"

"We met last week at his Virginia concert with XOXO."

Mitch gives Beau the eye, then turns back to me.

"So, you are from Virginia. I have family there myself. Oh, you are the woman from the concert. Are you a musician or singer?"

"No, I teach toddlers in a local community center."

"You must have a lot of patience."

"I hear that a lot."

"How did you catch the eye of this guy?"

"A dress." I feel Beau's thigh against mine and his fingers against my arm, when he intervenes.

"Yes. She was wearing an eye-catching watermelon red dress to be exact. We had lunch the next day, and we've been talking ever since."

"I'm getting a glimpse inside his world tonight, as he did mine today."

Mitch looks confused.

"Please elaborate."

I look over at Beau as he describes today.

"Amelia was surprised when I showed up at the center where she works, but she accepted my invitation to come to Nashville, and here we are."

"A new budding romance. I'm going to keep my eyes on the both of you, I feel this relationship is only going to grow."

"Thanks, Mitch."

When the session is over, we wait as Mitch holds up his finger covering the microphone.

"Was this the first time you both went public?"

"Yes, you got the exclusive. I've always admired your interview style and you've always been good to me in the past."

"Thanks." He reaches his hand over to Beau, then to me. "Amelia you will be fine with this guy, he's a good one."

"Thank you."

Beau pulls us away from Mitch's booth onto the next one. Cameras are flashing, and people are calling out his name. He leans in where only I can hear him.

"We just came out. How do you feel?"

"Surprisingly good."

We spend more time visiting booth after booth, then are off to a bigger party, and then the last party, which is over-the-top crazy. I see and meet so many country music singers that my cheeks hurt from smiling. Beau has been a wonderful date, keeping me by his side while making introductions.

We head back to the hotel about 2:00 in the morning, stopping at my room first. I lean against the door with my key in my hand, stalling not wanting to let him go just yet.

"Thank you. What an amazing night."

"I'm glad you accepted my invitation."

"Me too. I'm going in my room and get out of this dress."

He looks down at the carpet covering the floor. "Would you like to come over to my room?"

"You don't need to rest your voice?"

He takes the key, opening my door.

"We can watch a movie and just be quiet together."

"I'd like that. Just give me a few minutes."

CHAPTER 14

Amelia

I scramble to brush my teeth and loosely braid my hair, then slip into pajama shorts with a t-shirt. I rummage through my suitcase grabbing a travel wrap. All night Beau and I have been kissing, holding hands and talking about everything. We've covered so many years of our lives in such a short period of time. I find him totally irresistible and too good to be true. He has this confident way of handling every situation leaving me feeling safe and at ease. I grab my phone charger as well as the room key and head over to his room knocking one time, as the door opens and he's standing in cotton shorts and a t-shirt. *Would running into his arms, wrapping my legs around his waist and covering him in kisses be too much?*

"Hey, you, what took so long?"

"Sorry there was traffic." I brush off my joke.

As I walk by, I notice he's holding something in his hand.

"What's that?"

"Medicine for my throat. I have a routine at night to keep it healthy. For you I have a gift basket from the hotel. It's got good stuff in it. Want to see?"

"Does it have candy?"

"Take whatever you want."

I lay down my stuff then peek inside the basket, impressed. "It's all candy!"

"It is."

I take a bar of dark chocolate with nuts, and a bag of sour gummies. I hear him gargle in the bathroom as I open the bag popping in one candy.

"Beau, I need to tell you something before I lose my nerve."

He pokes his head out of the bathroom. "Should I be concerned?"

I sit on the edge of the bed. "No."

"Okay I'll be right out."

When he returns, he takes a seat next to me. "What's up?"

I take in a deep breath before starting. "There is something from my past I want you to know about."

"Okay."

"During my junior year of college, I met a baseball player who was a senior. His name was Chase Richardson, and he was a tall, quick first basemen. He had hopes of a pro career until the night of April 12, at a home game. A large guy from the visiting team plowed right over him at first base, and Chase shattered the elbow of his throwing arm. His college career ended that day and his pro career would never start. There were several surgeries and specialists, but he was never able to get the speed or the coordination back. Upon graduation that summer, he took a job working as a consultant for a travel ball team and rented an apartment in the city. When I was home for the summer, we were fine but when I went back for my senior year, things started to change.

I know he had a hard time accepting his new life, but I couldn't get him to talk to me or his parents about any of it. For Christmas break he asked me to spend time with him at his apartment, just the two of us. For three days he was the Chase I dated before his injury, which gave me hope he was doing better. He was sweet, we cooked meals together, and played video games. New Year's Eve we attended a party at Jordan's, and he saw two friends who had gone on to play professional ball. Seeing them ripped open his wound once again. I went back to school after winter break and he said he was applying for a new position with less travel. He said he wanted to see a doctor for medication, even seek out a therapist to help him get through his depression. I felt better that he was going to try.

By February he was calling less and when I did speak to him, he was preoccupied, agitated, and ended our calls quickly. He texted one day saying he was having a hard time adjusting to the dosage of his medicine. Another two weeks went by with even less conversation, so I drove into the city to his apartment one Friday to check on him. When I arrived, I used my key, letting myself in unannounced, only to find a huge mess in the apartment, and an unrecognizable smell lingering in the air. I called out his name but heard no response. He wasn't in the living room or the kitchen, so I went further in making my way down the hall finding him on the floor of his bedroom not moving. I shook him calling his name over and over; he was breathing but wouldn't wake up. So I called 911. While on the phone he opened his eyes but was clearly confused. In one quick move he stood up looking frantically around the room for something, and that's when he pulled out a knife from under the bed. It threw me off guard, why did he have a knife under his bed? What was he scared of? His pupils were huge, he was breathing heavy and was sweating. I stood up slowly trying to talk to him, taking two or three steps backwards, and that's when he lunged at me. I turned and ran, but he followed me. The force of the first stab grazed my arm but I kept running. When I reached the kitchen, he grabbed my shirt and I pulled away from him losing the hold he had on me, which sent me falling into the kitchen table then onto the floor. Stuff was falling around me, I screamed, and I tried to get up while fighting against each stab. I reached for anything I could get my hands on to stop him, when one knife stab took my breath away, and I blacked out."

"The fear you must have felt."

"I was terrified. He never said my name; I don't think he

knew it was me at all. He stabbed me seven times and five caused enough damage to keep me in the hospital for two weeks. I had surgery, then six weeks of physical therapy at home. I saw a counselor every week after getting out of the hospital, until three months ago. Now I see her when I need to talk. I see his face, the distant look in his eyes almost every day, but I keep moving forward becoming stronger inside and out. I also have a great family and friend support system."

"Sounds like a good mix to have when going through what you did."

"There is no substitution for family or friends who love you. I did something to remind myself every day of what I survived. I covered my scars with sea turtles, which represent long life and good luck." I pull up my shirt to show him five in the front and one on my side. Beau looks at each one, looking up at me for approval to touch them. I give him permission. He studies each one.

"What happened to Chase," he asks?

"He was in the same hospital as I was for a week, then he left to go to a rehab facility to detox and await trial. He was killed in a car accident on the way there. I never got the chance to see or speak to him again. I'm telling you because I feel you should know everything about me. I don't want something to come out and be a problem. It also keeps me guarded--at least until I met you."

He reaches for my hand. "Thank you for telling me and for trusting me."

"I don't want to go through my life questioning every man I meet. Chase was a good person who got lost and was unable to find his way back. He needed help and none of us knew how far he would go to find peace. The doctors said one day I might be triggered to remember more about that night but until that day, I refuse to let it consume me. You've changed everything for me."

"I like the way that sounds, but how?"

"You're open and honest about who you are, so I wanted to be the same with you. In one week, you've broken through a thick wall that protects me."

"This will stay with me, I will protect it, I will protect you. You have my word."

"Thank you."

He scoots back on the bed leaning against the headboard, patting the space next to him and I follow handing him the bag of gummies.

"Still want to watch a movie?"

"Still want to keep seeing me with my dark past?"

"Nothing will stop me from seeing you."

Wrapped in his arms and my secret out in the open, I feel lighter, I feel safe.

*

I leave about 5:30 in the morning to get some sleep before meeting for brunch at 10:30. I wear pixie style black pants with a floral top, and I put the final touches to my makeup when I hear a knock on the door. I sprint over to open it.

"Good morning," I gleefully say.

"Amelia, we need to talk about our new status."

"Did something happen, are we no longer a couple?"

"We are still very much a couple." He leans over kissing me. "Social media is buzzing with pictures of us and asking questions about you."

He hands over his phone and I scroll through what he's talking about.

"So, it begins."

"Are you still okay with the exposure?"

I hand back his phone. "I am; they are just curious."

"Good. Let's give them more to talk about."

CHAPTER 15

Beau

I didn't want her to leave my room this morning, but we both needed a few hours of sleep. She opened up to me about something very personal that happened in her life. Amelia was attacked, stabbed, and could've died, yet she walks around with a light in her eyes and continues to just look forward. I didn't get much rest after she left because when she's not with me my mind is busy thinking of ways to be with her.

At the interviews last night, we let it out that we are dating. I know what that can do to me, but for Amelia, I know her privacy won't be the same. The questions about us were handled last night but today and every day we are together, curiosities will rise—the downfall of being in the public eye. It's up to me to help guide her through the madness and do what's necessary to keep her safe.

*

We arrive downstairs to meet Jason, where we find him with his phone attached to his ear. The man works hard to make all this happen, but I do wish he would relax and maybe find someone. Listen to me. I sound like I'm in love and want him to feel the same. I look over at Amelia smiling and there goes that feeling. Maybe I am, I've never felt this strongly about a woman before. Could I be? Jason motions us over. I take another glance at Amelia. If this is love, then sign me up because right now she's the only woman I see.

"Well don't the two of you look like a hot summer day."

She looks at me, and I look at her, then at him.

"Dude, what?"

"Are you saying we look sweaty?" Amelia asks.

"No, oh sorry no I mean…"

She hooks her hand around his arm. "Jason, are you hungry?"

"How did you know?"

"Because your words are really messed up. Come on let's all get some food, hydrate, and enjoy the morning."

He pats her hand on his arm, and raises his eyebrow towards me.

I watch as he leads her to the car. Inside the car Jason fills us in on the plan for the morning. One spot, lots of food, and promotors taking pictures or short videos endorsing their products. Another waiting game for her, and test for me to stay focused on my job and not on the beauty next to me.

*

Breakfast includes a lot of laughter and stories from Jason about me. We aren't bothered by cameras as it is a private event. After breakfast we head over to the venue. I begin my rounds and by the third booth, I wave Amelia over to join me.

"Amelia, this is Charles Dewitt. He is the representative for Palmer Crackers."

She reaches over to shake his hand.

"Nice to meet you. My kids love your crackers."

"How many do you have?"

"Currently ten." He looks surprised.

"I teach toddlers at a community center."

"That part is good to know. Beau thought you might be interested in a program we host. Your center could receive free products if it meets the criteria. It takes just a little bit of time;

would they be interested?"

"Of course. How do they get started?"

"I can have information sent over to Beau's hotel room for you to take home. Everything they will need is in the packet."

"Thank you, Mr. Dewitt."

Beau extends his hand.

"Thanks Charles and I look forward to seeing the new promo. See you at the concert?"

"Of course, my daughter Salor is coming as an early birthday present. She is very excited. Nice to meet you Amelia."

"Nice to meet you. I'll keep my eye open for the packet."

Amelia tugs at my arm. "Thank you for the introduction. The kids love those crackers."

I try and speak but I need to clear my throat first. "Sorry about that."

"We stayed up late last night. All of the talking you've done and you still have a concert tonight. I have an idea. How about a nap? Your place or mine?"

"Very forward of you Ms. Mathews."

"So, you in?"

"I am."

"Good."

"My room?"

"Yes, because you have the candy basket."

"So, you like me for my candy?"

She steps in front of me. Her hand slides around the back of my neck pulling me down for a kiss. One that leaves me without a doubt how she feels about me.

"The candy is a perk, but you come first. Now, how many

more appearances do you have left?"

"None."

"Perfect. Can we leave?"

"Yes."

*

My alarm goes off, stirring her to stretch while squinting towards the light I turn on beside us.

"How much time do we have?"

"About two hours. I'm going to order some soup, what would you like?"

She sits up yawning.

"A salad with chicken. After we eat, I will go back to my room to give you some time to do what famous people do before appearing in front of thousands."

I roll over taking her with me as she giggles.

"I just drink tea and take a hot shower. Sexy huh?"

"Yes, actually. A guy with a cup of tea in his hands all wet from a hot shower, I'll take that visual."

"You are a witty girl."

I begin to tickle her, which leads us to falling off the bed shifting her shirt giving me a view of her tattoos. She's quiet as I trace over one with my finger. I look up at her then lower my head to kiss one, then another. Her belly retracts with the first, but then relaxes. I raise my head.

"They are amazing, just like the woman wearing them."

She places her hands on both sides of my face kissing me, then kisses my right cheek, then the left.

"We should probably order food."

"You're right."

She excuses herself to the bathroom, and I must remember why that intimate exchange didn't go any further. Respect. I want her comfortable, I don't want to push, and she should have as long as she needs to trust again. Our time will come.

CHAPTER 16

Amelia

Tonight's concert involves many singers who are allotted thirty minutes each to play. Beau's time is from 9:30 to 10:00 and it takes place on an outdoor stage right off music row. I don't have the alluring red dress from last weekend's concert, but I choose an off-the-shoulder red shirt with a pair of jeans and cowboy boots. This time I meet him at his door. He opens it and finds me tucking my ID and money into my back pocket.

"I thought red was fitting for our second concert together."

"You will have to wear red to each and every concert in the future."

"We'll have more?"

"I hope so. I have this backstage pass for you, and when I'm done performing, we have a meet and greet. After that we can go out and be tourist."

"Sounds exciting but how does that work?"

He shows me a t-shirt that says, "I love Nashville", then he holds up another one that says, "Hot Nashville Chicken" then two baseball caps.

"Are you in?"

"I am. This should be fun."

I wait with Beau backstage and when he goes out to perform, I make my way into the crowd in front of the stage, tucking the pass inside my pocket. I make friends with an exuberant group of girls. We are all bouncing up and down as they scream out Beau's name. He begins to sing his song, "Kicking Back" driving the noise level up a few more degrees. He spots me in the crowd and winks, sending a familiar warm feeling through me.

*

Sunday morning after the concert, brings a monster headache with an overall feeling of dread having to even open my eyes at this horrible hour. We went from bar to bar last night, drink to drink, and before I knew it, we were making out in the back of an Uber. I've never kissed as much as we kissed, and touching my lips with my fingers this morning reminds me of how much I enjoyed it. In the hall early this morning he went to his room and I went to mine, but it was a struggle to let him go. Beau sets off all the right buttons inside of me, but I need to be sure I'm ready. I've been with no one since Chase and didn't desire anyone in that way up till now, but I owe it to myself and to Beau to be sure. My phone buzzes as I scramble trying to find it. The floor lights up under the bed and I stretch trying to reach it until I fall out the bed onto the floor. I look at the screen, it's Jordan.

"Morning," I hoarsely say.

Jordan is screaming into the phone. I try and get a word in, but I can't. I finally scream back, "STOP!" while grabbing my head. "Please tell me what you are freaking out about."

"Shit, shit, shit. WTF Amelia. Have you seen any news programs or feeds today?"

"No, why?"

"You and Beau are everywhere in very hot embraces, kissing, and going into a hotel together. I'm so freaking happy and jealous. You are the new mystery girl on the arm of Beau Reston. What is going on with the two of you?"

"Slow down." I switch on the TV for the local Nashville news and then start scrolling through my phone. That's when I see it. Pictures of us in different bars, cuddled up together and yes going inside the hotel.

"Tell me, is he good in bed?"

"Jordan, no, we never..." There is a knock on my door. "Hold on." I walk over to find Beau leaning against the door. I open and wave him inside then peek out to see if anyone is in the hall. "Jordan let me call you back." I can still hear her screaming as I disconnect the call.

Beau looks hungover like I do, which probably means his throat is suffering. I pick up the phone and call for hot tea with honey and some food as he sits on the bed where I join him.

"We are the next best thing."

"Jordan told me then I saw it on my phone. They make our night seem tawdry."

"That's their business. Get pictures, make money. Maybe I let it out to soon."

I put my head between my legs feeling a wave of nausea.

"It's fine."

"It's not." He rubs circles over my back.

"The last time I was in the news was after my attack." The rubbing stops and the weight of my words are felt by him. I raise up leaning into his arm. "Some of the pics are pretty steamy."

He holds his head with his hand. "My brother sent me a text wanting to know who the new hottie was in the pictures."

"Seriously? Is this how it has always been for you?"

"It's been more frequent since I turned 21. Photographers would unexpectedly show up at any little or big event day or night. It got bad when a story broke about our backup singer, Ginger and me."

"Ginger?"

"Yeah, they had us dating, then married in secret when she got pregnant."

"Wait I remember reading that when I was stalking your social media accounts."

"It didn't scare you off?"

"No, I throw no stones."

"She was seeing Alden Rich, a promotor who was married at the time. He denied it at first in hopes to save his marriage I'm thinking, but he finally decided to step up and take responsibility. It cleared my name but ended his marriage. Alden and Ginger along with their twin girls, Scarlet and Reece now live in Florida."

"Oh."

"I'm not interesting at all when I am away from this business. When I'm off, I sleep, hunt, and fish. I enjoy various sports and grilling for my family. It makes me sound boring, but it's true."

"No, it sounds wonderful." My nose brushes against his arm. "I'm fine so don't worry about me. Will you stay while I shower?"

"Yes. I will get the food when it arrives."

I smile. "My treat."

*

We were promised an easy get-out-of-the-hotel-free card with extra security this morning, but fans always find a way to the people they love. Beau signed a few autographs, and then we left. I was taking a flight back home, and he was heading to New York tomorrow. We said our goodbyes in the car and he promised to be back in Virginia to see me in three weeks. He made me promise to clear the whole weekend so we could just hang out at my house with Poppy, which I happily agreed to. Sitting on the plane waiting to take off, I was reliving the past few days with only the sound of his voice through my ear buds, and I realized I miss him already.

I call Jordan to meet me at the airport, which she did because she wanted the scoop on my weekend. We pull up to my house about 7:30 in the evening. She let me out and as I walk towards the porch, I hear something to the right of me. I look but see nothing, so I proceed to put my key in the door knowing I wouldn't retrieve Poppy from my grandparent's until tomorrow. I hear the noise again, like bumping against the fence but I see nothing. I wave at Jordan after cutting on my light inside then lock the door. Looking into my living room I get a sense of emptiness. No Poppy, no Beau.

*

The next morning was like every Monday during summer hours at the center. I get up, dress in my khaki shorts and t-shirt, then throw my bathing suit into my bag because today is swim day for the toddlers. I pull up to the center and notice a police car without the flashing lights. Clearly no emergency, but what?

I grab my backpack and head to the front door when I'm met by an officer and my director, Mrs. Steele.

"Amelia thank god you are alright."

"What's going on?"

"We had some uninvited guests in the parking lot this morning."

"Who?"

"Miss Mathews," says the police officer next to her. "Were you home last night?"

"Yes."

"Did you notice anything unusual?"

"What is this all about?"

Mrs. Steele interrupts. "Pictures were posted Friday by a teacher whose name I will not say at this time. The pictures got out to the parents, which concerned them about the safety of their children, and then there was the announcement of you dating Beau Reston this weekend."

"So, you're saying I had something to do with the unwanted guest here at the center?"

Mrs. Steele touches my arm pulling me close to her. "Photographers were here in the parking lot waiting for you. I had to call the police."

I look at the officer. "I don't want anyone being affected by this, or the parents feeling their children are unsafe here. What do you suggest?"

Officer Banks speaks first. "I've informed Mrs. Steele that we spoke with the men, had them vacate the property, and posted a squad car nearby for a while. It might not be enough to deter them, so call us if they return."

Mrs. Steele moves in to shake their hands walking them to their cars. Before clocking in, I send a text to Beau letting him know that our new status has now resulted in the center having unwanted press on the premises.

I wait for Mrs. Steele to return.

"Amelia, I don't think this will be the last time we see them." She pulls me into her office and shuts the door so no one else can hear us. "With that being said, how was it, the weekend, Beau? I mean you went from preschool teacher to being on the arm of one of the cutest singers I've seen in a while, and he's so nice."

I'm beaming like a toddler on ice cream day, but I can't help it.

"He's amazing and he makes me smile all over. Am I moving too fast?"

She's shaking her head back and forth.

"Do you like him for who he is without all the fame?"

"Yes, he's wonderful. I only care about the fame when something like today happens. I told him about my attack. Maybe I'm in over my head."

She's looking at me with that motherly kind of expression when I realize what I was doing. She picks up on it and immediately chimes in.

"Don't."

"Don't what?"

"Amelia, you have worked here with me for some time now, and I've watched you grow into one of my best teachers, a leader and a warrior when it comes to keeping the kids safe. I've been here watching you heal from a devastating assault. Just give into how you are feeling. Look he's been dealing with these kinds of things for years, let him help you. Don't worry about who was in the parking lot this morning, I have the police on it." She hugs me. "Now I need you to get to your room. I see Maria is here."

"Thank you."

"I'm here whenever you need to talk."

"I know."

CHAPTER 17

Beau

I can't believe I have to wait until she goes to lunch to find out more about her text. I was so stupid to allow the press or anyone else know about her so fast. They are quick to act; I should've been more careful. She doesn't need this kind of attention to stir up a past memory or make her uncomfortable.

Jason comes in handing me a cup of tea.

"I have to say that she is different from the kind of girls you usually have on your arm."

"You mean the women who are *put* on my arm. Hell, Jason I've not been interested in or picked someone on my own in quite some time. I kind of forgot what it's like to be so open and honest with a woman."

"So, you're ready?"

I look out the window of the bus and smile. "I am. She has inspired three songs in one week and has taken possession of my heart." I clear my throat then drink the hot tea.

"You need to see the doctor before that gets worse. The visit won't take long; are you good if I call for an appointment in New York?"

"Sure, set it up."

"I will. Now no talking. Dreaming of Amelia is permitted, however."

*

I sit in my room alone on the bus drinking broth, when

Amelia calls. She explains to me what happened at the Center but says everything is fine, however, I don't think it's over either. Her voice makes me want to see her, so I ask to FaceTime. She tries to fight me due to the pool day, but I'm persistent. When the phone switches over, I see her smacking her lips together, evening out the product she just applied. She's embarrassed when she catches me looking at her.

"Tell me the words to the new song."

I try but start to cough.

"I feel bad I might have played a part in your throat being irritated."

"Come on, no regrets. It was the perfect weekend."

"I have a special tea recipe that one of my co-workers suggested. She says it might help with the irritation. Do you want me to send it to you?"

"No. I'd rather you bring it to me. Or I can come and get it from you."

"I'm serious."

"I am too, but I'll text you the address of the hotel so you can send me the tea."

"Sounds good. I need to get back to work. No talking to anyone." She blows me a kiss then my screen goes blank.

*

I was hoping to clear my throat of whatever has taken it over before calling her, but it is still not better yet. I throw back two pain relievers when I try her at about 9:00 pm. She answers the phone, clearly out of breath.

"Hi."

"Hello."

"Beau, you don't seem any better."

"I have a doctor's appointment tomorrow. Why are you out of breath?"

"Poppy needed a bathroom break, which lead to her not wanting to come inside. I tried treats but she was real interested in staying in the yard, so I chased her hoping not to miss your call. I'm making blue gelatin (ocean water) with gummy fish. So, you get front row seating while I mix."

"I can just watch?"

"Oh, you like to watch, huh?"

"Depends." She shoots her eyes at the phone with a half grin.

"I will be sure you see everything."

She props the phone up on the counter while she dumps out the boxes and begins to mix. When she's done, I see her open and shut the fridge, then the phone falls. She picks it up.

"Sorry Beau, I moved the bowl. I'm all done." She cuts off the light, then walks down the hall to her room.

"Your phone is sending a lot of friend requests."

"Your fans really want to know about me. Do you think they will soon forget?"

I shake my head no.

"That's what I thought."

We continue our conversation into the bathroom where I get my normal perch while she brushes her teeth. She picks up the phone as we travel over to her bed. Pulling down the covers, I can see white sheets with a floral blanket. She holds the phone up in front of her.

"Ready for bed?"

"Is that an invite?"

She hesitates, giving me hope she wants me there with her. "You need to rest and relax your throat."

"This is true."

"I'm going to say goodnight."

"Let me know how the project goes."

"I will. Thanks for watching me mix."

"Hot, so hot."

CHAPTER 18

Amelia

Today the temperature outside was abnormally warm, so this morning all the kids were outside playing. As I make my way to our playground, I'm met by six toddlers wanting hugs with plenty to tell me. I begin by taking roll and checking with the current teacher on the playground for any special instructions or concerns from the parents. There are big plastic puzzles close to the fence line, and it's one of their favorite spots to chat. Another student arrives, so I head to the gate to say good morning, when I hear a scream from behind me. I look to see a guy hanging over the fence with a camera that falls to the ground. I run towards the children assessing each one, then I send them inside with the other students and teachers. I run back to the man on the fence.

"What is wrong with you? Is getting a story more important than the safety of these children? What if you had hit one of them?"

"You're Amelia Mathews, right?"

"Get off the fence."

"Come on Amelia, meet me after work today, give me a chance to tell everyone who you are. What do you say?"

"No!" I pick up the dropped camera and begin to pull out the film."

"Please don't do that. It's how I feed my kids."

"What if one of these kids were your kid? No story is worth hurting them."

"You're right and I'm sorry if I scared the kids, it's just that Beau is popular with a large fan base who want to know about you. Getting the story out before anyone else will pay off my student loans." He reaches for his empty camera. "Please may I have my camera back?"

"Don't come here again."

"What about the story?"

"Go away!"

He disappears as Mrs. Steele makes it to the playground. He's right, this kind of behavior will not stop until they get the story they want. I climb the fence to be sure he's gone.

"I called the police; did he leave?"

"I'm so sorry. How are the kids?"

She notices my panic and grabs my arms.

"They are fine; no one was injured."

"This is all my fault."

"No, it's not. Come inside. You will need to speak with the police about what you saw."

I close my eyes fighting back tears. "I'm so sorry. That man was here because of me. What if more show up?"

Her arm is around my shoulder. "We will figure out something."

I walk away, feeling the heavy responsibility of this situation, thinking about the safety of my kids, and knowing this won't stop even if they do learn more about me. I spend the next 20 minutes going over what happened with the police, then they speak with the other teachers and one parent who was dropping off at the time. I return to my classroom trying to make the rest of the morning a good one-- flooding my students with music, centers, and my ocean sensory project. They've forgotten what happened earlier, but I'm still a little on edge. I want them to play "Catch a Bubble" after naptime, so I head out to the store on my lunch break to buy bubbles. The parking lot outside the center seemed quiet, nothing unusual, so maybe the guy understood the severity of his actions and he won't be back.

*

I arrive at the store and park my car looking around before getting out and when I feel comfortable no one is going to surprise attack me, I proceed to the store. I pass a few cars and a delivery truck, when I'm abruptly stopped by several people with cameras. My stunned reaction gives them a few photos before I pick up my pace, almost running into an oncoming car that was coming to a stop in front of the store. The car blows its horn and I apologize. I run inside and bump up against a security guard. When I glance back the photographers are gone, but I'm still holding onto the shirt of the security guard.

"Miss, are you alright?"

I look around shaking my head and answering, no. He asks me to follow him over to the manager's office where I am given a bottle of water, and I explain what happened. Once calm I make my purchase, and the security guard follows me to the car.

Back at the center, I once again start looking around to see if the next ambush is near, but luckily no one was around. I sit in my car for another ten minutes with hopes to pull myself together and start to think back on the day I left the hospital after the attack. I was in pain, and I'd just learned of Chase's death. I sat in the car with tears streaming down my face, waiting for my father to get in on the driver's side. He notices right away and covers my hands with his. "Breath in and out, Peanut, it will get easier," he said.

I take in a deep breath and blow it out. I repeat the action once more. I squeeze my eyes together not wanting to cry. Maybe I'm not ready for this kind of relationship if it means I'll have cameras around all the time. I need some time to think. I grab my things and head back into work.

After dinner, instead of going outside and playing with Poppy, we stay inside, shutting ourselves off from the outside world. I jump at every little sound and look out my window as lights pass by my house, wondering if a vehicle will stop. I try drinking a glass of wine, but it does nothing for this uneasy feeling. I text Beau around 11:30 telling him I wasn't feeling well and that I would speak to him tomorrow. It was the first night in a long time I slept with my light on all night.

*

Waking up the next morning having gotten very little sleep, I realize Beau is the best person for me to talk to. I figure he's been dealing with this kind of thing for over ten years, so he might be able to help me. I will call my therapist before going to work in hopes of getting an appointment today to try and squash this uneasy feeling. About 6:30 in the morning before leaving for work, I text to see if he is up. He calls back immediately.

"Amelia, how are you feeling?"

"I'm okay, it's just yesterday a photographer tried to get pictures of me. He was hanging over the fence at the center. He scared the kids when he dropped his camera, and the police were called for the second time. Then at lunch, I went to the store where a few of them tried to get more pictures, yelling questions at me. I stepped out in front of a car that was stopping near me. I was so preoccupied that I didn't see it. I kept hearing sounds last night and jumping up to check lights from cars. Beau, I need to..."

"Please don't say it."

"I don't know what else to do. The parents are upset about the incident at the center, and I get it because I would be too. I don't think they will stop even if I tell them more about myself or about our relationship. Tell me what to do to make them back off."

"I can post that we aren't dating."

I feel like the wind has just been knocked out of me, and I shut my eyes hoping for the right words, but I guess this could be the answer.

"It could work. You are on tour with a ton of scheduled appearances. Maybe it's not a good time for us to physically see each other. My job ends at the end of July, until then we just talk over the phone. Maybe you can announce we aren't seeing each other, and they will lose interest in me keeping the Center off their radar. What do you think?"

"I don't like it, but I can't be selfish. It could work."

"My feelings for you have not changed. I'm not giving up on us."

"I understand."

"You don't sound convinced."

"I hate that we have to do this, but I want you to be okay. I will do what you ask."

"Time apart won't change us."

"I'm going to hold you to that." He sighs. "It's only for a short time. I will do everything on my end to make it work, but don't believe what you might hear on social media."

"I won't."

"I'll speak with Jason and make a few social media comments about us later."

"Okay. I'm sorry to put restrictions on us, but…"

"I still want to spend time with you, even if it's just over the phone."

"You got it."

*

One week later...

Being a teacher is what I've always dreamed of; it's where my focus has been for years. Cultivating young minds, seeing the wonder on their faces when they learn something new, it's what motivates me. One week has passed since our new arrangement started, and I don't like it. I put limits on this relationship, and I want to take it all back. Celebrities meet and fall for non-celebrities all the time and it works out. I'm allowing my past to hold me back when I should be fighting for what makes me happy, even if it means a new direction for my life. I need help to be sure I'm heading in the right direction, so I call Jordan. We decide to meet on Thursday at my house for a dinner of shrimp and grits, and she requests bourbon for my therapy session.

*

Thursday has arrived, and as I put the seasoning on the shrimp, my phone alerts me to a message. It's Beau telling me to look at a video online. I find it and a familiar sensation moves over me, as well as a few properly placed tingles. It's him, singing a new song called, "All You". I text him back when the song is over, telling him how much I love it, and that I miss him. He sends back a drawing of two musical notes forming a heart. This distance relationship is hard, but I hope to find a resolution tonight.

*

Jordan and I eat, while sipping bourbon, when she informs me that what I'm doing is admirable in trying to protect the kids, but wonder if it would be easier for me to just quit my job. She also reminds me of how far I've come since my attack, that I'm stronger and can handle the press or whatever comes my way. Her words set comfortably in my brain as I begin to work out details. My therapist said I need to prioritize, and right now I want to make Beau number one on my list.

I go to bed that night with Jordan curled up next to me talking in her sleep. Looking over Beau's schedule, I'm trying to find a hole in it so that I can surprise him. Then, I remember the few days he has off in July. My vacation with the girls is also in July, which is a trip we take annually. Would my friends be okay if we all go together? I send off a text to Sophia and Lily. They chime in immediately. There will be some details to work on, but I think we can make this happen. The first text will be to Jason then, "Operation surprise Beau" just might have a shot. I grab my computer to start researching my plan, and with each email my excitement builds.

Two people can fall in love during all kinds of situations. Wait, I said love. It *is* love. I state the next words in my head, only for me. *I LOVE BEAU RESTON!*

CHAPTER 19

Beau

"No, I won't."

Jason comes over to me as the doctor excuses himself from the room. This is a second visit to a doctor in the last two weeks.

"You don't have a choice. Look, I know you want to meet with Amelia but if the biopsy turns up something, then you will need surgery which could put you out of commission for weeks."

"I heard what the doctor said."

I stand up, walking around the desk, looking out the window. It's raining in North Carolina today, making my current situation heavier than it already is.

"I've been steady at this since I was 14, and I am grateful for everyone who has helped me succeed." I take off my hat rubbing my head. "This time things are different, though."

"I know. Tell me what you want to do."

"Get the biopsy scheduled for tomorrow if you can." I say with a sense of urgency in my voice.

"If you need surgery, I will need to notify the label."

"Yes, but I'm not telling them anything until we know more. I want to tell Amelia and my family in person if it's cancer."

"You don't want to call her about the biopsy?"

I sit in a chair holding my head with my hands. "I'm not going to lie. I'm scared, but she's been through so much. I just want to be sure what I'm up against."

He nods his head accepting my wishes, then leaves to find the doctor. Can this be the end of my singing career? I look down at the floor trying to steady the flow of thoughts in my mind. No one is ever ready to hear that word from a doctor, but I just did, I could have cancer.

*

Jason...

Standing outside the doctor's office, I lean against the wall for support. It hit me hard, the words from the doctor, and Beau's grip on his chair. He's like my younger brother, and no one needs to face this alone. He's right, I'm his friend first, his manager second. I seek out Dr. Bishop, letting him know we want the biopsy. He makes a call then confirms the time. I pull out my phone and punch in the number. As the voice on the other end answers, I fill her in on what will happen tomorrow, she calmly responds, "I'll be there."

I've known for a while how he feels about Amelia, but there was no hesitation on her part about coming out here, which tells me she feels the same. She is what he needs, and I'm going to make this all work.

*

While Jason is gone, I decide to FaceTime Amelia. I just need to see her. She connects immediately and is wearing a blue faded shirt with paint smeared on her cheek. Her blue eyes look straight into my soul, so I try hard to hide what I'm really feeling.

"Hello handsome."

"I like the paint, new look?"

She rubs her palm across her cheek then smiles. "Embarrassing."

"No, I like it. What's the project?"

"I'm painting a cabinet for the living room, but I took a break to eat one of your favorite summertime treats." She shows me a bowl of watermelon balls.

"They look delicious."

"You know we have about eleven days left before we will see each other in person."

"Believe me--I have an alarm set on my phone."

"You are so romantic. You know you could probably write a song about that and make the girls swoon even harder for you. Oh, Poppy found a snake in the yard last night."

"What did she do with it?"

"She played with it until it slithered out under the fence."

"What did you do?"

"I let it leave in hopes it won't return." I hear the door fly open and her grandfather's voice. "Beau, I need to go, can I call you later tonight?"

"Of course. Tell Sid hi for me."

"I will. Are you okay?"

"Yeah, I just can't wait to see you in person."

"Eleven days and I'm all yours." She blows me a kiss then disconnects.

*

I disconnect with Beau only to immediately receive a call from Jason. He fills me in on Beau's doctor's visit. I don't hesitate to agree with everything he says, then I hang up to talk with my grandfather. Then it all becomes clear to me, and I call the director of the Center and put in for an indefinite leave of absence.

CHAPTER 20

Amelia

My flight leaves at 1:00 in the morning and Jason has set up a room for me across from Beau's. When he leaves for the biopsy, I will be there to go with him. He doesn't want anyone to know about the procedure until there is more information, but Jason felt I needed to be here. I'm grateful he did. Beau has left an imprint on my heart and put life back into the part of me I thought was gone forever. I want to show him just how much he means to me.

My grandfather is taking me to the airport, so I need to hurry because he'll be at my house to pick me up in 15 minutes. Waiting for him, thoughts of my parents enter my mind. We used to talk about everything, but now we barely speak. I want to tell them I've fallen in love and how wonderful Beau is, but I can't. They've distanced themselves from me and I don't know why. All I *do* know is that Beau's the man I want, and I'm prepared to fight alongside him through all the challenges we might encounter.

*

Getting up this morning, I felt oddly calm. This has to be a good sign that Beau will be okay. I shower and slip on a sundress with a red ribbon that details the high waist, and then I grab a sweater. I have five minutes to knock on his door before he leaves, and I refuse to be late. Quietly shutting the door to my room, I wait in the long hallway outside his door, while the next four minutes just drag. When his door finally opens, and he sees me; everything I did to be here was worth it. His arms are around me in seconds, and I hold him just as tight. He pulls back to look at me running his thumb across my cheek, then kisses me.

"Happy to see me?"

"You have no idea."

"I hope you don't mind Jason calling me."

"I'm grateful. Thank you for coming."

"We need to be downstairs per Jason's explicit orders. You ready?"

"I am now."

I kiss him, wanting to take away any concerns he might have, but I just hold on tight to his hand, letting him know he's not alone. Walking with our arms pressed together, we make our way to the elevator and down through the kitchen and out the back door. Jason is waiting inside the car. I wink at him then Beau addresses Jason.

"Thank you for calling her."

"You need our support; let us help you through this."

"I will."

*

I wait with Beau until he has to leave, but when it was time for them to take him for the biopsy, I couldn't hold back my tears. He kisses my hand and groggily says, "I love you." I repeat the words to him in hopes he will hear them and the double doors close. The whole procedure was to take only a couple hours and we are sent to a waiting room down the hall for a little more privacy as Jason finds coffee.

"Here. You need this just like I do."

I reach for the cup of coffee. "Thank you."

He sits next to me. "He's going to be fine."

I reach for his hand. "He will."

"You are all he talks about, you know."

"I didn't, but you can share if you want."

"No way. I'm sure in the next two days while he's resting his voice, you two will have lots to text about."

"We've talked a lot on the phone these past few weeks. I never wanted to stop seeing him, I just needed time to figure things out."

"He knew that."

"Thank you for helping with the vacation plans."

"He'll be excited to know he has you for a week on a beach, but I guess that depends on today's outcome."

Jason gets up and walks over to a table of bottled water then slams his hands onto the table knocking over some bottles. I go to him placing my hand on his back to comfort him. He turns and I see tears in his eyes. He tries to speak but can't, and I wrap my arms around him. We stand together like this as our tears fall and prayers are spoken.

About three and half hours after Beau left, Dr. Bishop comes in to talk with us. He explains due to the location of a lump on the right side of Beau's throat, he had to take extra precaution not to damage the vocal cord. He felt that the mass was benign, but the test results will determine if more procedures or treatments will be necessary. He gave us explicit instructions for him not to talk and get plenty of rest. Beau will have to have regularly scheduled visits for a while and be given tools to keep his voice from suffering problems in the future. We are called back twenty minutes later to sit with him while the anesthesia wears off.

Beau's discharge nurse comes in to go over instructions, while he is starting to wake up.

She hands the packet to Jason, then turns to Beau. "Now,

you need to do exactly as the doctor ordered; we need to keep that voice of yours in top condition. Do you understand?"

He shakes his head in agreement, while smiling at me. She looks at him then at me.

"I knew you two weren't done."

"No, we've just begun," I say.

After he's given the okay to leave, he sits in a wheelchair as Jason pulls the car around. He asks me for his phone and begins to type when my phone pings. I read his text and giggle.

"We can do one, two and four, but number three will have to wait until you recover." He kisses my hand.

Inside the car Beau sits with a goofy smile on his face and a tight grip on my hand. Jason and I talk while he just looks between the two of us. Taking in a deep breath, he exhales grabbing his neck, then holds up his hand that it's okay.

We enter his hotel room where he changes out of jeans and into shorts. I order up some doctor-approved liquid choices because he is hungry. Jason excuses himself, leaving us alone to get some much-needed rest. Beau is sitting on the sofa and pats the space next to him. I sit and he leans over kissing the top of my head.

He types on his phone. "*I've missed touching you.*"

"I surprised you, didn't I?" His eyes widen and his arms stretch out, nodding his head. "You could have called me."

He types, "*I know, I didn't want you to worry, plus we had an agreement.*"

"Which was necessary but no longer needed. I'm sorry I got scared about all the things that could've happened. If it's okay with you our agreement is over."

He claps then types. "*I wanted you to be alright and would have done whatever was needed.*"

"I know. I'm here because I can't be anywhere you are not. I love you."

He types. *"I love you too."* He pulls me closer to him as we get cozy and wait for room service. He begins to type again. *"I wish I could kiss you properly."*

"We will in time. I'm not going anywhere."

Room service comes and when we are done eating, I ask if he is tired. He makes a motion with his thumb and pointer letting me know *a little.*

"Naptime it is."

He types. *"Will you join me?"*

"As long as you behave. I don't need you straining."

His eyebrows dance up and down, which makes me giggle.

*

He's asleep with his hand resting across my stomach and for the first time since leaving the hospital, I think about today. He's a songwriter, but the words he writes are brought to life by his voice. Beau is a natural storyteller and a wonderful entertainer. I slide down in the bed gently putting my hand on his not wanting to wake him. He's mine. I can feel it, as I am his and whatever the diagnosis is, I'm right where I need to be.

After waking from our nap, he takes another pain pill and we play chess while we wait for dinner to arrive. Jason comes by to join us, but he's been on his phone most of the time.

"Maybe you need a break from your phone for a couple of days. What is so important?"

"I have to respond to emails, requests from promotors and marketing. Beau's popularity right now has soared off the charts. The new songs are powerful, fun and filled with emotion. Companies want him to be their spokesperson; events want him in their lineup. I have a few requests from fans for him to sing at their weddings in September and two more marriage proposals today."

I jump up going over to him. "May I see?"

Beau sits back, shaking his head holding his hands up towards Jason in an attempt to ask him why. I flip through Jason's phone, seeing everything.

"I've seen proposals before, but I never realized how often he gets them." I look over at Beau. "Do you answer them yourself?"

He shakes his head yes.

"We've always believed to be a great singer you start with being a great person and being good to the people around you who brought you this far. Beau has always wanted to tend to his own social media. He hasn't posted in a couple of days, and the regular followers are waiting, so they are posting all kinds of concerns."

I hand the phone back to Jason and glance over at Beau.

"Do you want to post today?"

He picks up his phone and waves me over. I join him on the sofa. He types.

"*Will you be in the picture with me?*"

"Of course."

He pulls me close, snapping a photo. He checks it then hands it to me for approval.

"Try again." This time I tuck myself even closer to him. He prepares to take the picture, when I raise up to kiss his cheek. He snaps the picture then shows it to me. We both shake our heads as he gives it a caption. He turns his phone to show it to me; I smile and tell him to go for it. When I get the ding on my phone, I give it a few minutes before looking at it. The picture leaves no doubt that I'm back with him, especially with the caption, "In good hands with Amelia".

I look over at Jason. "Good?"

"Excellent. Now watch it blow up for the next hour with questions. Thanks guys, thanks a lot."

Beau and I start laughing, but know it is true. Everyone will want to know more about us. I don't mind because the word "us" means everything to me.

CHAPTER 21

Beau

Amelia is lying beside me and it's not the dream that I've had on repeat for weeks, she's real. I notice she smiles in her sleep, which leaves me to wonder just what it is that she is smiling about. I move her hair away from her ear, revealing three tiny earrings adorning the upper part. I notice her arm with the tiny mark where she was grazed during the attack. I had to let her go until she was ready, but now that she's back, I know I never want to be without her.

I lay back on my pillow thankful to have her, yet feeling anxious about my diagnosis because I am worried that today could put an end to my singing career. Dr. Bishop feels fairly certain it's not cancer, but I can't just go on that, I need assurance. I get out of bed and walk to the bathroom for a shower. I look back at Amelia, knowing I will get through whatever comes my way today because of her, Jason, and my family. Today's results could affect a lot of people, especially the band members. Looking in the mirror I realize no one is exempt from bad news, but how its handled is up to the individual. Amelia is a perfect example, and an example I want to follow.

As I'm drying off, I hear a faint knock on the bathroom door. Wrapping the towel around my waist, I open the door. Amelia's eyes fall to the towel but come back up to meet mine quickly. She clears her throat.

"Good morning, feeling better?"

I nod, yes.

"I'm going to my room to shower and change. How about

breakfast when I return?"

I walk past her to get my phone and type out my response.

"Did you sleep?"

"I did." She glances in the mirror touching her face. "Why do I look tired?"

I type. *"No, but you seem restless this morning."*

She raises her left eyebrow letting me know she's on to me, then she swats at my side making me jerk. I play like it hurts.

"Oh, I'm sorry."

I begin to type. *"No just playing. Do you know you smile while sleeping? It's damn cute."*

"No, I've never been told that."

I type. *"It probably only happens when you're beside me."*

"I will agree with that. I'm going to shower; think about what you want for breakfast." She goes to pull away, when I catch her arm turning her to me. That's when I sign, "I love you."

She says the words to me. Her voice, those words--nothing is better than that in my book.

*

Jason walks into the room as I sit strumming my guitar. I nod hello.

"Amelia gone?"

I stop to type. *"To shower."*

"Didn't invite you?"

I type. *"Asshole."* He belts out a sound that makes me stare at him. Then I type, *"You are a funny guy."*

He takes a seat. "She really cares about you."

I nod in agreement.

Jason continues, "She came here without any reservations. What's it been, about a month, month and a half since you guys started talking?"

I type. "*It feels damn good being able to touch her and hear her in person.*" I put down my guitar making my way over to grab a bottle of water.

"I heard her say I love you yesterday."

I touch my chest and mouth, me too.

"For you, was it the drugs?"

I type. "*Nope it's real. I'm in love with her.*"

"I'm happy for you both."

I take a seat next to him in the chair and begin to type. "*I just wish I'd said it without being under anesthesia.*"

"I'm sure she felt every word."

I smile. Then type. "*Today could change everything for me and so many others.*"

"It could, but let's wait and see what Dr. Bishop has to say before we get crazy."

I type. "*I've been thinking about it. No matter what he tells me today, I want to make some changes.*"

"Like what?"

I type. "*Writing and singing have been all I ever wanted. Hearing my songs on the radio and traveling to so many different places has been an amazing opportunity that I've never once taken for granted.*"

"But."

I type. "*But sharing my time with the people I love needs to come first.*"

"So, we might need to make a label change, freeing you from the constraints of a contract. We've talked about it before;

maybe now is the time for that conversation. I don't want you giving up, we don't know anything yet."

I type. "*I'm not giving up. I just want to make changes. One life, do it right.*"

He smiles. "Words to live by. Your grandfather did just that, and so will you."

CHAPTER 22

Amelia

Back in my room I drink from a bottle of water, and in my mind, I run through different outcomes for today. I believe he will be okay and will continue to pursue the career he wants. I repeat the words three more times. I sit on the side of the tub. We both said, I love you. Three small words that sing to my soul. I turn on the water, letting it heat up, slipping out of the clothes I slept in last night, when my phone pings. It's Beau and he's trying to FaceTime me. I cover with a towel and answer.

"Can't wait to see me, can you?"

He's on the other end smiling while pushing Jason out of the view of the phone. I hold my breath because I think he just flipped over a chair. I can hear him scrambling to get back up. Jason pops back into the picture.

"Sorry Amelia, someone was being impatient."

"It's fine, give me about 20 minutes. We're still cool on time, right?"

Jason looks at Beau who is giving the most adorable pout. He points to his stomach that he's hungry, then he winks at me, and I give in immediately.

"Okay, you win, fifteen minutes. Now let me go, the clock is ticking."

I shut down my phone. One short shower, a quick blow dry and I've got three minutes to spare. I hear the knock and run over to open the door, seeing both men. "Wait." I remember the most important part. I grab a pair of plastic watermelon-shaped glasses putting them on. Beau smiles and Jason looks confused.

"Watermelon red is our good luck."

Beau leans in kissing my cheek. *I would dress as a watermelon if it would guarantee good news for him today.* Jason interrupts.

"We need to go if we are going to eat. Ready?"

Beau takes my hand, and I grab my bag. "Let's go."

*

Beau is still on soft foods, so he has broth with warm tea. We are to arrive at the doctor's office by 10:00 and when we pull up, we see people outside holding up signs of well wishes. We also spot a few cameras. How the press or the fans find out the exact location of something so personal blows my mind, but they do.

Out on the sidewalk we aren't rushed. Everyone sees him get out of the car and they give him the respect that's needed this morning. He smiles as he passes each one. It's a touching tribute to how much they care about him.

Once inside Dr. Bishop's office, we find him seated behind his desk with a rather thick folder in front of him. He stands, greeting us.

"Good morning. Please come in. Beau, may I speak openly in front of everyone?"

He nods, yes. He motions for me to sit next to him, then points to another chair asking Jason to join us. Once we're all seated, Dr. Bishop begins.

"Beau, during the biopsy I removed a small tumor and a sample was sent for testing. I felt positive it was benign and pathology confirmed it. No cancer was present."

Beau turns, hugging me, kissing my cheek then he turns and hugs Jason. He excitedly looks around until he finds what he needs. He writes on a pad in front of him. "Can I talk?"

"No, not yet. You are a singer, so I'm going to ask that you not talk for three more days and then come back in for a follow-up where together we can test your voice. I want to be sure you are healed completely."

He types a text to Jason then asks him to read it. He thanks Dr. Bishop for taking such great care of him. He also wants to thank the staff for their professionalism. The doctor stands, extending his hand to Beau.

"You are most welcome. Follow the instructions for your recovery and you will be back to singing in no time. Nice to meet you all."

He stands and leaves. It's just the three of us and Beau turns to me.

I put my arms around him, hugging him as tight as I can. "You are okay. I'm so happy you are okay." He cups my face giving me a kiss, and I can feel the tension flow out through our kiss. He turns to Jason shaking his hand.

"I knew you were good," Jason says. Both men exchange a grateful smile.

Beau grabs the note pad then turns it to us.

"Time for a vacation?"

Jason shakes his head in agreement. "I will send out a message to the band and the label. An announcement will need to be made to the public about the cancellation of Friday's event.

Beau turns to me and types. *"Do you need to go back home?"*

"No, I'm good to stay." He has no idea we will be leaving for Folley Beach in South Carolina on Sunday--a surprise I will keep for now.

*

When all is done, we leave to discuss the next few days but

not before getting ice cream to celebrate. The first call is to his parents, and Jason reassures them Beau is fine, but Beau's mom wants to talk to him, or rather talk and he listen. The next call is to the label where Jason fills them in on the results of the biopsy and that they need to find a date to set up a new concert to accommodate Friday's cancellation. Then Beau posts to social media and the response is crazy, blowing up his feed. His fans show their support of him over and over.

The plan for the beach is that Beau and I will arrive two days earlier than my girlfriends, giving the two of us time to just be alone. Jason will come the day after the girl's arrival, and the band members are to arrive on Wednesday. Our two worlds are getting ready to meet on a beach and I can't wait.

On the last night before his follow-up visit with Dr. Bishop, I decide to fill him in on our covert beach getaway. It is about 10:30 p.m., and he is reading over some papers Jason had delivered earlier before dinner.

*

"Beau. We, need to talk."

He lays the papers down on the sofa waiting for me.

"One night during our 'break' I had dinner with Jordan, and I made some decisions. I then called Jason and he helped me with some plans and secured a vacation house on Folley Beach in South Carolina. It's away from the public with lots of things to do, and we're leaving Sunday. I know we've been talking about a trip together while you are on hiatus from the tour, so I hope what we've done will be okay."

He texts. "*I'm intrigued.*"

"Keep an open mind because it's also the annual vacation I take with my friends every year and when I told them what I wanted, well they were all for it."

He texts, "*You have my undivided attention.*"

"The first two days will be just you and me. Then the next day the girls are coming, which will give you time to be around them, then Jason will arrive the next day with the band members after that. Oh, did I mention everyone is bringing a significant other?"

He texts. "*Seems like a full house.*"

"Yes. I want the opportunity to spend time around the band, and you can spend time with my friends. One big happy, crazy but loveable family."

He scoots me down under him in such a quick motion I gasp. Running a finger down the front of my shirt, I eye him intently. He moves the shirt up slightly to reveal my belly. He leans in kissing the skin above my navel tenderly. He reaches over to grab his phone.

He texts. "*I think it's going to be great.*"

"Really?"

He nods assuring me he approves. Who knows what will happen once we get there, but those first two days will give me a chance to show him just how much I want him in my life.

CHAPTER 23

Amelia

Beau's follow-up was by-the-book perfect. He began talking, and I realized how much I had missed the sound of his voice. After the visit, we boarded the plane and soon after, landed in Charleston, South Carolina. We drove a car over to Folley Beach. The house was tucked away in the most heavenly, secluded spot. We had our own boardwalk out to the beach, a pool, and a crow's nest. There were huge balconies on two floors, a game room with a pool table, and a promise not to talk business while we were here.

My annual girls' trip usually includes us lying out on the beach, taking walks, and visiting bars, as well as visiting the stores along the boardwalks of whatever beach we landed at, but this time we had everything we needed at the house. I even had Tim arriving to surprise Sophia. They've been talking a lot lately, and this will give them an opportunity to get to know each other better without her parents around. I feel having Beau's band here will keep Jordan busy with his drummer, Wade, and Lily will have her boyfriend Zach. I also gave the band members the choice of bringing their significant others, but decided--no kids, so adults can be adults. I selected a room for Beau and I that had a mini balcony looking out over the beach where we could enjoy the sound of what looked like our private ocean. It was a smaller room with a small bathroom, but it was all we needed.

I leave him upstairs to unpack as I prep food in the kitchen for us. We had breakfast on the way here but now a limeade out on the balcony is going to hit the spot, and it is spiked with a little vodka. As I finish the last squeeze of a lime, he walks into the kitchen wearing a dark blue pair of trunks with a yellow t-shirt. He leans in grabbing a slice of cheese from the platter while propping himself against the counter next to me.

"What are those?"

"Fresh squeezed limeaides with a touch of vodka. Want one?"

He reaches out for the glass but leans in to kiss me first.

"You had a sip already, delicious. How did you find this place?"

"I began the search, found it, and Jason ran through a checklist of things to be sure we wouldn't be interrupted. It seems taking a vacation with a famous person requires a special skill set."

"I don't like that we have to do that, but it makes for a better vacation. My guys are easy to get along with. What about your friends?"

"Real easy." We start laughing. "What was I thinking putting all these people in one house?"

"That you are totally into me, and our families need to get used to being around each other."

"Yes. Now, ready to eat?"

He turns, carrying me piggy-back style outside. I grab the tray of food and he takes the two glasses. Teamwork has never been this sweet before.

*

Our first day together is full of touching, kissing, and heated looks, fueling the restlessness that has been building between us. We go for a swim, take a walk down the beach, and play chess. We even take a nap in a large hammock on the deck. We soak up the shade with a much-needed rest.

After a dinner of grilled shrimp and roasted corn we decide to take our dessert out on the deck as the sun is going down. I can see the moment the sun hits the water and imagine it sizzling as the two meet. The breeze moves the fabric of my beach cover up and my hair sweeps around my face as I spit out the loose stands that land in my mouth.

He laughs. "You okay?"

"Yes." I flip my head over and put my hair in a knot. I pop back up, and Beau sits next to me in a lounge chair holding two bowls.

"Oh, wow that looks delicious. Thank you."

We settle into to enjoy the sweet peachy goodness of the cobbler as the ice cream melts and I begin to moan at the sinful dessert. Beau eyes me, with his spoon half in his mouth.

"What?"

"Do you like it?"

"No, I love it. Oh my god it's so good." I take in another spoonful, filling my cheeks, and after swallowing I lick the spoon plunging it in for another taste.

"Amelia."

I turn to look at him cradling his dessert. "Beau, I'm almost done, and you are still sitting with an almost full bowl."

"I can't."

"You can't what?" I scoop up another spoonful with my eyes locked on him. I moan again, savoring the mix of warm cobbler with the cold ice cream, like I've never experienced such sweetness before.

"I want to be your peach cobbler."

I know what I'm doing, the moans, the licks. His need for me must be as strong as mine for him. I set my bowl on the lounge chair, straddle his lap and begin to feed him his dessert.

After the first bite, I kiss him taking my time before offering another bite. His body reacts, abs tense, his hands move up under my cover-up heating a path where his fingers touch. My tongue licks a dab of ice cream off his bottom lip and a wonderful growl escapes him as his hands move up over my bikini bottom pulling me snug against him.

"More?"

"Please."

I scoop up another loaded spoonful and some ice cream drips on his shirt, and it is like blood to a vampire. I want his shirt off! In one movement he stands with me holding my legs around his waist and the bowl drops to the deck. We make our way inside, lock the door and proceed to leave pieces of our clothing throughout the house.

The next few hours we give in, give up, and give everything we have to each other. I feel his tongue tease the dip in my back as his lips trail up and over to my shoulder with a light bite. I giggle glancing over at him. He flips me over where I'm below him and I tug at the scruff on his face. His eyes call out to me and I answer happily. I'm lost completely and utterly hypnotized by him. My legs tighten around him as he takes me further into our newly discovered place of euphoria.

*

I wake first, needing to make coffee and wanting a large breakfast. I can't stop the feeling I have rushing through my body, which is making me blush just standing next to the bed watching him sleep. I grab one of his tees laying on the floor, holding it first to my nose. I head downstairs pulling it over my head. Flashbacks of last night flood my brain and I can't stop smiling. After scooping the coffee grounds into the pot and filling it with water, I pull out the bagels, ripping a chunk of the soft chewy bread, savoring the blueberry goodness.

"Morning."

I turn to see Beau shirtless, walking towards me. Leaning against the counter, I look over him from his messy hair to his bare feet and my body experiences a wonderful flashback. He takes a huge bite of the bagel from my hand.

"I'm hungry."

He kisses my neck. "You must be tired because you didn't sleep much last night."

"No, I'm not tired, besides while awake I found out what makes you..."

I playfully cover his mouth with my hand. "You did. How about breakfast?"

"Eggs?"

"Okay, I will assist." I peel off his shirt handing it to him. "So, you don't burn yourself."

He turns to see me completely naked, holding his shirt.

"Breakfast can wait."

*

Outside on the deck we watch as birds make a graceful dance above us. We listen to the peaceful calm that Mother Earth is offering up this morning. He turns his chair towards me.

"You know we've entered another layer of our relationship."

My chin rests on my folded hands, propped up on the table by my elbows. I tilt my head towards him. "I would agree."

"Do you feel we are moving too fast?"

"No, not at all." He exhales as if I just put to rest some concerns. "What's on your mind?"

"When we took the time apart and only talked on the phone, it gave me time to realize so many things."

I bury my face in my hands. "I'm sorry I even suggested

it." I cover his hand with mine. "I always wanted *us*; I was just scared of the unknown. I want to give you the best of me all the time, but I needed to know I was strong enough. I can handle all the media excitement, the privacy intrusions, and big moves to come because I know I'm ready."

"Which is why the time apart was important to both of us. I know what I want in my life."

"Which is?"

"You. This next part is important."

"Okay."

"I'll wait until you are ready, but…"

Beau lowers himself to the deck on one knee taking my hands in his.

"What are you doing?"

"I want to share every part of my life with you, and I want you to share every part of yours with me. I promise to stand by your side, to love you and make you laugh every day for the rest of our lives. I will be your voice if ever you are lost, and I promise to protect you against anyone or anything. I want to grow old right beside you no matter where we are. Amelia Elizabeth Mathews, will you marry me?"

Tears fall down my face, hitting the top of his hands, which are wrapped around mine.

"Amelia, I realize it's only been a couple of months, but I feel this strongly about you, about us. I don't want another day, another decision or trip made without you."

I stand bringing him up with me. I'm completely lost in the man standing in front of me. I've never experienced this kind of love or this kind of friendship with any guy before.

"Yes, yes, yes!" We fall into multiple wonderful kisses feeling this high together.

"I didn't expect to propose in this way, but last night I laid awake for a long time just thinking about us. I don't have a proper ring at this time to offer you, but I didn't want to wait any longer."

"It's what's in our hearts that ties us together."

"I agree, but I still want to get you something that symbolizes us."

"I love that idea."

"Should we tell everyone when they arrive?"

"Let's wait."

His smile fades. "You don't want to tell them?"

"I do, but I want this moment to be just ours for a little while. Is that okay?"

He rests his forehead on mine. "If you have any doubts."

"I have no doubts."

He pulls away but doesn't let go of me. "What if I get drunk and blurt it out later in the week?"

"I will pass it off as you kidding around."

"What if I'm caught in town picking out a ring?"

"That could be more complicated."

His hand slips behind my neck as I tilt my head up.

"What if I catch you up in a moment like this, look into your brilliant blue eyes, and confess my love in front of them all?"

"That's easy, I will confess I love you too. What would really throw them for a loop is if we got married while we were here."

It only takes a moment for him to respond.

"Let's do it."

I'm equally surprised I said it, but I like it. "How, we will need a license, and doesn't that take time?"

"We can figure that out. It would be a small wedding with our friends, but how do you really feel about it?"

"It would be like eloping. I think I love it."

"You and I can tend to all the details."

"No one will know about our secret until the day we say, "I do.""

"Say it again."

"I do."

*

We spend the rest of the day planning our surprise, along with swimming, cooking, and finding ways to express how happy we are together. Tomorrow morning will bring people into the house and our mission will be to keep our wedding plans hidden and our feelings in check.

*

The girls arrive ready for beach time, drinking, and learning more about Beau. He has in a short time turned my world upside down for the better. I'm still not sure about all that goes along with being involved with someone like him, but I sure as hell will give it my all.

Jordan bounces inside the house loudly bringing her "A" game.

"Amelia, Beau, where the hell are you?"

I walk out of the pantry trying to be cool. "Why are you being so loud?"

She smiles, making her way over to me. She looks me over then speaks.

"You had sex with Beau, didn't you?"

"This is how you say hello?"

Sophia and Lily join her. Now all three of my friends are staring at me. Shit this is going to be hard, but I'm saved by Beau who comes in from the balcony.

"Ladies, we've been waiting for you."

Their smiles broaden as they rush over to him. All three of them give him the once over and start circling around him. Jordan stops in front of him placing her finger on his chest.

"Fess up, did you deflower our innocent friend?"

He lets out a spontaneous sound or laugh then he swallows looking over at me for help. I just fold my arms over my chest watching him struggle as I just did. He can handle thousands of fans, but three women are now leaving him speechless. I can't have him struggle anymore, so I reach inside their circle for his hand.

"Come on, some things are left private between two consenting adults."

Sophia jumps up and down while saying, "This week is going to be amazing. I can't wait to get one or both of you drunk to confess all your secrets."

I shake my head. "Seriously?"

"We all know that's when you speak what's really on your mind," Lily says.

"Enough with this inquisition. Sophia, I have a surprise for you. A special guest is arriving on Wednesday just for you."

She straightens. "Me, who would be coming here?"

"Tim."

"Stop, I thought he had plans?"

"You are his plan. Lily, Zach will be here on Wednesday as well, and Jordan, Wade is also coming with the rest of Beau's band. Now stop getting in my business and get some business started of your own."

They rush in hugging Beau and I and off they go to find their rooms.

Beau's arm slides around my shoulders. "I like your friends, but they scare me a little."

"They're harmless."

"I'm going up on the deck from our room so you can have some time with them."

"I'll come get you for lunch."

He kisses me, and up the stairs he goes speaking to them as they randomly move from room to room finding their spot for the week.

CHAPTER 24

Beau

I'm sitting on the balcony of our room enjoying calm ocean sounds all the way down to the swaying reeds just below me. I shut my eyes and say a little prayer for my health and for giving me Amelia. She has agreed to marry me with no ring and in just a few short days from now. Her friends are protective of her, and my guys are not going to be ready for the news either, but I'm sure they will all support us.

My phone rings and I see Jason's picture.

"Hey, you miss me already?"

"No. I'm actually getting a lot of business done without my diva singer."

"That hurts."

"How are you doing?"

"Great. I'm relaxing. This place is really nice."

"And Amelia?"

"She is currently with her friends, getting them settled in their rooms. I think I just heard someone scream about a bathing suit while someone else popped someone's bare bottom. It's a big house and sound travels.

"Maybe I should come down early; seems like a good party. I do have someone coming with me, I hope that's okay?"

I set up in my chair. "What? Who?"

"A friend from school who divorced her husband about two years ago, Anna. She works for Mendoza. She called me about your contract with them. Don't worry she'll be cool. Besides you said I needed to get out and find someone."

"I'm proud of you."

"I promised Amelia no business talk, so keep relaxing and give her a hug. Not that you haven't already. She's special, don't drive her away with all your demands."

"I will try to behave myself. See you soon."

I can't wait to tell Amelia about Jason. I can't wait to tell Jason about Amelia and me.

*

I must have fallen asleep but I'm now being awakened by my loving fiancé standing beside me wearing the sexiest red bikini I've ever laid my eyes on. I reach out touching the side strap.

"Is this new?"

"I don't want you to lose me in the midst of all the beauties in the house this week."

She swings one leg over my legs, taking a seat. "You've been asleep for almost an hour. Are you ready to eat, we've prepared lunch?"

My fingers move gingerly over her thighs. "Like what?" I watch her lips move with each word.

"Chicken salad sandwiches, Sophia's specialty. You're watching my lips; did you hear anything I said?"

"No." I kiss her tasting the sweetness of her last drink, when I hear a loud voice coming from the lower level, it's Jordan.

"We're hungry and you both need to keep up your strength for that kind of action. Get your asses down here!"

We both smile and Amelia stands up.

"Let's hope you still like them once they're drunk later. They are good at loud talking and singing, lots of off-key singing."

"Do you do the same?"

"I have been known to, yes."

"Then I will tend to the bar."

*

After lunch we decide to play cards, then a game called Guess It. Getting to know them in this setting, I see why Amelia loves them so much. Laughter is plentiful, and I watch Amelia laugh multiple times to the point of crying.

Later after another trip out onto the beach, I grill tuna for dinner. Lily shows us how to properly cut a pineapple, while Sophia makes whipped cream from scratch. They beg me to play my guitar while sitting around the fire pit, which I do. Amelia's knees are tucked up under her arms; she listens, closing her eyes while taking in the song I'm playing. I watch her closely and when she opens her eyes at the end, she looks at me and winks. Sophia stands teetering a bit as I reach out trying to steady her.

"I want to make a toast. Come on now pick up those bottles and glasses. First, let me start by saying, thank you to this guy." She holds her bottle up to me. "Beau, you have made our girl here happy again. Look at her, she melts on the inside every time you look at her. We've been with her through some tough times, and we have shed many tears. But looking at her now, we feel she will be smiling forever. So, a toast to the spell you cast on her and to the one she cast on you. Cheers!"

Lily stands up next. "I'm willing to share her, just don't break her heart. Ask Zach, I will hunt you down. Cheers!"

I reposition myself in my chair leaning my guitar against the railing. "Duly noted."

They all break out in giggles, looking over at Jordan who seems to be the boldest, most outgoing of them all, but she's now quiet. Laughter dies down as all eyes are now on her.

Amelia touches her leg.

"This is your moment to speak up. It was your insistence on those bright colored dresses at the concert that got me noticed by Beau. You are kind of responsible for us getting together."

She shakes her head, wiping off a tear that had fallen on her arm. I stand reaching for a napkin, handing it to her. Her eyes are fixed on me as I do and she smiles.

"The four of us are very close. We've been through things no one should have to ever endure. These are my sisters, my heart. Will you promise to keep the light in her eyes that she has today?"

"I will do everything in my power, yes."

"Are you taking her away from her family and friends?"

"She will never be far from you." I felt this needed to be the time I spoke up. I look over at Amelia hoping she agrees, and she does. "I'm in love with her."

The three girls look over at Amelia, stunned by my words and wait for her to say something.

"I'm in love with him; in fact, he has asked me to marry him."

They all drop their drinks and start jumping up and down, then tackle Amelia with hugs. One by one turn to me as I stand welcoming their congratulations. Jordan comes over to me last. She doesn't kick me in the knee or power punch my arm, she just hugs me.

Amelia walks over, slipping her arms around me then she reaches for Lily's hand, and they all reach for each other holding hands while including me.

"This is our little secret. He just asked me yesterday."

They all have tears in their eyes but are smiling.

"We'll have another time during the week to fill in the others."

Lily grabs my hand. "Where's the ring?"

Amelia looks at me. "The proposal was unexpected, so he didn't have one. I don't need a ring to say yes."

"Well don't tell Zach that," Lily says.

We all burst out laughing at her comment.

Sophia clears her throat. "Okay, another toast. Here's to Beau and Amelia, may you have a long, happy, and fruitful marriage. Cheers!"

*

We take our leave of the girls about 1:30 in the morning, falling asleep as soon as our heads hit the pillow. About 5:30 in the morning I look over to find Amelia curled up on her left side with the sheet pulled up to her chin. I spot a throw, laying it on her for extra warmth. I lean against the back of the bed and plan our list of what to do today. Keeping 'operation wedding' a secret from our friends will be difficult, but so worth it.

CHAPTER 25

Amelia

I meant what I said last night and so does Beau. In my wildest dreams would I ever think I'd be ready to marry this soon after meeting someone, but I am.

Beau received a text today that Jason is coming in at about 3:30, and Zach texted Lily that he'll be arriving with Tim about 6:00. We decide to make it a pool day, so we fill the cooler, turn on the music, and put on our bathing suits. All the girls are by the pool when Beau makes his appearance. I admire the look of a well-fit man any time of the day and obviously so do my friends.

We use a pump to inflate a few pool floats, hook them together, and make Beau our center of attention. It's good he's wearing sunglasses because he's probably rolling his eyes at the idiotic but hilarious things we are talking about. He excuses himself to grab some quiet time upstairs, and I offer to walk up with him. I tell them I will be back, and we take the opportunity to make some phone calls. We make an appointment at the courthouse for 1:00. We tell the girls we are going for more booze, and with that, they turn their attention to draining the pitcher of margaritas. Everything works out, and we are back by 2:30. Undercover surprise wedding is underway, and we could not be more excited.

*

Lily and Jordan are on the beach, while Sophia and I start marinating chicken for dinner. Jason has arrived. Beau opens the door, and who I see with Jason is a very attractive redhead. She shakes Beau's hand with the normal greetings then both turn their attention to Jason. He enters carrying two bags; he is wearing shorts and flip flops.

"I like this more relaxed side of you," Beau says.

"I'm going to try, per Amelia's instructions."

"Good. Come on in."

The woman walks over to where Sophia and I are standing.

"Hi, I'm Anna, you must be Amelia."

I dry my hands. "I am. Have we met before?"

"No, but being associated with Beau, social media is ablaze with your beautiful face."

"Well I hope they do me justice. This is Sophia."

Sophia grins, says hello, then offers Anna a spiked lemonade.

She accepts taking a big sip. "Keep them guessing Amelia, it's more fun that way. This is a good drink, thank you."

"We have plenty of everything. We have rooms all over the house. If there is a ribbon on the door, it's full. Park your bag anywhere you want. We have lots of people coming, and we are crashing all over. If you want something more intimate, choose your spot well and hang your ribbon." Jason comes over and Beau gets him a beer, but he gives me a hug hello first.

"How's he doing?"

Before I can answer his questions, Beau's hands slide around my waist pressing me against his stomach. "

"I'm better than I've ever been."

"Throat is good?"

"Yes."

"Well let's start this vacay!"

*

Sophia heads outside while we wait for Jason and Anna to settle in, which gives us a moment alone.

"What have you done to my manager? He listens, holding up his end of the "no business rule," and is ready for a little vacation. "You've charmed him."

"I'd like to say I have, but it's you. He cares about you, your health and happiness. He's your friend and it shows on his face when he looks at you."

"Do you think he will guess our secret?"

"Oh definitely, you are full of Cupid's arrows with those dreamy eyes you keep looking at me with, so obvious. Do I appear to be a woman in love?"

He leans back just a bit. "Gushing. Your eyes and the blush on your cheeks is a giveaway. Your body language says you are into me."

"Really."

"Your breathing changes when I'm near you." He touches my arm and the hair stands up. "Now that is electricity between two people. When I kiss you, you just fall."

"Fall?"

He kisses me, feeding that need inside that only he can fill. I push away from him noticing he's right.

"See, very physical, very natural reactions from a person who is attracted to another person."

"You're right."

He places his finger on my chest. "Your heart beats for me."

"It does. And your heart…"

"Beats only for you."

We hear someone clear their throat only to find Jason standing a few steps away.

"Was I meant to hear that?"

We both smile like we've been caught making out by our parents. Beau glances at me.

"We need to tell you something."

He places his hands on his hips. "Am I going to need a stiff drink."

"It's all good." Beau goes over putting his hand on Jason's now tight shoulders. "Amelia, maybe he will need that drink. You are tense buddy."

Jason sits on a bar stool then takes his glass, turning it up drinking it straight. I pour him another and he grabs my left hand, then looks at Beau.

"Okay what else?"

"We are engaged. I asked her and she accepted."

He stares at Beau, then looks at me. Anna joins us.

"Jason say something. They want your support."

A light bulb goes off in his head, I guess, and he stands. "Yes, yes of course I'm happy for you both, I knew it was only a matter of time. I wish only the best for you both, I really do."

I walk over to Beau then look at Jason. "I feel there is more you need to say."

Beau senses it too. "Jason what is it?"

"As your friend, I'm all for it. As your manager we are about to hit a shit show of craziness, not to mention the news of your biopsy and proving to the label that you are as strong as ever. Besides all of that, where is the ring?"

Beau just looks at him for a moment, then at me. His face softens as he kisses the top of my head. "We are back to the ring thing again."

"I know."

"It was a spontaneous proposal, and I didn't want to wait any longer."

Anna reaches for glasses from the drain. Takes the bottle of bourbon and pours four shots sliding them to each of us.

"What Jason is trying to say is, congratulations. You are in love; this should be celebrated and respected by everyone. As far as the ring goes, I had a huge diamond for 12 years, now I am getting a divorce. Put your energy into each other. Cheers to you both!"

We pause at her frankness, then start laughing and turn up our glasses.

"This will work, engagements are good," says Jason.

"Are you still in shock?" says Beau.

"Just a little."

I glide my hand through Anna's arm. "I like you, how about we go out and meet the other girls while Beau talks to Jason?"

She kisses Jason's cheek, gives Beau a congratulatory hug, and heads out with me. I look back as Beau smiles at me. Crap, he's right. I do gush when he looks at me.

CHAPTER 26

Amelia

My friends are enjoying their vacation a little more than usual this year as we are joined by some pretty special guys. Everyone has someone, which helps a lot when Beau and I disappear a few hours over the next two days. Jason is probably the one who is more concerned about why we leave, but he never asks what we are doing.

*

"Beau, stop, I can't breathe." I giggle again.

He rolls off to the side, laying on his back. "One more tickle spot to add to the list."

I roll over on top of him, pushing up off him with my hands on his chest.

"I'm surprised the whole house is not climbing the steps to check on us."

"Give me a few minutes and they might." His finger slides down my stomach. "You look good in this color."

I look down at myself, naked. "What are you talking about?"

"Your natural coloring."

"Are you making light of my odd tan lines?"

He tightens his abdomen as I grip his sides. I lunge forward as he catches me before our faces crash together. Our eyes meet giving me the motive to make a bold move. I use my tongue to tease his bottom lip first, then give him a light kiss moving onto a soft bite on his bottom lip. My hand moves and he curls his body into me when I hear him murmur.

"Amelia."

I leave my soon-to-be husband completely satisfied and sleeping soundly in our bed. I sit on the balcony looking up at the moon, when I see a shooting star. I close my eyes and make a wish, then send a kiss to the sky. I look back as he moves, picking up his head to look for me. I stand when he sees me.

"Come back to bed."

Climbing under the sheet I put myself as close to him as humanly possible.

"I love you."

He kisses my head. "I love you too."

A few months ago, one night in my backyard, I wished for someone like him. I wanted to find a person and feel the way I do now, and my wish came true. I have everything I could want, so tonight's wish was for him, for his voice, and for his health.

*

Today is the day. Standing in front of the mirror this morning I run over what we've secretly accomplished this week. Everything has been worked out and all that's left is telling the others in the house. Beau sneaks up behind me laying his chin on my shoulder.

"Are you ready for our reveal?"

"I am, but I'm a little nervous. What if they freak out?"

"They won't."

"But they could."

"Only one way to find out."

We lock hands, and he leads us down the stairs to meet with our friends to inform them of our wedding day details. The first to see us and say something is Lily.

"What's wrong, you both look a little green."

I look at him and wonder if we do.

Jason sits at the bar now two stools away from us when he addresses Beau. He's so suspicious with his raised eyebrow and crossed arms.

"You're about to tell us something that is going to make me finish a bottle of some kind of alcoholic beverage today, aren't you?"

That comment must have made others a little curious bringing them closer to us. Lily and Sophia join Jordan and smile. They start to figure out something is up, when Jason grabs a bottle of tequila. Beau rushes to him grabbing the bottle.

"Don't do it. I need you to be conscious." Beau reaches for my hand. "Amelia and I have an announcement." We both notice the boxes on the bar. "The donuts came this morning to soften the news we have to share with everyone. Amelia and I are getting married, *today*."

What played out next was priceless and should have been on video. My friends jump, yell, and make their way to me, as his band mates join him. Jason lowers his head on the counter. Anna places herself next to him, waiting for his response to our news with her hand on his back. After a few exciting moments, Beau sits beside Jason, and the room is quiet, again. Jason peeks at him then sits upright. He reaches over hugging Beau, and the whole room lets out the loudest cheers. Tears sting my eyes seeing the brotherly love between the two. Jason holds open one arm and invites me into their hug, whispering in my ear.

"From day one you had him."

"I'm his voice and he's mine."

He kisses my cheek, as I hug him. I turn my attention to Beau and the shots of tequila that are making their way around the kitchen. I look over to Lily who is arm in arm with Zach; she's smiling. Sophia stands by Tim, who also sends a nod our way. There are a lot of tears as the emotions begin to overtake our friends. Wade steps up to make the first official toast.

"I just want to say I've heard this guy be sappy about this woman for months now." His bandmates all agree. "He missed her when they were apart and would not stop talking about her. Amelia and Beau on behalf of the band, your brothers, we wish you both the best. So, cheers to Amelia for becoming a part of the family, and here's to this smiling SOB who finally landed a proper woman!"

Beau and I kiss, turning up our glasses. As everyone collects themselves, Beau speaks next.

"Let me start by filling you in on what's going to happen. First breakfast, which Amelia and I still need to do. Then a bachelor celebration will begin 11:00 sharp, out on the beach with a volleyball game. Then for lunch BB&B Company will bring us, Brats, BBQ and Beer" He turns to me as I fill in the ladies about the bachelorette festivities.

"Ladies we are being pampered by Lucy's Salon, anything you want they will do, then we will enjoy a catered lunch with the guys."

Beau continues.

"At 3:00 p.m., we will separate with ladies on the second floor, guys on the first floor, and prepare for a beach ceremony, which will take place at sunset. Wear what you want, and then we will enjoy the rest of the night with many Carolina favorites and kegs out on the beach. Tomorrow there will be a much-needed brunch."

I watch Jason take it all in, and I'm sure he's wondering how we got it all arranged without the press knowing or even the house knowing. Once all the plans are revealed, everyone goes their separate ways until 11:00. We ask them not to mention this to anyone, no social media or pictures are to be shared with anyone outside the house.

Breaking the news went better than expected. Jason stands asking us to follow him to a small side porch to talk. We take our seats, giving him time to prepare his thoughts.

"I knew you were up to something; I just didn't think it would be this week. Amelia was this the reason for the trip?"

"No, I had no idea he was going to propose or that we would move this fast to get married."

"Are you official with a license. Who is officiating?"

Beau answers trying to reassure his friend. "We are legal, and the Folley's municipal clerk will serve as the officiant. There will be another family gathering later once the tour is done." Beau takes my hand. "I don't want to put off spending another day without her being my wife. This is important to both of us."

Jason looks at me. "I guess you feel the same."

"Yes, I do. I love him and my heart is all his. Maybe a piece of paper is not needed to declare our love, but we want to be married."

"Are you okay with his lifestyle? I know you had reservations before."

"I clearly don't know what it's like to be so public all the time, but I'm not afraid anymore. I'm ready for what's to come."

"I think I just got a few more grey hairs, but I'm truly happy for you both."

I walk over to him. "Um, Jason, we aren't having people stand up with us because we want everyone to be a part of this day, but would you consider walking me down the beach to meet Beau?"

"I would be honored."

CHAPTER 27

Amelia

I chose no shoes and shiny red toenail polish for the beach ceremony. My dress is a high-low design with spaghetti straps and ruching around the waist. It is cut low in the back and is made of taffeta. My makeup is minimal and my hair is up with a few wispy pieces.

We had ordered white roses, hydrangea's, lamb's ear and silver brunia for my bouquet, and for him we chose a rustic rose boutonniere.

The catering company will set up on the beach, then they will leave once we begin eating. Tim offers to take photos because we find out he does photography on the side.

As the time for the ceremony approaches, Sophia, Lily and Jordan take me aside for that special moment between best friends, before one takes the important step into marriage. Lily has a box cradled in her hands.

"Look, I know you aren't concerned about traditions tonight, but we wanted you to have a few tokens." She hands me a box. "This is from me, something new and blue."

I open the box to find a blue wrapped condom, and my face speaks for us all.

"We said we would do pregnancy together, so use this tonight and give me some time to convince Zach about getting married. Deal?"

"Deal." I hug and assure her I'm not in any hurry. She's right; we always said we would be pregnant together, but today proves the unexpected can happen. Next was Jordan. She removes a bracelet from her arm.

"This is the something borrowed."

"Jordan, you've worn this every day since we've met. I remember when your parents gave it to you when you were cancer free."

"It marked a special occasion for me, as it will for you today."

She places the diamond bracelet on my arm.

"I will take good care of it tonight, thank you so much."

Sophia moves closer to me.

"This is really emotional. Ok, mine is the something old." She hands me a small ring. "This belonged to my grandmother. She got it when she was 16. I wear it every day and it reminds me of her strength in how she approached life, business and family, but today it reminds me of you. Amelia you deserve a lifetime of happiness and I truly, truly feel that lies with Beau."

I hug her, thanking her because I do feel that way about him. I know what she's talking about. What I went through with Chase could have broken me, kept me from going out and meeting someone else. I have lived with the fear I felt after waking up in the hospital, and it makes me grateful for family and these girls who kept me out of the darkness.

"You are all the best women I know. Thank you for your love, your support, and being my friends. This was not what I expected would happen on our vacation, but I am so happy it did."

Jordan starts a chain of hand holding. "Enjoy your life with this new man. The possibilities are endless, oh, and by the way, we would like front row concert tickets forever!"

We all laugh wiping tears off our faces. "I will make that request."

*

When we get outside, I don't see Beau; everyone does their best in keeping us apart for just a little while longer. Jason steps beside me.

"You ready?"

I look at him with much confidence. "I am."

The music we hear as we walk out is coming from Beau's bass player, Jeff. Our walk across the sand over to Beau still doesn't give me a clear look. As I get closer, our friends part, allowing a path to open for Jason and I. That's when I see him, and he sees me for the first time. Our eyes lock and he mouths, *I love you*. I mouth the words back to him. When Jason and I reach the front, I hand my bouquet to Jordan. Jason kisses my cheek, then turns to shake Beau's hand, and soon finds a place by Anna. Beau and I join hands.

"This is really happening."

"Any regrets?"

"None."

His thumb rubs back and forth over my knuckles. "Let's get married."

The ceremony is simple, as we choose to speak from our hearts, but we don't sacrifice saying, "I do" or the traditional kiss after. Many congratulations, hugs, and photos follow our ceremony, and later we travel up to the house for our reception.

Sitting next to my new husband after eating dinner, I'm being fed peach cobbler with vanilla ice cream, a throwback to memories of our first official night together.

"I might be a little tipsy," I say after swallowing the last bite.

He swipes ice cream across my nose with the spoon then kisses it off. "Me too."

"You are the sweetest man I've ever met." I take the spoon putting some ice cream on his lips. "Oops."

Without hesitation I boldly kiss him. With a sigh, I break from him as he drops his face to my chest. I look out at our friends, when I notice Anna sitting across Jason's lap.

"They seem to be hitting it off."

Beau looks at them. "She's snarky, he needs that. He needs a distraction to take him away from his job."

I run my fingers through his hair messing it up just a little. "We have so much to discuss."

"Eventually."

"We can't stay tucked in this house forever. We both have houses in different states, and you have a tour to get back to."

"One day we will decide where to call our home, but for now we'll gravitate to your house because of you attending school. I hope you will be able to join me for some of the tour."

"Me too. Now no more serious talk tonight. How about a beer?" I stand up kiss him then head to the keg. Yep, I'm avoiding that decision. I don't know if I want to continue with classes right now, but I also don't want him to think he's getting me off track. Anna comes up next to me as I pour Beau's beer. Deep in thought I allow foam to overflow the cup.

"Oh shoot."

"Here let me help. Are you okay?"

"I don't know." I shake off my hand. "I have 'just got married' fog in my head. Here let me pour yours, I promise to do better."

"Just married is a wonderful feeling to have. My marriage wasn't always bad you know. We just grew apart, and he grew to like other women more and more. We now only speak because of the finances we are still settling."

"I'm sorry."

"Don't be." She looks at Jason. "I'm looking forward to getting to know Jason better now that we've reconnected. I work for a company that relies on entertainers to promote products and events. It's a busy, complex world that needs good people in it with a strong support staff. You and Beau will do fine; just be flexible and keep communicating. Just don't lose yourself."

"What do you mean?"

"It's easy to get lost when you are involved with someone like Beau. He's famous; a big name can overpower things sometimes. Be true to yourself, follow through with your plans, and speak up if it gets to be too much."

"Thank you." I give some thought to her words while walking back to find my husband sitting with Zach and Lily. I've been kissed by a man from North Carolina, married him after knowing him less than two months, and I'm about to enter his celebrity lifestyle. I hand him his beer and he smiles, instantly melting away any of my concerns.

CHAPTER 28

Beau

We spent our wedding night in the room at the top of the stairs, while the others kept the party going until late. We have a few days left before I head back on tour, and we vow not to waste any of it. The wedding, my wife, and this feeling I'm having as I wake up this morning tells me how hard it's going to be to separate from her.

"Good morning," she says softly then begins to stretch.

"Good morning. How is my wife this morning?"

She smiles. "We did get married yesterday, didn't we?"

"We did. I've been lying here thinking. I'm leaving my new bride for the next three weeks and how it does not seem right? I'm sure there is a law or a written statement somewhere that we shouldn't separate."

She giggles. "We have two days to fit in three weeks of newlywed bliss." She climbs over me and stands by the bed wearing nothing but a wedding band. "Honeymoon in the shower?"

*

When we were back at the beach house, Jason was not kidding when he said he dreaded going back to work, because now I understand. The media goes nuts after I announce the results of my biopsy, then add my disappearance for a week, along with the news I have married Amelia, and everything blows up more than I expect. The media had her pregnant, and I was trapped in a loveless marriage. One even stated she was a gold-digging fangirl after my money! What the hell? Now sitting in the office of my label, I notice Jason is on his third cup of coffee. We flew in last night as the band continued to the next venue. I look over the email sent from the record label yesterday. *Mandatory meeting at Spot on Records. The board requests your presence to discuss recent events.* So my life has become an event. Why am I not surprised?

"Why does the coffee always taste better here," he asks?

"Maybe just take in some deep breaths and lay off the coffee."

He paces in front of me. "We have no idea what they are going to say. Do you have any idea? I mean this could get tense?"

"Jason, I got married, I didn't quit. I'm still doing everything they want. How could they possibly find a problem with any of this?" He has a wild look in his eyes as I reach for his cup of coffee. "Maybe switch to decaf."

"Have you told Amelia about the meeting today?"

"No, she's looking into signing up for classes and setting up interviews with perspective schools, along with worrying about possible wedding fall-out from her parents. She doesn't need more to think about, besides maybe they just want to congratulate me in person."

Right then, Cara, the Spot On Record receptionist opens the door to the big office, where six men and four women are waiting for us. Jason is usually the go- between with official label business, but today I've been requested. I walk in ahead of him and everyone stands to greet us. Richard, CEO of the label and Marcus, head of promotions, meet us first. Everyone else sitting at the table is introduced next. We all take our seats, when Richard begins to speak.

"Beau, on behalf of the board we want to express our relief that you are healthy, and that the biopsy results were negative. I'm sure it was a hard few days for you. We also want to say congratulations on your recent marriage, to…" He looks inside a folder in front of him, "to Amelia."

"Thank you."

"Let's get to the business at hand. Everyone at this table represents a part of you with this company. Your brand, your contracts, and the advertising are choreographed by a number of people, as I'm sure you are aware."

"I am."

"As an artist, for you to concentrate on your craft, a team like this helps to guide you through the legalities, make new contacts, and arrange tours. We also help to facilitate studio time covering the cost to make albums, which I am sure you also know."

"Of course."

He straightens in his chair, then clears his throat. "When we received the word of your biopsy results a few hours before your official announcement, you have to know how confused we were that you didn't fill us in sooner."

"To clarify, it was my choice not to tell anyone, as it was a very personal situation I was handling."

"Yes, I agree, but one that could have been dealt with better. You have people at your disposal to get you through important matters such as this one."

"You mean my possible cancer diagnosis? Richard, if I announce it, then the information is correct and straight from me, which is how I've always done things with my fans. You know how things can get construed when it comes from a third party."

"We invest a lot of money on our artist." He clicks a control lying on the table. Up on a large screen is a display of remarks made on social media. Bethany, the social media rep stands up pointing at the comments.

"Beau, I know you handle most of the comments on your

social media account, which is great, but my team needs to know more, preferably before you post something so important as a medical diagnosis or a marriage. We have a legal team of lawyers to help you out, but we can't help if we don't know it's going up on media"

"So, I'm to notify you or your department when I have a personal issue that can be clearly handled by me because it only pertains to me?" I start to tense.

"Just a heads-up is all we ask when you are going to announce it to your fans. The other comments, fun facts, and pics you post have been fine, but this was more serious. Now let's talk about the impromptu wedding."

I set back in my chair crossing my arms over my chest.

Richard leans into the table. "You got married in South Carolina."

"I did."

"We had no idea you had proposed."

"It was spontaneous."

"You met her, what, two months ago?"

"Your point?"

"Well, you can see from a legal point of view that it may hurt you in the future."

"How?"

Randall Forsythe, the lawyer for the label, begins to tell us all about the ramifications of my sudden marriage. The longer he speaks, the hotter I get.

"Wait, this is all about a pre-nup?"

"Yes."

"How does this affect the label?"

"If your marriage ends suddenly, Amelia stands to get

more than you think, which affects our business with you."

"This is bullshit."

"Come on Beau, how much do you know about her? What if the two of you break up in a few months, what if she has someone in her past that could be a problem? It could cripple you financially as an artist having to deal with a divorce, but also the stress of it all could keep you from performing at your peak."

Jason, up until now, had been silent, allowing me to respond to them directly. But now, even he is getting annoyed, tapping his fingers on the table. I look at him wondering if I've missed something in my contract. Then he speaks.

"Where in his contract does it say he has to get a pre-nup? Where does it specifically say he has to tell you he's getting married?"

Randall answers. "It states that we, Spot On Records, need to be contacted in the event of sudden changes that could affect the relationship of the artist and Spot On Records. Beau can marry whomever he wants, but from a legal point of view, this is a train wreck." He looks at me. "Currently, you are one of the top five male country singers. Your concerts are sold out, sales of your previous albums have sky-rocketed, and the new one is smashing records all over. We are putting extra people on your website for the merchandise that is flying off the shelves."

"So, my fans are supportive, they come to the concerts, they still follow me, and they buy my merchandise, but you have a problem because I didn't get a pre-nup?"

"We know nothing about her," he says.

"You don't need to know her, she didn't marry you, she married me. My personal life is separate from my business with you."

"It is to a point."

Richard leans on the table. "We are concerned about your health, but more about your mental health."

Jason stands up. "Enough. The guy fell in love; he's happier than he's ever been. He has been cranking out songs faster than ever before and damn good ones. If you knew him, you would know how dedicated to his craft he is, how diligent he is to follow up personally with his fans, and how big his heart is when it comes to everyone on his team. He is not out there jeopardizing himself or his career. It's clear to me you don't know him at all."

"Jason that's not true," Richard says.

"Beau has a medical condition with his throat, and you all knew what could happen, but you took a chance on signing him because at that time you saw the kind of entertainer he was and still is today. He's never wavered in his duties to the label."

I look at him as he reaches over to pour a glass of water for himself, splashing a little on the table. I stand pushing my chair away from the table.

"I'm not having a mental break down; my mind is clearer than it's ever been. I had a medical scare that was no one's business. I took one week off from social media to have a vacation and regroup, which lead me to marrying a woman I love with my whole heart. And, don't forget, my contract has a clause stating that I can leave the label if I choose to, but I will be penalized. I don't want this situation to escalate more than it already has. I'm still here, none of my private trips, or the expense of the impromptu vacation/wedding was billed to the label. I appreciate Spot on Records for signing me knowing the risk of my medical condition, but I've never given you a reason to doubt me or my responsibilities to the label.

"Beau we don't want you to leave the label, but you have to understand our concerns," Richard says.

"I do understand from a business point of view your concerns, but I'm telling you there is nothing to be concerned about."

I turn to walk away, getting a nod from Jason, who puts down his glass of water to follow me. Richard calls for me to wait.

"Beau we had to have this conversation, and I hope you will understand the importance of it all from our side."

I extend my hand, which he takes.

"As long as we are in agreement about the difference between what's private and what is for the label to worry about."

"Agreed. Bring Amelia by sometime, I would like to meet her in person."

Jason and I walk out of the office and get into the elevator, down fourteen floors, to get in a car and head to the airport for the next concert venue. He slams his hand on the seat in front of him.

"I was so close to letting them have it. I've been in the business for a while, and it's not right how they keep their artists so tight. You have proven you're talented, committed, and a hell of a nice guy. You get married and they're concerned about a prenup."

I look at my phone to see a few texts from Amelia, the last one stating she got signed up for classes and has an interview at one of the schools she wants for a student teaching position. I lay down the phone and look out the window.

"She just told me she got signed up for classes."

"You knew her dream was to teach."

"I know."

He smacks my shoulder. "I guess you need to have a talk with your wife."

My phone pings. She sends me a picture of her eating a slice of chocolate pie. Her cheeks are full and there is whipped cream across her lips. I turn the phone to Jason.

He leans in to see it. "I'm kind of hungry for pie now."

This time I slap his shoulder playfully, knocking him against the seat. I knew about her dreams of being a teacher before, and of course I will be supportive in the direction she wants to take, but longing to be with her is a real thing.

CHAPTER 29

Amelia

The pie picture was to remind him of our last night at the beach house, but what it did was make me realize how long we will now be apart. Last night Lily asked me if I missed him. I didn't respond, I just turned up my wine glass, drained it, then set it on the table with a sad face, and she poured me another. We knew it would be this way, so I can only complain so much, but I ache to have him with me. Waking up in my bed alone the first morning, fixing breakfast for one, makes me wonder about other choices I could make in my life. I just registered for classes, but is it what I really want right now?

Lily tries to reason out the pros and cons, but she comes back to my following him on the road, living out our honeymoon one town at a time. She's a romantic, so yeah, that's what she would think, but I need to follow through with my plans and just be rational and stay on track, I think.

*

My grandma isn't the least bit upset that Beau and I got married. She says love will appear when it's needed, so I guess it was needed by the both of us at this time. My grandpa is very happy to have Beau become a member of our family. He likes him and thinks he's a down-to-earth man who would protect me and keep me safe. Grandpa has always been concerned about me, especially since the attack. I reached out to my parents, but I have heard nothing back from them so far. I don't even know if they've seen any kind of social media, considering I don't really know what country they are in right now. I miss them, but I guess some things need time to work out, even though I wish they would just tell me what's going on with them. The not knowing is worse than any bad news they may give me.

Everyone at our wedding has sent me their photos and I'm sending them off to the printers. I looked over Beau's social media last night and it was full of congratulations, best wishes, and only a few haters, which I'm getting used to. I guess that's not bad considering most people think I hijacked him because I'm pregnant.

*

His concert tonight is in Kentucky, and he promised to call me after. But for now, I'm home with Poppy. I greet her while looking around the house, and I decide to make space for Beau. I want this house to feel like his home when he's here, so I turn on some music and for the next few hours and do just that. I'll add some of his favorite foods in the kitchen and toiletries in the bathroom. I want him to keep a guitar or two here, so he will need the corner of the living room. It's going to be good; I convince myself that he will be here before I know it.

*

The next two weeks don't fly by. Every day seems longer than the day before. My concentration is terrible, but the amount of energy I have is crazy. I paint my bedroom then add a fresh new quilt with less flowery accents. Beau is due to come in on Friday and weirdly enough my parents, are coming by on Saturday. I can't believe they texted me because I've heard nothing from them in months. But today is Thursday, giving me one more day to finalize my plans to welcome my husband home. Lately I've been able to elude the press by calling in food orders or calling in for groceries and having them delivered. I spot a few photographers outside my house, but they've been considerate of my space, especially at the Center. But today I need to pick some fresh veggies and stop by Bevins, the little country store in town. While picking over the tomatoes, a woman and her daughter walk up to me smiling.

"May I help you?"

They apologize for the interruption but want to know if I am Amelia Reston, and I reply quietly that I am.

The older woman asks if her daughter could have my autograph. Her daughter May is a huge fan of Beau's. She is about twelve years old and she hasn't stopped smiling at me.

"May, are you a member of his fan club."

"Yes ma'am, he is a great singer and very cute."

"Yes, he is. What do you want me to sign?"

She hands me a brown paper bag from the produce section, and her mother gives me a pen.

"Sorry, it's all we have."

"It works." I sign the bag. "I know it's not from Beau, but I could see if maybe I could get you a real signature. Would you like that?"

Her face lights up. "That would be awesome. Thank you."

"You're welcome." I pull out another bag handing it to May's mom. "You can write your email on this."

"Thank you." May holds the bag to her chest.

"You are welcome."

"Goodbye, Mrs. Reston."

"Bye May."

She and her mom walk away and no one else is even aware of what just happened. That was the first time someone has asked for my autograph and in such a sweet, non-evasive way.

I pass a display of magazines, when my eyes divert to one of the tabloids. The picture looks familiar, at least where it was taken. I pick it up, studying the location, then look at the two blurred people in it. It's Beau and me sitting on the beach the night of our wedding. The caption states, "Quickie Wedding". I don't recall this photo in the ones I just sent off for printing. I pull out the magazine and flip to an article about us. What the heck? None of this is true! I shove the magazine back in the rack walking away to retrieve the items I came here after, when I'm startled by a loud scream.

A group of young girls are coming at me with enough enthusiasm to knock me into the produce display, so I brace myself. "It's Beau Reston's wife," they say like there is another somewhere, but I also hear, "She's so pretty, she's so lucky!" Then they all stop in front of me which piques the interest of the others in the store. They are firing off questions faster than I can answer them. I did what any country girl would do, I whistled, loudly and everyone stopped.

"You are an excited bunch. Who are you?"

One of the girls takes charge. "We are involved in the cheer-leading camp at the college. I can't believe this. You are Amelia, Beau Reston's wife; am I right?"

"You are."

The noise level goes up a bit, but quickly comes down. A girl dressed in a blue dress holds out the magazine I just put away. "Would you sign this for me, for all of us?"

"Sure, but don't believe what you read inside. Follow our sites to get the real story."

The first girl responds. "We knew you lived in town, but never dreamed of seeing you today."

Before I can respond, all have a magazine in hand. I sign one magazine after another, answering only generic questions about myself. They want to know about me, how Beau and I met, his favorite foods, and more. When everyone finishes, the manager is standing with his copy of the magazine as well. Walter Sims has been a friend of my dad's for quite some time, so I know he wants it for his granddaughter, Delaney. The girls get what they wanted then headed over to check out.

"Amelia, you handled that crowd like a pro."

"Thank you, Mr. Sims, I guess working with children pays off in mob situations. They were sweet and I didn't mind. I need to get used to it, I guess. Would you like a signature?"

"If you don't mind. Delaney told me the other day on the phone if I saw you to get a signature. I haven't read the article yet, have you?"

"No, but what I did see is speculation."

He reaches over grabbing a ball cap off the rack. "Here you may need this if you have more shopping to do. We can always pull your order in the future, if you prefer."

"Thank you, but I'm embracing my new role one day at a time."

"Well either way, just let me know."

CHAPTER 30

Beau

The last concert did a number on my throat. Besides that, there was hard rain mixed with lightning, and we had to cancel part of my performance. However, I was able to catch a flight home to Amelia sooner than planned.

I have a service drive me from the airport to her house. The porch light is on, and I can't wait to surprise her. With my bag in hand, I take the steps in one leap then ring the bell. I can hear music from inside that she turns down just before opening the door. Seeing me, she squeals and jumps into my arms wrapping her legs around my waist. I drop the bag kissing her over and over. She tastes like mint and feels amazing in my arms.

"How did you get here so fast?"

"A storm cancellation."

"Welcome home Mr. Reston, I've missed you so much."

I squat to pick up my bag, not letting her down, not wanting to let her out of my arms.

"You look beautiful! I've missed you too."

"Are you going to carry me all night?"

"I might."

"Put me down, I'm sure you're tired. Are you hungry? I made food, but it won't be ready for another 45 minutes."

"I smell cookies, what kind?"

"Snickerdoodles and mint chocolate chip."

I clear my throat. "Maybe some tea for now?"

"Hot, with honey?"

"Yes, please."

We enter the kitchen where the best smells are lingering in the air. Poppy comes running to greet me, wagging her tail and jumping up on my leg.

"I've missed you too girl." As Amelia gathers a few things, I notice her place looks a little different. "You've changed something?"

"I made room for your things. I figured we will be living between our two places, and I want you to be comfortable. I bought a stand for your guitar if you want to leave one here."

"Do I still get the right side of the bed?"

"You do and your own dresser with space in the bathroom, and look." She opens the pantry door where I see some of my favorite foods.

"You've been busy."

"You're my husband, and I want you comfortable in *our* home. I went to the store today and people wanted my autograph. Seems I'm popular because I'm married to you. Don't worry everyone has been good; there have been no surprise visits to the Center and no stalkers in my yard."

"What? Stalker?"

"That was from before we got married. I didn't know, but Poppy knew someone was hiding in the bushes to get pictures. Everyone's been exceptionally nice since I returned home. They love you and getting close to me puts them closer to you. But I'm pretty sure I love you more."

The teapot whistles. She pours two cups of water over tea bags and drizzles mine with honey.

"I hope that never stops."

"Me loving you more, fat chance buddy. I've claimed you as mine, so you are."

"I wouldn't have it any other way."

She sits next to me. "How are you really feeling?"

"Tired. It's been a busy three weeks and I'm looking forward to doing nothing with you for three days. By the way, can I fit in your tub?"

"Yes. Do you want a relaxing soak before dinner?"

"I would."

"Let me get the water started while you drink your tea."

I can't let her go quite yet, so I pick up both cups and follow behind her. Three weeks apart is too long to not be with her as much as possible.

*

I finish my chicken sandwich with apple slaw and a side of jalapeño macaroni and cheese, as she sets down the plate of cookies. I grab one taking a big bite.

"The meal was delicious, and this cookie is really good."

"I know you miss home-cooked meals."

"That I do."

As we make our way to the sofa, I have questions to ask.

"Okay truth time. Were your parents upset their only daughter got married without them?"

"Mom found out from a magazine, not from any of the texts I sent, and she didn't say much to me about it. My father said congratulations and that he can't wait to meet you."

"Meeting the parents after the wedding. I guess we did this a little different than most."

"Yeah, but it suits us."

She takes my left hand moving my ring with her fingers.

"We should engrave a special message inside one day when we have time."

"Don't move. I'll be right back." I find my duffel bag then return with a small red box. "I know an engagement ring was not something you needed, but I saw this in Indiana; I hope you like it."

She pulls the ribbon off then opens the top just staring at the ring.

"Beau I love it." She raises up on her knees to kiss me. "It's the most beautiful ring I've ever seen."

"I saw it and thought of you. Do you like the rubies?"

"I do. Would you put it on me?"

She holds out her left hand wiggling her ring finger, and I slide on the new ring. I lift her hand placing a kiss on both rings, then kiss her.

"It compliments your band."

Her arms wrap around my neck and I embrace her back. "I love you, thank you for wanting to do this for me. I will cherish it." She kisses me.

*

The next morning we're in no hurry to leave the bed except for letting Poppy out to do her business. That's when we make our way to the kitchen for coffee, toast and eggs. When breakfast is done, I carry her over my shoulder back to bed. We emerge hours later to fix lunch. I opt to prepare BLT's and we eat on the sofa going over details of the meeting I had with Spot On Records. We FaceTime my parents then fall asleep while watching TV. She wakes me up in a way I always want to wake up, and then I show her the same kind of attention while appreciating the privacy of our home and this time together. At 6:15 we decide to make flat bread pizza.

We are in bed by 10:00 on a Friday night. I feel her arm

tighten around my mine. "I love having you to myself. Is that selfish?"

"Not at all. Is it weird I want to bottle your scent and take it back on the road with me?"

She smiles showing her dimples, which I've missed.

Not at all."

"I'm not looking forward to leaving you here while I finish the tour."

She sits up in the bed. "Actually, I want to come out with you if it's allowed. I've given this a lot of thought lately so hear me out. When I met you, my life changed in a way I never dreamed. You completely take me to another world, and I want to be in it with you. Tell me what you're thinking because I won't go if you don't like the idea."

"I want to be selfish and say hell yes, come out with me, but I know how much teaching means to you. I don't want you being disappointed that you didn't follow through with your plan."

"I can do it later. I'm not giving up, just postponing it."

"Are you sure?"

"Yes, 100 percent."

"Then let's do it."

"Will everyone be okay with me on the bus, I mean I don't want to cause problems."

"They already love you. I will call Jason tomorrow."

"If I become a distraction…?"

"You will be the best distraction."

CHAPTER 31

Beau

Tonight is the first time I meet Amelia's parents, and I have to say I'm not sure what to expect. They haven't been as open as her grandparents about our marriage, but maybe tonight will change everything. They are the ones responsible for making the enchanting woman who is my wife and to that, I'm grateful. I finish buttoning my shirt when I hear Amelia call out my name.

"Beau, can you come in here, please."

I make my way into the kitchen where I see her with two towels on her hands trying to find a place to set down the hot baking sheet. I run over clearing a spot for her, when she says, "Ouch!"

"Did you burn your fingers?" I examine them, kissing the two that seem red."

"That was hotter than I thought."

"Let me help you. What can I do?"

Her hands move down the front of my shirt popping open a button then another. Her nose brushes against my bare chest.

I see the bottle of bourbon with an empty glass. How many have you had?"

She giggles. "Not enough. Want one?"

"Can't have you drinking alone." She pours one for me, and I turn it up. I reach over wiping flour off her cheek. She picks up a cherry tomato popping it in her mouth. I take her chin between my fingers getting her to look at me. "How many?"

"A few."

I fill a glass of water for her. "I should be the nervous one."

"I feel they've been avoiding me and I'm a little concerned as to why."

"They will tell you soon enough. Besides once they get here and see how charming I am and how happy you are, they will be over-the-top excited for us." I pour another shot for myself and we tap glasses.

She reaches her hand up under my shirt looking up at me with innocent eyes.

"You smell so clean."

Once again, she buries her face inside my unbuttoned shirt. I grab her hands. "Let's change the subject before they arrive, and before I have you in a compromising position."

She giggles, slipping her hand back out. "Ok, fine, subject changed. What did Jason say about me coming back with you?"

"He's good with it, but we might need to meet a few board members at Spot On Records."

"They are unsure about me and want to be sure I'm legit, right."

"You have nothing to prove to them."

"I understand where they're coming from. I did kind of take possession of their star singer during an important tour."

I hand her half of a ham sandwich. "I'm not concerned about them or their thoughts on our life choices. Now will you eat this before your parents arrive?"

"I will, thank you." She kisses my cheek, leaves with the sandwich in hand, and goes down the hall to take a shower. With a sexy little look, she taunts me. "Too bad you've already showered." She licks mustard off her finger.

"That's not playing fair, Amelia." I hear her giggle all the way down the hall.

*

She comes out wearing a floral dress, and she appears to be more relaxed.

"Feeling better?"

"Yes." The doorbell rings, her eyes meet mine, and she reaches for my hand. "You ready?"

I follow her to the door. "I think so."

Amelia opens the door and her mother is holding a platter. She is petite like Amelia with the same hair color. Her father is little shorter than me, but he's stocky like a wrestler. Amelia ushers them in and shuts the door.

"Mom and Dad, this is Beau."

Her mom cautiously approaches me. "You mean your new husband? Nice to meet you, I'm Pamela."

I hold out my hand. "It's nice to meet you." Her father moves over to me with his hand out as Mrs. Mathews hugs Amelia, which doesn't seem at all right.

"Good to meet you, Beau. I'm Cole. I've done some research on you and have a few questions."

"Sounds good, ask me anything."

He walks past me to Amelia.

"Hi, Daddy." He kisses her cheek then gives her a loving hug.

He speaks to her in a whisper, but I can hear him say, "You look happy."

She winks at me, "I am. We have strawberry lemonade in the kitchen, would you like some?"

Her mom moves in that direction only after her husband takes her by the elbow. She keeps looking at Amelia then to me.

172

I can't read her, and she seems sad, maybe even a little agitated. I take the lead to pour the glasses, then hand them out. Amelia had already set out a couple of dips with chips and some cut-up vegetables. Her father goes in right away at the appetizers as her mother sits on a stool sipping her drink--not smiling. Her father dips in a carrot stick and breaks the silence.

"Your grandparents will be here in about 30 minutes, which gives us some time with the two of you. Beau, how did you know our daughter was the one? I've seen pictures of you with many different women over the past few years; you've dated a lot."

Beau looks at me. "Most of those women were arranged dates and were only for show. I've not seriously dated anyone in years. I've been concentrating on my career, promoting, and writing. I signed on to a new label about four years ago and the record label has kept me busy.

"So, what's different now? Where are you finding time for Amelia?" Her mother asks.

Amelia's dad interjects, "Pamela."

"No Cole, if she is going to go starry eyed over this boy and get married, we need to know if he will support her in the life she's been working at for so long."

"Mom."

"Amelia, this is not like you."

"No, it's not but…"

"Exactly. He's famous; his picture is everywhere. What precautions have been set in place for your safety against all the eager fans who want to get to him? Where are you going to live? If he's traveling are you traveling with him? And if you are does that mean you are no longer finishing school?"

Amelia's expression changes. "You haven't been keeping in touch with me for over a year. I can't reach you, and you think coming in here asking all these questions is okay? It's not. I won't have you berating him the first night you meet him."

"Sweetie, I just don't want you to be swayed by a good-looking boy you know nothing about."

"Do I have history of that?"

The look her mother gives is now confusing me. Is this questioning out of concern or is it something else?

"How about we table this conversation until after dinner," her father says.

Mrs. Mathews stands straightening out her dress. "Fine. Where's Poppy? Is she outside? Cole, why don't we go see her."

He smiles, taking his drink with him and as her mother reaches the door, she turns to Cole then to us.

"Amelia, dinner smells delicious. Is it lasagna?"

"Yes, it's one of our family Friday night favorites, remember?"

"I remember."

What is going on here? I wonder. They step out, and Amelia begins to put the last-minute touches on the salad. I take the tongs from her.

"I don't understand. Did I do something wrong?"

"I'm sorry. She's being ridiculous."

"If there is something I can do or say just let me know."

She buries her head on my chest as my arms circle her, willing my strength into her deflated body.

"We should have kept drinking."

I laugh. "Maybe they are tired from the flight; let them rest, then eat this wonderful meal, and maybe we can start over."

She shakes her head agreeing with me, when we notice her grandparents walk into the back yard. Her grandpa Sid comes in after greeting his daughter and son-in-law. He reaches for my hand immediately with a wide smile.

"I see you survived the inquisition."

"So far."

"You can count on there being more; in fact, I'm sure there's more. My daughter is a strong-willed individual." Grandpa Sid goes to Amelia. "How's my girl?"

"I'm okay, but she's being weird. I've never seen her so combative."

"Maybe she's tired."

"That's what Beau said, and I hope you're both right. Would you and Grandma like a lemonade?"

I pour two glasses and he sips out of one. "Tastes like it might need a little bump." He reaches over grabbing the bottle of bourbon, carefully adding some to the lemonade. He then sips and smiles. "Perfect."

Grandpa takes ours then pours bourbon into our glasses, handing each one back.

"You both need this. Come on let's go outside. Have no fear; back-up is here."

*

Her grandfather is right. We sit down for dinner and the questions continue. Mr. Mathews says very little other than to change the conversation a few times, and even Amelia's grandma tries to address her daughter but she doesn't understand her daughters tone either. There is a brief lull in the conversation, when Amelia's parents drop an unexpected piece of information about selling their house.

"Why sell? I mean you're not really here most of the year, but where will you live when your mission work stops?" ask Amelia.

Her father speaks. "We just decided to do it, so we are still discussing the details."

"So, you plan to live where, out of state or out of the country? What are you running away from?"

Her mother stands. "That's absurd."

"No, it's not. You've been gone since I showed the slightest bit of recovery from the attack and you have been distant ever since."

"Let's not get into that right now. Does anyone need more wine?" She walks to the kitchen.

"Mom, we can talk in front of Beau, I've filled him in on everything." Amelia follows her to the kitchen.

Both women are standing in the kitchen on opposite sides of the island when her mother's wine glass hits the counter. I go to stand when the others at the table suggest otherwise. Her grandmother lays her hand on mine.

"They need to do this."

I reluctantly sit back down.

"Amelia, you told him about Chase? Does he know the details, I mean does he know you don't remember part of that night and that you don't need to be stressed?"

"Yes, I told him everything. He's my husband; how could I not tell him?"

"I guess now it will be in every media source out there. You don't need any publicity about that night, and Beau probably doesn't want that kind of information out either."

I couldn't just sit there, so I walk into the kitchen. "That information belongs to Amelia, it's for her to tell. I would never put her in that kind of position."

"Yes, but you are very public. It will get out."

"But it won't be either of us letting it out," I say.

She walks over, putting her hands on Amelia's arms. "Listen to me. You don't need to be around situations that could trigger you."

"He's a singer, what kind of harm will I be around?"

"Your fans can be persistent when it comes to you. How do we know they won't come after Amelia?"

"Her safety is and will always be my priority."

Amelia's dad enters the kitchen. "Dad, what is she talking about?"

"Peanut, your memory about that night could resurface without warning. We don't know what that could do to you."

"I am aware. I saw a therapist who tried many ways to get me to remember, but nothing helped to trigger it. I just figure it's gone forever."

"I hope you don't remember. That night was a traumatic one, and one night I don't want you to ever relive," says her mom.

Amelia reaches for her mother's hand. "But it happened to me. I was attacked by someone I trusted, my boyfriend. He hurt me, but I've come out from under the pain. I won't let it stop my life. I opened myself up to Beau, and I see kindness in his eyes. I feel his gentleness when he holds me. He renewed my excitement for the future and my ability to love someone again. Mom, he means everything to me. I've moved on from that night, you need to do the same."

I slip my arm around her waist leaning in to kiss the top of her head in hopes she feels my love and support.

"I can't Amelia. I've tried, but I can't."

She pours another glass of wine and leaves for the backyard, taking Poppy with her. Cole follows behind her. Out the window I can see them embrace, which means there is more to this than what is being said.

Estelle, Amelia's grandmother, walks over to the both of us. "You both didn't deserve all of this emotion spilling out tonight. Amelia, I will talk to your mother, maybe she will open up to me."

"Isn't my moving on important?"

"It should be all that matters. Bring out dessert, let's try again."

Outside our conversation is calmer over dessert until her dad asks about my next album. Pamela's eyes cut to me with a stare that makes me regret my response.

"I finish this tour in September, by October I will be in the studio."

"Where do you live when you are not touring?" she asks.

"North Carolina. I've built a log cabin on my parents' farm. I can't wait to take Amelia there to see it."

"Do you record there?"

"No, usually I record in Nashville."

"Amelia how can you travel from state to state if you are teaching?"

"I'm putting teaching on hold for right now."

"So, you are putting your life on hold for his career?"

"I've worked double time to catch up with my studies since the attack. I've spoken to my advisor and he says I will be fine. Besides, I think it will be fun and it will give me a glimpse into his world."

"It seems like a lot of change."

"Yes, but good change. We are excited about the next chapter in our lives."

Mr. Mathews clears his throat in a way to diffuse more questioning. "How are you feeling, Beau?"

"Good. My voice is back to normal. Thank you for asking."

Amelia squeezes my hand. "I'm going to get the coffee. Beau, want to help?"

Before I can stand, her mother speaks up, "I'll help her."

I'm sitting below the kitchen window and able to hear their conversation from inside. I don't know why I feel the need to protect Amelia from her own mother. I wonder what is not being addressed?

"Mom, I thought you might want to spend time with your parents. I can get the coffee," Amelia says.

"You need to be careful, Amelia."

"What is up with you? I'm fine. I'm not stressed being with Beau. He makes me happy. He's not Chase, you don't have to worry."

"You will never understand."

"Then tell me."

There is silence inside the kitchen as I wait for an answer, but there's nothing.

"Excuse me, I'm going to use your bathroom. I'll meet you outside."

When her mother returns, everyone is laughing from a joke that Sid just told us. He reminds me of my own grandfather. A family man, who has worked hard his whole life, and you can see the love between him and Estelle even after all these years. They are the couple I aspire to be years from now--with Amelia.

Her mother is still a little on edge, which is showing in Amelia's body language. About 9:30 her parents say their good-byes, and her grandparents stay for one more glass of wine. When they walk home, I let Poppy outside while trying to help Amelia in the kitchen. She covers a dish of leftover lasagna, seemingly lost in her thoughts.

"Now that we're alone, tell me what you are really thinking."

"I don't know. I'm sorry for the way she behaved, how she made this night into a huge tension-fueled dinner. It's like every time we spoke about our future, she seemed sad. It's not fair. Why can't she be happy for me, for us?"

"Maybe she doesn't like me."

"You are very likeable."

She moves around me brushing my arm with her shoulder. We finish the last dish, and I lean on the counter wanting to take her mind off tonight.

"Ready for bed?"

"I'm too amped up to sleep."

"Then we won't."

I walk to the back door and let Poppy in. I lock the door then go to Amelia, reaching out my hand for her hand. She takes it, smiles then follows me down the hall to the bedroom as we turn off the lights. I kiss her and I don't stop kissing her until the tension is released from her shoulders and the smile is back across her lips. She pushes away from me.

"We need music. May I?"

"What do you have in mind?"

She looks over her shoulder at me. "You'll see."

She walks over to the nightstand picking up her phone and scrolling through it until she finds what she wants. She wiggles her hips as one of my songs, "Heat of Summer" begins to play. I wrote it when I was 21.

"I found this when going through all of your earlier songs. It has a sexy feel to it."

She walks to me, slipping out of her dress while performing a slow rhythmic movement of her body that's burning a hot memory inside my brain. Her fingers are up in her hair undoing the tie that's restraining it, and she bends her head slightly as it tickles her back. I swallow hard. I can't hide what she's doing to me and when the second chorus begins, she makes her way to me lifting my shirt up and over my head. Her fingers make their way across my chest, as she kisses my arm and works her way behind me. I can feel her breath on my back. Her hands slide around to the sides of my shorts as she proceeds to ease them off. I step out of them turning to face her then pull her body to me feeling the heat between us. I reach up moving her hair from her face.

"I'm not sure I will be able to sing this on stage ever again without embarrassing myself."

"Why is that?" she playfully asks.

"Because I will envision you just like this."

"Let me give you more to think about. Take off your boxers." The directness of her request gets her the results she wants. She removes the last bit of clothes she is wearing as her hand touches my cheek. "I'm all yours."

No words could ever mean more, no feeling could ever feel this strong. I'm hexed by this woman, and I go gladly.

*

The next morning while she sleeps, I make bacon waffles. I put maple syrup in the microwave to warm and then cut some fresh fruit. I pour myself a cup of coffee when my phone vibrates.

"Jason."

"Beau, how's it going?"

"Amelia and I are doing great. It's good to be at home with her."

"How was meeting the parents?"

"Her mother was not happy at all."

"Why? America's boy next door couldn't win over the parents."

"I'm not sure it's me. I mean of course they have concerns because of my lifestyle and they don't know me, but it seems to be directed at Amelia, which is odd."

"Maybe it's a family thing. I'm sure you two will weather it just fine. Hey, I checked with the label, they said since your sales have spiked with the new record and social media is favoring your marriage, they agree Amelia on tour with you would be good."

"I'm gad they approve. She's really looking forward to it."

"I'm for having Amelia on the last leg of the tour and so are the guys. I went over the last two songs you submitted and have been keeping up with your social posts. Did I tell you how goofy you look all in love, smiling all the freaking time?"

"Well I've seen a few smiles from you since you started seeing Anna."

"Yeah, she's pretty easy on the eyes and knows what this business can be like, which makes it easy to be in a relationship."

"In a relationship? Jason, are you falling for her?"

"I didn't say that. We're taking it slow."

"She's getting to you so just admit it."

"You're hopeless. I just wanted you to know we're all set. I'm also detailing the bus; you guys are nasty, and she doesn't need to come on board with all that. We will see you both on Monday morning. Now get back to your wife."

"Thanks man."

*

Poppy makes a small noise next to me then leaves to meet Amelia coming up the hall putting up her hair.

"Good morning, my husband."

"Good morning, my wife. Coffee?"

"Yes, and what did you fix for breakfast? It smells scrumptious?"

"Bacon waffles. Come, have a seat while I warm the syrup."

She moves over to the stool but not before kissing me. I take my seat next to her, watching as she inhales the wonderful sweet and savory smells.

"Babe, these are fantastic; my tummy thanks you."

"I thought you might need extra fuel this morning."

She smiles while chewing, knowing exactly what I'm talking about. Hell, we both need extra fuel after last night.

"Um, about my parents. I don't think any of what my mom was saying had anything to do with you. They've been different since my attack; well mostly she's been different. It's like she's afraid of something. I mean, when and if I get my memory back, then I will deal with it. She needs to stop worrying about all of it."

"You are her girl and she will never stop worrying about you. I do feel something is not being said, and I hope they'll come around soon. On a positive note, Jason called, and everything is all set for us on Monday."

"The label approved?"

"It seems they are now supportive of our marriage."

"That's a good thing, right?"

"I'm not pro-label yet."

"Well on another note, I spoke with your mom Wednesday. She mentioned me bringing my pound cake recipe."

"Pound cake is her weakness. She likes to taste everyone's recipes. Do you talk to her a lot?"

"Yes, she tells me stories of when you were little."

"Well you're still here, so I guess they aren't too bad."

"It's all good, she loves you; no doubt about it." She reaches over squeezing my cheek. "You were such a cute little boy."

"That was a pure Mom move."

She shrugs her shoulders, sipping her coffee.

CHAPTER 32

Amelia

My parents never came back to say goodbye to us before we left to go on Beau's tour. I can only hope someday they will tell me what's wrong, but for now I'm following my husband to see what his life on the road is about. I married a singer/songwriter--a much-loved entertainer who gets recognized wherever we go, and today is my first day living on a tour bus. My friends came over Sunday night for burgers on the grille. They were sad I was leaving, but ecstatic that I was embarking on my new life with a man who is crazy about me as I am him.

We fly into Alabama for a festival on the beach tonight. XOXO had already arrived and are in the middle of a sound check by the time we arrive at the venue. There are people moving about doing various things, and I want to talk to them all. We don't stay through the whole XOXO practice, but we will be returning in about an hour for his warm-up.

Beau leads me through a maze of buses, finally coming upon his. On the side are big black letters spelling out his name, and I'm reminded again how big he really is. We climb the steps and are met by streamers and balloons with lots of cheers coming from inside the bus. I stop on the platform while Beau stands behind me and Jeff moves towards us.

"Amelia, welcome to the bus."

"Thank you for this lovely welcome. I will try not to get in anyone's way while I'm here."

"You make the bus better already," says Wade.

Beau urges me to walk towards the back. "I'm going to get her settled before we need to be on the stage." I stop remembering my gift for them.

"I brought you all something." I pull out the bags of cookies. "Enjoy!"

If I had timed it, the cookies are gone in minutes, so I make a "note to self in the future" to make more. Beau tells me the bedroom on the bus is small, which it is, but it also feels like home.

"That's not the same bed cover I've seen in our video chats."

"No, I asked Jason to pick up a few cleaner things."

I cup his face. "You didn't have to." I kiss him. "I'm pumped to see you perform tonight. The last concert I attended was in Nashville. I know we are different now, but I don't want you worrying about me when you need to be focused on your performance."

"Once people know you are here..."

"They know already. Look."

I pull out my phone showing him my social media pages. He looks it over flipping through them while shaking his head.

"You've become quite popular, which makes me even more concerned about your safety."

I give him a look, and he slides my phone into my back pocket, kissing me as my hands settle between us.

"I'm a wife here today supporting her husband. We are normal people doing normal things on a tour bus with thousands of people about to merge onto a concert scene where you are the headliner." I nervously giggle. "I see what you mean."

"Are you ready to go?"

"I am. Let's do this."

*

The festival stage is ready for the performers and it is Beau's turn next to practice. He has me walk up onto the stage as the guys all check out their instruments, rundown the list of songs and their rituals of sorts. The lighting team is also practicing, as I see the lights twist around and change color often. Beau prompts me to follow him on the stage as he stands behind me, hooking his fingers in my belt loops. I lean against him.

"I remember feeling very scared when you had Jason bring me up on stage at our first concert. This is still very intimidating."

"I've never had an issue being in front of people performing. I'm told as a child I was fearless when it came to singing in front of others."

I turn to face him. "That's because you're a natural." I kiss him then find my way to the side of the stage where Jason provides me a stool.

I look at him arranging his guitar, messing with the mic when he turns his hat backwards and winks at me.

"Amelia, are you comfortable? Can I get you anything?" asks Jason.

"Nope I'm fine. Thank you for making it possible for me to join the tour for a few weeks."

"It's a no-brainer for me, I mean, look how happy he is. This will be fun for you both."

The practice begins and I'm glued to my stool. His voice is strong, and the connection between all the band members is fun to watch. They communicate with looks and gestures that no one else would know. I notice someone standing to my left when I realize it's the lead guitarist of XOXO.

"Amelia, congratulations on your marriage to Beau, you

guys are so cute together."

"Thanks, Darcy."

"He's a good guy; you are very lucky. I hear you are the only girl on a bus full of testosterone."

I laugh. "I am."

"We'll have you over to our bus for drinks soon--a girl's night."

"That'll be nice, thank you."

After the practice is over it is time for dinner. Sitting around the bus with the other guys gives me the opportunity to learn more about them. At the beach they were funny, relaxed, and playful. They play pranks on each other all the time. Wade asks me about Jordan, and I fill him in on some of her likes and dislikes. They've been talking over the past three weeks with hopes of meeting up when the band returns to North Carolina. We all talk about our families, and I get to see many photos. I excuse myself to get ready for the concert when Beau arrives soon after to shower. I do my hair, put on a little makeup, and lie across the bed waiting for him. He gets out of the shower with a towel wrapped around him that he's holding with one hand.

"What are you wearing tonight?"

"Jeans and that blue tee."

"How do you pick what you wear for each concert?"

"Today the blue in your eyes seemed brighter. So, I'm going with blue."

"Any rituals?"

He grins at me. "We could start a new one." He strips off the towel tossing it to me.

"What would you do if I wasn't here?"

"Call you and we would get creative." He plops down on

the bed beside me after pulling on his boxer briefs and jeans. "What do you think so far?"

"It's all well-organized. Everything runs so smoothly."

"It does because everyone has a job. The label oversees hiring of the crew, leaving us to write music and perform without worries. Jason will be able to help you with anything you need while I'm performing. Are you okay to be on the stage tonight?"

He stands up pulling on his shirt. "Wait, what did you just say about being on stage? Beau what are you talking about?"

"It's the first time my wife has joined me on tour. I'd like to bring you out for a proper introduction. Is that okay?"

"When were you going to tell me? I need to rethink what I'm wearing; I mean I would've spent more time on my hair or picked better shoes."

He sits beside me. "You're beautiful in anything you put on. Come on, what do you say?"

"I mean, I will."

"Really?"

"Yes. But remember I'm not like you, this is not easy or natural for me. What if I freeze or pass out?"

"You won't. Besides if you do, I'll be right there next to you."

I hop off the bed giving him a kiss on his cheek. I need to find concert appropriate clothing to wear in front of thousands. "I will be out in 20 minutes. Is that good?"

"Yes. Don't worry." He kisses me then grabs his cap and leaves me to prepare. My twenty minutes is up, and I descend the stairs to meet him. I'm met by the band and Jason. I decide on a hobo halter dress with black sandals. My hair is left loose, and I hang my credentials around my neck. I look up to see everyone looking back at me. Wade winks, causing me to smile as he turns to walk away with the others following but looking back at me. Jason puts his hands in his pockets and walks away smiling. I stop in front of Beau.

"Is this okay?"

He turns snapping a picture of the two of us. "Very much so. Now let's go wow the crowd Mrs. Reston."

Wow is exactly what happens. He starts his intro song, then when it is done, he begins talking to the crowd. He speaks about how his heart was lost at a concert back in June, how a Virginia girl made him the happiest man in the world in July, and now that its August, it's only fitting that she be properly introduced. Please welcome onto the stage my new bride, Mrs. Amelia Reston. He turns to me standing to the right of him off stage. I feel Jason's hand on my back nudging me towards Beau. I come out in view of everyone; I am smiling not wanting to trip or throw up on the stage. I look out at the crowd cheering then back to him where he's smiling, willing me to him. He swings his guitar to his back and meets me in the middle, wrapping his arms around me as I grip his side like my life depends on it. I know the cameras are on us both, so I'm very conscious of what my face is doing. We separate just enough for him to bend to kiss me, then hand in hand or as I see it stuck like glue, he leads me to the mic.

Phones are flashing, the audience is screaming, and as I try to look out at them, they begin to fade because of the bright lights of the stage. I feel the energy; I see women smiling not yelling or booing, at least where I can hear them. He takes the mic with his available left hand and begins to speak. He asks everyone to quiet down. He whispers in my ear that he wants me to say a few words. Fear grips me, but I don't want to let my husband down, so I take the mic with my right hand and every-one immediately quieted. *Yeah, no pressure.*

"Hello. Thank you for welcoming me tonight." I look at him still smiling. "A red dress brought us together, and through our many phone conversations we fell in love. This man has run away with my heart and I couldn't be happier." He places his hand on his chest. "He's very special to me and I know he's in good hands with you for the next hour. I'm not going to keep him from you any longer, have a great concert!" I look at him and mouth, *I love you*. He says it back then leans in, kissing me before I depart off the stage. I wave out at the audience, and my heart is pounding so hard in my chest, I'm sure others can hear it, right?

Beau flips his guitar around and states, "That's my beautiful wife, Amelia. Let's get started with one of her favorite songs."

I turn, blowing him a kiss, then I disappear off stage collecting myself, pushing air back into my lungs as Jason hugs me.

"You did great." My eyes express how nervous I am and it makes him laugh. "Here drink this." I throw it back, handing the glass back to him. "First one is always the hardest."

For the next hour Beau is like a god, belting out one song after another. He interacts with the crowd, keeping them pumped up. The energy up on the stage is fueled by the fans on the beach. Add the warm breeze coming off the ocean and the warmth of how proud I am of him, and I could not have asked for a better first day. My husband is talented, funny, and in love with what he does, giving himself back to the fans who are here for him. His love is big and it's felt.

I post a few pics on my accounts and soon I am singing and moving to the songs, while Jason tends to other details and occasionally joins me. Beau gives them two encores. After the concert, he does a meet and greet with some children from a local charity called, "Hands Up". There are about 35 of them ranging from five to sixteen. They all receive press bags and take pictures with him and the band. All the members are at the event and are hanging out with the kids. I stand off to the side just watching the special event when one of the parents approaches me holding a baby about eight months old.

"I'm sorry to bother you, but are you Beau's wife, Amelia?"

"Yes, I am."

"I know this is a big favor to ask, but would you mind holding her. I need to get my phone to take pictures of my son, Corey, and it's lost in the diaper bag."

"Of course."

"Her name is Stella."

I take Stella and place her on my hip then begin to talk to her. She smiles reaching for the strings on my dress.

"You look very comfortable with her."

"I spend my days with toddlers." The baby bends her head down resting on my shoulder. I cuddle her, swaying back and forth. "She's adorable. Which one is your son?"

She points at the boy standing next to Beau with two other boys. "That is Corey wearing the green shirt with a turtle on it. He's five."

"He's excited."

"My husband is in the Air Force, and having Corey involved in this program is wonderful. He gets to participate in so many activities I would never be able to give him. I mean, look at him, he's playing cars with Beau Reston. May I?" She holds up her phone to take pictures of Stella asleep in my arms. "My husband will love this. I'm Margo by the way."

"Nice to meet you."

"So, tonight was your first official appearance as Beau's wife?"

"Yes, other than social media pics."

"You didn't know him before June?"

"I knew of him from his music." Beau smiles at me while I pat Stella on the back.

Margo snaps a few more pictures of Corey before putting her phone away. "I'm so sorry I've kept you from joining in on the fun." She reaches for Stella. "Thank you for holding her."

"Oh, no problem."

"I knew my husband about four months before we got married. Eight years later, here we are with two kids, a dog, and a life I wouldn't change. Sometimes you just know."

She's right because that's how I feel with Beau. A bell rings signaling time for everyone to say their goodbyes. The kids give high fives and lots of hugs. I find my way over to Beau after his last goodbye.

"Whose baby were you holding?"

"Her name was Stella, and she was so freaking sweet, especially when she laid her head on my shoulder and fell asleep. Her older brother was one of the kids you met tonight."

"You're so comfortable with kids."

"It's in my blood. Now, where to next?"

"Are you hungry?"

"I am."

"Good, there is a big spread for us at the hotel next door."

I hook my arm in his. "This is a good thing. It's a unique experience for the kids and the parents who wouldn't normally have this kind of opportunity."

"We hope the kids enjoy it. How many do you think *we* will have?"

"I don't know, two?"

"How about four?"

"That's a good even number."

"Agreed. We can practice on making those babies later, but for right now let's eat."

CHAPTER 33

Beau

I notice Amelia holding a baby and it's a sight I could get used to, and one I hope will be our reality when the time is right. Soon she will meet my family and see the side of me that only they know. Dirty boots, hunting and fishing gear strewn around the cabin, and slow, peaceful nights out on the porch relaxing to the sounds of nature. It's why I built back next to the creek, and until I met Amelia, that farm was home but now it's wherever she is. Back here at the bus, I kiss her shoulder, and I see her breathing steady as she falls asleep. The journal that I've written in most every night of my life lays on the table next to the bed, but tonight my words are quiet in my head as they are sleeping soundly beside me.

*

Although touring can be fun, it's laced with long days and a kind of restlessness, but the last three weeks have been better since Amelia joined us. She's cooked a few times, had us all make pizzas one night in this cool pizza oven she found at a stop in Mississippi. We've enjoyed brownies, pies, and a multitude of cookies. We've enjoyed a few hotels and pools, found some out-of-the-way bars and did an impromptu concert next to a bus dealership, while waiting for parts to repair an electrical issue. But nothing feels better than the last leg of a tour.

*

End of the summer tour...

We're in Florida about to finish our last concert until next year. XOXO is more than ready to get back to Nashville, and we are ready to go home to North Carolina. My parents call twice a week, sometimes three, to check on us, and my sister has arranged a party so Amelia can meet everyone right away. Jason will be flying into Nashville to prepare things at the recording studio for the next album and spend some time at his own apartment and maybe time with Anna, I hope.

We are currently in a resort in Florida, which gives us many things to do, but we promised each other that a reconnection away from the band was a priority.

"Amelia, don't do it." I raise my hand towards her.

She walks around the sofa with one purpose and a child-like playfulness, as she jumps onto my lap resting her legs on both sides, pinning me against the sofa.

"Are you afraid of a little pie?"

As the words come out of her mouth, I'm hit by a pile of meringue right in my face. *Oops* is all I hear her say, followed by a giggle. I clutch her to me, rubbing my face all over her chest. She wiggles about trying to break free from my grasp, but she's mine now and I'm not letting go. Pie is everywhere as we roll off the sofa and onto the floor with a thump.

"Amelia?"

"I'm good." She giggles while reaching up with her finger removing some pie off my face, but I grab her hand tasting it for myself. She moans. "See, desserts can be fun."

"When eaten off each other?"

"Yes."

I roll over on my back as she lifts her head looking around the room, and then lays her head back down.

"We probably should clean up, we've made a mess during our playtime." She rolls to the left and is now above me. "I will start with you." She lowers her face close to mine, licking off the topping residue on my cheek. She continues her quest down my neck to the top of my shorts. "You taste delectable."

She pushes off me, stands up and goes to the cart of food we ordered, grabbing some grapes and a towel. I watch her move and notice the hem of her pajama shorts sweep ever so slightly against her skin leaving me to admire her toned legs. This woman crushes me with each step, a toss of her hair or her sweet smile. I stand, following her to the bed, grabbing a bowl of strawberries to join her. I use the towel she hands me to wipe off any remnants of our shared dessert. She smiles, twisting her hair up as the wheels in her pretty head are thinking of her next attack. I bump against her on the bed.

"Have I told you today that I love you?"

"Yes, but I can hear you say it again."

I pop a strawberry in her mouth as she tries to bite my fingers. "Not quick enough."

"This working honeymoon has had lots of perks, but the last two days holding up here in this room are hands-down the best perk of them all."

"Should we go out and see the resort?"

We both look at each other and shake our heads in agreement that we will not leave the room. I set the bowl of strawberries on the table beside me and pull her down in the bed.

"Let me show you why I think staying in is a good idea."

I hold true to my statement. Our fun playtime with dessert leaves her moaning my name through those perfect lips of hers and me getting lost in the love I have for her.

*

I am not sure if the weather is going to cooperate, but finally the clouds move out and the rain stops. People are filling the venue at a steady pace. The local radio station is hosting a contest, and Amelia and I are scheduled to take pictures with the winners before the performance. When I'm scheduled to do events, the fans want her with me now because they've fallen in love with her, and the reviews of the concert since she's been with us have been incredible. We've gotten comments about our undeniable chemistry. The fans sense that we are a normal couple that they can relate to. This has been a tour to remember, for sure.

When we are done with our responsibilities, we go backstage to a dressing room to chill until it is show time. I am talking to Wade who is filling me in on flying Jordan down to North Carolina for a visit before we all head to Nashville. I can't be happier that he's connected with her, and Amelia will enjoy having her friend near. I turn to get her thoughts but she's busy reading a text, frowning.

"Something wrong?"

"My grandfather said Poppy was stung by a bee. She does have a curious nose."

"Is she alright?"

"She had to go to the vet; it's a little swollen but she'll be fine." She shows me a picture.

"Yep, that's a big snout."

She puts her phone away. "I can't wait to see her. Can I get you something?"

"No, I'm good."

"I'm going to get a bottle of water."

"Do you want me to go with you?"

"No, it's right across the hall." She kisses my cheek then leaves.

Jason comes in telling us we are up in 30 minutes. Wade seems distracted, focusing on a paper cup a little too long.

"What's up?"

"Beau, how did you really know Amelia was the one? I mean you moved along really fast, but you seem happy," asks Wade.

"It was a feeling. It's an indescribable feeling you get when you are with them and not with them that makes you want to be with them. Now I don't know what my life was like before her."

"You know I'm the oldest band member here, and I've always been very single, but you guys take care of each other, you put each other first. You seem content only being with her. Do you think I'm ready for that?"

"Not a question I can answer, but I have to believe if you are open to receiving love, then it'll find you."

"Good advice. I'm going to talk to Amelia. Maybe she can tell me more about Jordan."

"She would be the person to talk to."

"Thanks."

*

The last show brings everything out of us all. I guess in our minds, we are done and will be going home, so why not bust loose. We give the tour the last bit of ourselves, and for us that means extra pranks. A bottle of tequila makes its way around the room, as we all take shots. Amelia sits next to me when she's handed the bottle. All eyes are on her and she turns it up. The guys all cheer for her as she shakes her head. She has not turned down one challenge while on tour. As our five-minute warning is given, I take her hand.

"This is our last concert. How do you feel?"

"Better than I could ever imagine. I will never regret having this time with you. Thank you."

"It's just the beginning."

The guys take their places as one more announcement is made before my introduction is made.

"See you in three songs?"

"I'll be right here. I love you."

I kiss her. "Love you more." The look on her face makes me smile, and I head into the first song.

*

We close the concert with a few encores, throw out merchandise, and thank everyone a few more times for attending. We begin our walk back to the bus when one of the guys suggests hitting up a bar nearby called Slammers. It would have been easier to go back to the bus and start the drive home, but everyone is pumped and neither Amelia nor I want to let them down, so we all go to the bar.

At first everything is good. We order drinks and food out on the deck, overlooking a wide beach leading out to the ocean. The stars above along with good company make for a perfect night. Wade is getting a few looks from a couple of ladies on the dance floor, but he holds back, which makes me think he might be ready for a relationship after all.

The bar is a local's dream, with tons of history on the walls. We've been here before and as Amelia and I begin looking at the graffiti on the walls, there's a commotion over by the rail facing the beach. A woman and man are arguing and some of the guys raise up from their stools to look. We try and keep a low key status when out, not wanting to cause problems, but things seem to heat up between the two. Then another guy runs up and screams what I assume is the woman's name, and fists begin to fly. The chaos that is erupting around us has me tucking Amelia behind me as more people begin to crowd around us from inside the bar. Security comes over to break it up, but it doesn't deter anyone. A stool is hoisted and then thrown into the crowd or off the deck, and then a trash can full of ice is thrown in the center of the fight, but even that doesn't dissolve the crowd. We can't move but I think we are okay in the back close to the wall, until someone yells, "Knife!"

Jason yells my name, pointing over all the chaos towards the railing next to us as someone throws a full bottle of beer that sprays all of us. The deck shifts under our feet from the extra weight, and I feel Amelia's fingers grip my arm and the back of my shirt, as she says my name. Suddenly I hear a loud crash as the deck falls breaking free of the building. We are now standing on a ledge trying to figure out how not to fall to the sand below us. People are lying everywhere. I hear Amelia whisper my name and feel her breath on the side of my cheek as I catch a glimpse of blood trickling down the side of her face, and I realize she's hurt. Adam calls from the side of the bar that is still intact. "Beau, can you get her over this way?"

"Amelia, I need you to jump towards Adam, can you do that?" I turn my head to see her nod. "Tell me if you can."

"I, I can."

"Good. We need to change positions so you are in front of me. I'm right behind you. I need you to make it a good long jump and reach for Adam. Can you do it?"

"Okay."

She does exactly as I ask, and he catches her hand as her feet dangle below. I jump right behind her to the side and pull her up onto the ledge. They pull her over the rail, and I jump over myself until we are both on solid floor. I take off my shirt pressing it to her head to stop the bleeding, not knowing how deep the wound is, but she's pushing the shirt away.

"Beau, I'm okay, it's just a scratch."

"We need to get you out of here."

She's still pushing at the shirt and seems confused. I have

one arm around her and one on her head as we rush towards the door. I see everyone except for Wade.

"Jason, where's Wade?"

As we reach the exit, I see him outside. Wade's shirt is ripped, and he's supporting a woman who is limping.

"I broke her fall. Shit, what happened to Amelia?"

"I don't know exactly, but I need to get her to the hospital." Wade hands the woman over to an EMT, who is now on the scene. We get in a car that belongs to a patron who gives us his keys. In the backseat I tend to Amelia and she's beginning to shake. Her head has stopped bleeding but she's very pale, then her eyes shut as her body goes limp against me.

Adam has been in the band for a long time playing guitar right next to me. He is a former fire fighter and is married and has two boys. "Beau, keep her still and hold her head." He reaches over checking her pulse. "Jason, how much longer to the hospital?"

"GPS says six minutes."

Adam looks back at me. "Talk to her. Say her name, let her know you are here. She could be in shock."

I do as I'm told, saying her name, talking to her, and holding the folded shirt to steady her head. She regains consciousness just before pulling into the emergency room parking lot. She is groggy and seems disoriented.

*

We arrive at the hospital, and she is taken to triage immediately, but I am not allowed to go with her. I'm pacing the floor waiting for word on her condition as my mind begins to think the worse. I make my way to the nurse's station asking them again about her, and they go in search of a doctor. Jason comes over offering coffee.

"Here, drink this."

"Something is wrong, really wrong."

"They are doing tests and all we can do is be patient. She's in the best place right now."

"She was so pale."

"Beau, I know you are upset, but whatever it is you need to be calm for her."

I hear my name.

"Mr. Reston?"

I turn to see a nurse.

"I'm Beau Reston."

"The doctor wants to talk to you."

"Can I see my wife?"

"Not until he speaks with you. Please, follow me."

I look at Jason who seems to be just as agitated as I am. "Remember, stay calm for Amelia."

I follow the nurse into a room with a sofa, and two chairs. "What about my wife?"

"Dr. Samuels will be right in. Please have a seat."

I can't sit, can't think of anything as I'm flooded by all the horrible reasons he has me in here. The door opens and he reaches for my hand.

"Mr. Reston."

"How is my wife, when can I see her?"

"Please take a seat."

"Is she okay?"

He sits down in a chair prompting me to take a seat as well, which I finally do.

"Your wife is going to be fine. The cut on her head needed four stitches, but they will be hidden in her hair so there will be no noticeable scarring. We are going to keep her overnight because I'm concerned about something else."

"What?"

"Has she had a traumatic event happen to her recently?"

"She was attacked by her boyfriend over a year ago. He stabbed her seven times. Why are you asking?"

"I saw the scars and I needed confirmation. Does she remember the attack?"

"Yes, I mean parts of it she can't. They said that some event, stress or a situation could cause her to regain it." I stop as fear races through me. "Is that what's happened? Does she remember something from that night?"

"Did you know her then?"

"No. What has she said?"

"I would like to speak to someone who has knowledge of the incident. Do you know of someone who could answer some questions for me?"

"Um, her parents or friends. Dr. Samuels, what's happening to her?"

"I believe you wife has PTSD, Post Traumatic Stress Disorder. She is experiencing painful memories from that night. She was very upset when the techs started taking her blood. She kept trying to push away from them. She began crying uncontrollably like she was fighting at someone, holding up her hands trying to block them from treating her. We had to sedate her."

I stand. "What?"

"It's just to calm her so she doesn't struggle with what's coming to the surface. To get her through this, talking with someone who was there or saw her afterwards might be helpful. If not, we will need to take other measures to get her through this."

"What did she say?"

"She mentioned Chase, then started pulling at her clothes where she was stabbed and she said, "No one heard me" over and over. The sedation will wear off and when it does, we hope she will be calmer, but that's not guaranteed."

"I can call her parents."

"Amelia may need more help in getting through this. I would like to talk to them if that's okay?"

"Sure."

"You can go sit with her once you've reached them, then let the nurse know, and she will page me. Amelia began to relax as the medicine took effect, but she did ask for you."

"Why didn't someone come get me?"

"What's important is that you are here for her when she wakes up. Mr. Reston, we will do everything we can to get her through this. The more we know the better we can help. She's in room 26. I've asked for security; I hope you don't mind."

"Thank you, Dr. Samuels."

I realize I don't have her parent's number, so I pull out Amelia's phone and find it. She changed her password to the month and day of our wedding giving me access if I needed it, and I did the same for her on my phone. Her mother answers immediately, which gives me hope things are calmer now. They are in Virginia going through their house, her mother tells me, so I fill her in what happened. She is silent on the other end, and I can hear her breathing. I offer to get her a plane ticket here, then I hear the phone fall to the floor. I call out her name, but Mr. Mathews picks up the phone and I repeat what I had told his wife. I can hear her crying in the background. He accepts my offer and thanks me for calling them. I tell him Jason will call him back with flight details.

"Beau, she's going to need you now. We will be there as

soon as we can."

*

I've been sitting by Amelia's bed for hours. She's stirred a few times, but never fully wakes. Her hand is limp, not holding on to mine. I can't help her; all I can do is sit and wait. After making the call to her parents, I spoke with Jason, filling him in, and he is going to inform the guys, then head to the airport to pick up her parents upon their arrival.

*

A few hours later the door opens and I expect to see a nurse, but instead it's Amelia's mother and father. Cole, her father, is supporting her by the arm and she is clearly shaken by what's happened. I stand but never let go of Amelia's hand. Her father reaches over putting his hand on my shoulder, and I see tears in his eyes. I realize I need to let go to give her parents a chance to be with her, but I'm feeling protective. Why am I feeling this way about her own parents?

I watch as Cole walks back to Pamela at the end of the bed, moving her to the other side of Amelia. She takes her daughter's hand and bows her head in what I thought is a prayer, but she keeps saying, "I'm sorry, I'm so sorry." A nurse comes into the room to take vitals. Cole takes Pamela by the shoulders, getting her to let go of Amelia's hand. She wipes her eyes with a tissue when she speaks to me.

"Is there somewhere we can sit and talk?"

"Can't we talk here? I don't want to leave her alone."

"No."

"I don't understand."

She waves me over to the door and I reluctantly follow.

"What I need to tell you I don't want her to hear, not yet."

"If you can give clarity about that night, then it might help her."

"It's going to hurt her."

I look at Amelia and the nurse assures me she will be fine. I walk out to the waiting room where I see Jason. He stands.

"Jason, will you sit with Amelia until we return? We need to talk and then find Amelia's doctor. I will be close, if she wakes up, please text me."

"Of course," he responds.

I ask at the nurse's station for a quiet place to talk and she sends us to an empty room down the hall. The press had figured out we were at the bar during the accident, and photographers are beginning to show up at the hospital, which is what none of us need right now. I walk into the room first, turning to them as Cole shuts the door.

"Please, I need to know what happened that night so I can get her the help she needs. Whatever you can tell me."

Cole turns to his wife and begins to talk first. "There are details about that night Amelia was never told."

She lays her hand on his arm as tears fall down her cheeks. "This is my fault."

"Pamela."

"No, Cole. You went along with it because of me. I should never have let you lie or keep the truth from her."

I feel the heat rise in my body and my muscles tighten as my mind cannot fathom what I'm about to be told. "What have you kept from her?"

She is startled by my tone.

"The night of Amelia's attack broke all of us. Our daughter had been stabbed and left to die at the hands of her boyfriend. We were told over the phone that she had multiple stab wounds that had punctured organs, and she had lost a lot of blood and was in critical condition. When we arrived at the hospital, she was in surgery to save her life."

"But there's more. What are you hiding?"

She walks to the window and begins to tell the events that night. "Chase was out of his mind. We don't know how long he had been like that, but when she got there and woke him up, he never really knew it was her, he didn't know what he was doing, or so the doctor's said. Amelia fought hard to stay alive. When I think of the fear she experienced, it just rips me apart. She was able to hit him right before she lost consciousness. It was the only thing that saved her. One of the knife punctures went directly into her uterus." She pauses. "She was eight weeks pregnant."

I take a step back absorbing her words. "Amelia never told me that."

"Because she didn't know, and I decided not to tell her."

"What? You never told her she was pregnant?"

"No."

"Why the hell not? How could you keep that information from her? How did you keep the doctors from telling her?"

"She was in a lot of pain physically and emotionally. I couldn't tell her she was pregnant with this monster's baby. Losing the pregnancy was the best thing for her."

"Are you serious? That information was not yours to keep. Your daughter was pregnant, lost a baby, and you didn't think to tell her anything?"

"No. We might have lost her twice. Her not knowing was better."

I'm shaking my head in disbelief. "Were you ever planning to tell her?"

She looks at Cole. "No, I mean not right away, but when I read she had gotten married, I knew I had no other choice."

"It would have been hard, but she needed to know."

"You didn't see her. She was pale, bruised and had just come out of surgery. A surgery to save her life. Beau, it's possible she may never have children."

I turn away from her dragging my hands through my hair not believing what I have just heard.

"Amelia talks about having kids, we've talked about having kids."

"I know, I thought we had time. I didn't expect her to fall in love this soon, or to get married."

I look back at them both. "There's more, isn't there?"

Cole steps beside his wife and they exchange a look. "Chase didn't die in a car accident," she says.

Now I sit on the side of the bed in the room. Tears sting my eyes knowing what my wife is about to learn. "Where is he?"

"He's been moved out of state. She hit him on the side of his head with a wine bottle, so his skull was fractured. There was swelling, and in addition to the drugs he took, it left him unable to speak and he's paralyzed. He hasn't regained much movement and is confined to a wheelchair. Now he speaks with a device. He has 24-hour nurse care and is monitored by the state in which he lives. One day if he recovers enough to be held accountable for his actions. He will go to trial."

"Why did you tell her he died in a car accident."

"If she had known what she did to him, it would have crushed her. She loved Chase--not like she loves you, but he had a place in her life back then. His family moved him to the mountains where he lives out each day knowing what he did to her. He's also aware he caused the miscarriage. His parents were devastated by what Amelia went through because of their son, but they are also grieving the loss of their son. Cole didn't want any part of this plan to lie to Amelia, but I needed to buy some time because once she knows everything it will change her. She won't be able to accept what I've done, and I don't blame her.

She's been triggered, things will be coming back to her, so I have no choice but to tell her, and I hope with your love and support she will recover from all of it."

"It saddens me to think you don't know your daughter at all. She's strong, determined, and loves with everything she's got. It's the reason she went to see him that night. You could have prevented the pain she's going to face now."

Cole reaches for his wife's hand. "It's time Pamela, we need to tell her. She has this young man ready to fight by her side. She is strong, we need to tell the truth no matter what happens."

I go to leave when she stops me. "Beau."

I turn around. "Yes?

"Will you be in the room when I tell her."

"I wouldn't be anywhere else."

*

Amelia didn't deserve the attack and she didn't deserve to be lied to by her parents or the staff at the hospital. How and when do you forgive this kind of betrayal? I know they kept it from her for fear of losing her, but they never gave her a chance to fight for herself, to deal with the loss of a baby, or to confront Chase. I want to take her away from all this pain, but I would be no different than her parents. I said I'd be her voice, to love and support her, and that time is now. I enter Amelia's room seeing Jason holding her hand.

"Did she wake up?"

"No. Is everything alright? Are they coming back to see her?"

"I sent Doctor Samuels to speak to them, then we just have to wait until she wakes up. I think it's best if you and the guys go home. We might be here a couple more days."

"What did they say?"

"I'll fill you in on everything later, right now she needs your prayers."

"She has them. I'll send everyone home and tell them she needs to rest a few days. I want to stay until I know she's in the clear if that's alright?"

"Sure, it is."

"We need to release a statement to the press about what happened at the bar. There's a picture out with blood on Amelia's face and you escorting her out of the bar. I can send out a blurb about it."

"Thanks Jason."

I take my place next to her. Taking her hand in mine I kiss it, as my heart breaks knowing what she's about to face now and maybe later down the road.

CHAPTER 34

Amelia

My eyes open to the light coming through the window. Things are blurry at first but then I focus, aware I'm in a hospital. Memories of my attack flood in like those slide shows in elementary school. One still frame after another, how I fought him, the fear that consumed me as I tried to get away, and frantically reaching for anything I could to defend myself. Chills form on my arms as I tuck them under the blanket but not before touching the top of my head feeling strips over what I guess are stitches from being hit in the bar. Beau is asleep in the chair next to my bed, leaning his head against his hand, and I'm sure he's been here the whole time. I need to talk to him, to let him know what I remember.

"Beau." He doesn't move. The next time I'm a little louder. He realizes it's me and now he's awake.

"Amelia." He comes out of the chair rubbing his eyes. He kisses me. "Are you in any pain?"

"I'm sore. That was a crazy night at the bar. I hope everyone was okay."

"It was a mess but all of us are fine. My concern is you."

"Did you speak to the doctor about what happened to me?"

"Yes."

"Did he tell you I remember what happened during my attack?"

"He did. Do you want to talk?"

"I don't know if it was the bump to my head or being in the emergency room with all the lights and stuff, but I began to get short pictures of what occurred that night. I couldn't really hear or feel anything at first, but then it hit me hard, and I could see his face and the knife in his hand. I felt the stabs, and I wanted the pain to stop. The nurses were trying to help me, but I just freaked out and fought against them."

"I'm sorry I wasn't with you."

I take his hand in mine tracing his fingers. "I was told this could happen, but I didn't expect..." My eyes begin to fill with tears. "I kept seeing the rage in his eyes and being so afraid I was going to die. I was crying, pleading for him to stop, but he held me down with his legs and his hand pressed against my throat after I was knocked to the floor. He didn't know me."

He takes me in his arms hugging me as I cry. "What can I do?"

"What you are doing right now. As things come to me, I just need to talk about them, get them out."

"I'm so sorry you have to re-live any of it."

"I want to go home. When can we leave?"

"Amelia, your parents are here."

I look up at him confused. "What? Why?"

"Dr. Samuels felt like you were remembering a traumatic event from your past from the way you reacted in the emergency room. He wanted to know more, and I only had what you told me, but he needed details. I did what he asked and called them."

"But they weren't with me during the attack."

"You're right."

"I don't understand."

"They're waiting outside. I'm going to get them. I'll let Dr.

Samuels know you are awake. Is that okay?"

"Sure."

When he returns, my mother and father are both with him. Mom's been crying, her eyes are swollen, and Dad looks worn out. The door then opens and a doctor walks into the room.

"Doctor Samuels?"

"Yes. How are you feeling this morning, Amelia?"

"Tired."

"Your parents are here to help you with any questions you may have about the night of your attack."

"But they weren't with me, how can they help?"

"When our brains block a memory and it returns, our reactions to the memory can be severe."

"My therapist told me that, but my parents came to the hospital after my surgery. I don't know what they can tell me that I'm not remembering."

"Let's just hear what they have to say. You can call the nurse if you need help."

"Help? Why would I need help?"

"If they tell you something to upset you, we can give you medicine to relax you."

"Oh, I see."

"So, are you ready?"

"Yes."

"Good. I'm going to set up some tests for today, order food, and see about getting you out of the hospital. Sound like a plan?"

"It does, thank you." As my parents walk closer to me, I realize all of this is probably very hard for them, seeing me in the hospital once again. They are upset and I don't want them to be. "Sorry you guys had to come all this way, but I'm really fine."

My dad walks to the side of the bed kissing my head, but my mother doesn't move closer, which makes me nervous. Dad takes my hand.

"Peanut, we need to talk."

"You are scaring me, what's going on? Mom why are you so upset? I'm fine, really I'm fine."

My mother walks towards us and sits on the bed.

"Amelia, I want you to know everything I'm about to tell you is all on me, your dad had no decision in the matter at all."

"What are you talking about?"

"When we arrived at the hospital after the attack, your doctor filled us in on your injuries, the surgery, and your prognosis. We, I mean, *I* held back information on your condition from you."

"I don't understand." My father puts his hand on her shoulder. "Just tell me."

"You were pregnant."

I look at her, then at my dad. My chest feels heavy and a wave of nausea rushes through me when I look to Beau. Our eyes meet and from the look on his face. I can tell he already knows. I look back to her.

"What? No one told me I was pregnant while I was in the hospital or even during my follow up visits."

"I asked them to not say anything. I felt your present state of mind and physical condition couldn't handle that kind of disappointment."

I shake my head at her words. "That wasn't a decision for you to make. Legally, how did you get them not to tell me? It was private information that should only have been told to me?"

"In the ambulance ride to the hospital you started bleeding and when you arrived in the emergency room that's when they knew you were losing your baby. During your surgery they removed your appendix, fixed a tear in your liver, and they had to repair damage done to your uterus. I wanted so many times to tell you."

"But yet you didn't. How far was I?"

"Eight weeks."

My mom is looking down at her hands and not at me. Tears fall, hitting her clinched hands.

"There is more isn't it?" I raise my voice. "Tell me everything."

"I don't know the extent of your healing. I'm not sure if you can ever have children."

I take in her words feeling the sharp edge of a knife all over again. "How long were you going to wait before telling me?"

"Amelia, I didn't expect you to fall in love so soon. I was trying to give you time to heal."

"Heal? How can you heal if you don't know everything? I lost a baby and I never had a chance to acknowledge that life. Did Chase know? Did he know about the baby?"

"Yes."

"So, he knew he had caused the miscarriage?"

"Yes."

"Oh my god, what he must have been feeling knowing what he had done?"

"Amelia, he could have killed you."

I close my eyes and when I open them, tears run down my face.

"And he killed a part of both of us in the most horrible way possible."

"You don't blame him for what he did to you?"

"I've resolved and forgiven him. He's not here to speak on his behalf, so I've forgiven him and let it go, so I could heal."

My father walks away from the bed. "Tell her Pamela."

"What else are you not telling me?"

"Chase is alive."

"No, I don't believe you. I heard them say in the hospital that his heart stopped, but then *you* said he died in a car accident. So which is it? "Did you lie about that too? Why keep this information from me?"

"To protect you from that monster."

"He was no monster! Chase could not control what he did that night. He was under the influence of a drug that altered his mind. If he's still alive what happened to him, why haven't I heard from him?" I fold my arms around my body unable to stop the flood of tears or the ache in my heart.

"He's different."

"How?"

"In trying to fight him off, you hit him on the side of his head with a wine bottle. His skull was cracked, there was swelling, and it's left him unable to process thoughts or speak clearly. He has limited functionality from the chest down. He lives with his parents up in the mountains where he is under watch of the state. Amelia, he knows what he did to you and he knows the part he played in you losing the baby. Your dad wanted to tell you the truth then and every day since. I just wanted to give you time to get stronger. It's been hard lying to you, and when you married Beau, I knew I couldn't keep this from you any longer. This is why I had to distance myself from you."

I look away from her. I've always trusted my mother and I've always been able to talk to her about anything, but now I don't know who she is. My father reaches for my hand.

"Peanut."

"No Daddy, I want to talk to Beau, alone. Please."

Mom stands. "We can wait outside."

"Don't. Go home. I need time to think about all of this."

"Amelia, please, let me help you."

"No. That time is gone. Go home, let me decide what to do next."

I know my words are breaking her heart, but I can't focus right now with all of the information she's just told me. My dad comes over kissing my cheek, then guides my mom towards the door. As it shuts, I begin to cry, and Beau sits beside me on the bed, wrapping his arms around me. I'm overwhelmed and devastated by the lies, the loss of a baby, and knowing I could be the reason Chase will never recover. My future prognosis is ripping out my heart because I know how much Beau wants children-- how much I want children.

*

Breakfast is delivered, but I only touch a few sips of coffee. Jason comes by to check on my release and to speak with Beau. I force a smile and thank him for being so supportive. When Jason leaves, I ask Beau to lie in the bed beside which he does. Surrounded by his arms and feeling the weight of his body brings me peace.

"You had no idea that the woman you married was so broken."

"Don't say that, you're not broken."

"You and I have talked about kids, what if I can't have them?"

"We know there are options if you can't carry a baby."

I tuck myself closer to him.

"I'm sorry, you don't deserve any of this craziness."

He guides my chin up to look at him.

"You have nothing to say sorry about. Amelia, I'm in love with you, and I'm ready to face all of this with you."

"Yes, but kids were going to be a part of our life together. If I can't…"

"Do you have any idea how blessed I was to find you? How honored I am that you said yes and married me? Do you know my heart is fuller and that I love deeper because of you?"

I reach up kissing him. "I feel the same about you, but I don't want you regretting marrying me."

"We are going to have an amazing life whether it's the two of us or more of us. I'm never letting you go."

"Promise?"

"Promise."

With a kiss, my concerns get a small vacation of sorts. I fall asleep knowing I was strong before, but with Beau's love and support, I will be even stronger now.

CHAPTER 35

Beau

We stay another day in Florida after Amelia's release, just the two of us. We talk every time she has a memory flashback or needs to discuss what she now knows. I can see the tension leave and the smile I love appear, then disappear again. We are leaving today for Amelia's home in Virginia for a few days before heading to North Carolina where she will meet my family.

She hasn't spoken to her parents since they left the hospital except to text that we would see them when we return home. She struggles with the decisions they made, but to move on she knows what needs to be done. She's been quietly looking out the window of the plane when she turns to me.

"Are you sure you want to go with me to see Chase?"

"Yes, 100%. Why?"

"It could be difficult for you to see the man who hurt me."

"It will, but if you are ready to see him, I want to be there with you. Is it what you want to do now?"

"When I thought he had died, I spent the last year forgiving so I could move on with my life. Now knowing he's living with so much pain from what he's done, I just need to address it. Then I think, will he be able to forgive me?"

"Amelia, I don't think he's ever blamed you. My guess is that he lives everyday knowing what he did to you and that he caused the miscarriage. He probably thinks he deserves what life he has now."

"He doesn't."

"I know."

"I wonder if he knew this whole time that I didn't know about the baby or even that he was alive."

"I guess we will find out when we see him. I do think he's going to be happy to see you."

"Really?"

"Pretty sure."

"Thank you." She leans over giving me a kiss. "You have been my rock through all of this."

"Beside you is where I always want to be."

*

Amelia's grandmother makes us dinner, leaving it in the crockpot when we arrive home that night. We eat, soak in the tub, and bring life back into our tired bodies. Poppy is happy to see us this morning. I'm outside tossing her a ball as Amelia joins me with coffee.

"She loves the attention."

"I think we should take her to North Carolina when we drive home."

"No plane?"

"No. Besides we can see so much more driving."

"Did you hear that Poppy? You are going to meet Daddy's family." She licks Amelia's cheek. "Doggie kisses."

Poppy runs off into the yard as I pull out my phone.

"Amelia, I want you to read some of the comments about our post yesterday."

She begins to read as I slip back in the house to refill my coffee cup. I see her out the window of the kitchen smiling. She's the most important person in my life. I can't shield her from any of the pain she's experienced or will experience, but I will always be here to love and support her. Her phone pings on the counter with a text from Jordan. I know Wade has spoken to her about coming to North Carolina, which she accepted excitedly, he said. But before I can take Amelia away, she will confront her past one person at a time.

*

Amelia's parents live about 45 minutes away, on five acres of land in a subdivision where she grew up. It's a charming white two story well kept at the end of a cul-de-sac. Kids are riding bikes, and people are out watering their lawns. There are two women with strollers walking, and Amelia eyes them, waving as we drive by. I pull up in their driveway and turn off the engine. Looking up at the house then back to my wife, I see her eyes are closed, and she's taking in a breath then letting it out. I wait until she opens her eyes.

"Ready?"

"Yes."

Hand in hand we walk up the five steps to the front door. Her father answers, giving his daughter a hug.

"Peanut, your mother is down by the garden. She wants you to come out there if that's okay with you?"

"Sure." She turns to me "I'll be back." She kisses me. "Dad, offer Beau some water; this might take a while."

"I will."

I follow Mr. Mathews to the kitchen where he offers me a beer, but I take water instead. He throws me a bottle, taking one for himself. I look out the big picture window to see Amelia walking a path to a flower garden where a vine covered trellis leads her out of sight. I turn back to see him looking out the same window.

"How heated will the conversation between the two of them get," I ask.

"Pamela has always been protective of her daughter. We tried for years to have a baby before Amelia. We went through five miscarriages and almost lost Amelia at the sixth month mark, which could be why she was so worried about her. They've always been close, able to tell each other everything. They will find their way back to each other." He rubs the back of his neck. "I was standing right here in this kitchen and we fought hard about what Pamela wanted pleading with me to give Amelia time to heal, but I felt she needed to know. It put a strain on our marriage, but I love her, and I knew the day would come where Amelia would know the truth. All Pamela could comprehend was how devastated Amelia would be to find out she had lost a baby. Not to mention feeling responsible for Chase's current condition. You were right back at the hospital."

"About?"

"We didn't give enough credit to our daughter that she was strong enough to handle everything at once. So, I guess all we do is wait."

CHAPTER 36

Amelia

Walking towards the gazebo reminds me of my childhood. Flowers were something that gave mom and I one-on-one time to sort out life's issues. I played mostly in the dirt when I was younger while she did the hard stuff, but as I got older, she taught me the art of solving problems. This is the perfect place to regain clarity.

She's sitting in a cushion-lined wicker chair. There are two glasses of tea, and a plate of cookies. It's what she would do when I had real problems that needed her loving hand to help me through them.

"Amelia."

"Mom."

I walk over sitting in the chair next to her, as she picks up the plate of cookies.

"Would you like one? They are frosted lemon."

"Thank you." I reach for a cookie.

She sets the plate down taking her seat.

"You look good."

I flip the cookie around in my hands contemplating where I want to start.

"Beau has been supportive, we've talked, and I've cried, mourning a new loss. I'm really trying to understand, but I need you to tell me why you kept all of this from me even after I got better."

"I told myself every day that I was going to tell you, but every day I found one reason not to confess the truth. The guilt of holding back information from you weighed heavy in my chest and on my mind. I was scared that you would have a setback or that the pain would be too much for you to ever forgive me. My fear overtook my common sense and I am so sorry."

"It was going to hurt me *then*, just like it's hurting me now. Mom, no one could've kept me safe that night."

"I know."

I stand walking to the other side of the gazebo. "What about the miscarriage?"

Her eyes are glassy, as she wipes off her cheek with her hand.

"You should've been told so you could have grieved. I'm surprised your doctor didn't say anything at your follow up visits. I held my breath that whole visit."

"Remember the fire alarm went off and it was cut short. I didn't feel the need to go back, so I didn't. I was seeing a therapist and that was all I needed. My body was healing, it was my mind that needed to figure out how to move ahead. What about Chase? What will happen now?"

"He could still have charges against him, but his prognosis has kept him out of jail, he is unfit to stand trial at this time. He's watched and visited by the representative in the town where he lives for signs of improvement. They didn't expect him to recover at all. His brain has been permanently damaged."

"What does Chase know about me?"

"That you are living your life."

"I work every day to move past what happened, but I feel you will be stuck blaming Chase."

"Well, he hurt you."

"Yes, he did and so did you, but I want to live for the future, not the past. I don't want to be angry with you because it will keep me in the dark, and I owe it to myself to live every day to its fullest. I fell in love with an incredible man, and I want him to know how wonderful you can be. I need you to stop wallowing in the past and embrace the future that is right here. Mom, can you do that?"

She stands. "Amelia you are so strong, and I love you so much."

"I love you too."

I move to her, opening my arms needing to feel her hug. When we finally let go, she looks past me towards the house, wiping off her face.

"I owe Beau an apology for giving him such a hard time when we first met. It wasn't that I didn't like him, I was coming face to face with the person who was pushing my secret to the surface." She moves a piece of hair behind my ear. "I'm also sorry for not being happy that you found love. It's a special time for you and I let you down."

"Well let's stop the cycle. I've got good bones and a solid foundation to bring into my marriage, and he deserves the best I have in me."

"He's a lucky young man to have you."

"We are both lucky. He's an amazing man who you have yet to get to know."

"You are right, so let's change that."

"Good. Are you still selling the house?"

"Yes. We want a smaller place, maybe in town near your grandparents."

"They will love that." I add, somewhat reluctantly, "I'm going to see Chase."

She forces a smile. "Okay."

We walk back to the house with our arms around each other. We were close before all of this, and I know we will be again.

*

The next day Beau and I drive over two and half hours up into the mountains looking for the house that Chase now lives in with his parents. When the GPS indicates that we have arrived at our destination, I strain to look up at the house, and Beau is just as surprised.

"Are you sure this is the right address?"

I look at my phone once again from the text my mom sent me. "Yes."

We both get out of the car, walking along a paved path to large glass front doors. I reach for the doorbell, when I see Chase's mother walking towards us. She looks at me, then at Beau. We can hear her call out to her husband, and in seconds he appears. She opens the door for us and I immediately sense their pain mixed with relief. It is an odd mixture of feelings, but I understand. I feel Beau's hand on my back giving me a reassuring rub, when Mr. Richardson speaks.

"Amelia, it's good to see you."

"Thank you, Mr. Richardson. This is my husband, Beau Reston."

Beau reaches out his hand and the two men shake, greeting each other as I walk to Mrs. Richardson and give her a hug.

"You look so good," she says to me.

"Thank you."

"Beau, it's nice to meet you. Oh, my goodness, where are my manners. May I get you both something to drink?"

I look at Beau and we both say no that we are fine.

"Thank you for allowing us to come by today. I know it's short notice."

They exchange a smile. "May we talk in the sitting room before you see Chase?"

"Sure."

We are led to the room Mr. Richardson had come from, seeing a table with a pitcher and four glasses between two sofas. We take a seat across from them.

"Amelia, we've thought about you every day since that night. We want you to know how sorry we are for what happened to you," says Mr. Richardson.

"I appreciate you saying that. I didn't know Chase was alive until a few days ago. I also didn't know it was me who put him in his current situation, and I'm truly sorry for what he's going through."

Mrs. Richardson reaches for her husband's hand. "No, no dear. You were fighting to survive that night--the fear you must have felt. Chase regrets his actions every day and is very sorry for what he did. What he's experiencing now and maybe for the rest of his life is nothing compared to the pain he caused you."

"We both lost a lot that night."

Mr. Richardson wipes his eyes. "I said I wasn't going to cry, not very manly, huh."

Beau hands him another tissue. "It makes you human."

Mrs. Richardson continues. "Chase once told me that he thought of marriage, and he thought you could be the one. Now, I'm not telling you this to make you upset, I want you to know he did care about you."

"I know he did."

Mr. Richardson hands me a folder.

"We want you to take this; don't read it now, but after you

see him. We want only the best for you, Amelia. We're here if you ever need anything."

I take the folder from him. "I appreciate that, thank you. May I see him now?"

"Yes."

We all stand up and Beau takes the folder, tucking his other hand in mine. Walking to where all the natural light is coming from the back of the house, we see a line of windows from floor to ceiling, giving a view of the property behind the house. There are trees to the left, a pond, and open fields to the right with a few horses. There is exercise equipment, a big screen TV, a sofa, and a couple of chairs. There are large spaces for a wheelchair to pass easily. Beau squeezes my hand and I look over at him. He winks, letting me know he's right here for me.

An aide comes out from another room pushing a wheel-chair towards us. The guy doesn't look like the Chase I remember. He's thinner now, wearing sweatpants and a pullover long sleeve shirt. His hair is longer--not his normal buzz cut. She pushes the chair over by the sofa and when she turns him to face us, he locks his eyes on me and the power of our first look is surprising. The aide places her hand on his shoulder as if to comfort or calm him. Mrs. Richardson moves over to him.

"Chase. Amelia wants to talk to you. Remember we spoke about her coming by today?"

I see tears filling his eyes and he rubs a partially gloved hand over his face. Thoughts of us before the attack, the intimacy we shared, is quickly replaced by the brutality of the attack. My fear and not knowing if I would survive, all hit strong as a chill passes through me. I swallow hard trying not to lose it by breaking down.

Chase's mother reaches out for her son's arm. "Are you okay?"

He types on a keyboard then a voice says the words. "Can I

have time alone with them?"

"Of course." His mother walks back over to us. "He communicates easier through the computer. He'll type it, then it will say his words just like you heard. If it's a short response, he will say it. We are going to leave. Please take your time." She calls back to the aide still with Chase.

"Jenny, why don't you come with us."

The woman touches his arm before walking past us. I don't know if she knows who I am or why we are here, but she seems protective of him.

"Do you want me to leave?" Beau asks.

"No. I want to introduce you." I take his hand and we walk over sitting on the sofa next to Chase. "Chase, this is my husband Beau Reston. Are you okay if he stays?"

He types then we hear his response. "The country music singer?" He looks past me to Beau then types. "You are welcome to stay." He types again but stops. This time he says the words, but they come slowly. "I'm sorry for what I did to you."

"I'm sorry, for what I did to you."

He types. "Please don't apologize. How I am now is nothing compared to the pain I inflicted on you or the time you lost at my hands." He types again. "I'm sorry about the loss of our baby. I will never be able to erase that night for you or for myself. I remember enough to know the damage I caused. I don't blame you if you hate me."

"No. Chase I don't hate you. What you experienced that night wasn't you, it was what you were taking. I wish you had opened up to me or to your family. I came that day to talk to you, to see if I could help you. The Chase I loved would never hurt me, and it's the truth." Tears fall on his keyboard.

I pass him a tissue and our hands touch. I see the wounds he carries with him. Some physical but the ones trapped inside need to come out. I kneel by his chair.

"I forgive you Chase, but I need you to forgive yourself." He begins to cry, and my instinct is to comfort him. I stand wrapping my arms around him, laying my chin on his head. His free hand comes up to touch my arm, but he hesitates. I notice and take his hand in mine. "I'm not scared for you to touch me. If you don't forgive yourself, how can I ever forgive myself for putting you in this chair."

He types. "I deserve worse."

"No, you don't." I stand up straight pulling up my shirt to show him my scars as he closes his eyes unable to see the reality of what's left behind. "Chase look at me. I covered each of the seven scars with sea turtles because I had to find my strength, my courage to move on. I have to be patient in my recovery however long it takes, but I want to be present in my future. Each turtle makes me stronger. I reach for Beau's hand. I'm happy, I've found love and I want you to get stronger and be happy too. Can you forgive yourself?"

He looks up at me then types. "I don't know if I can."

I take his hand. "Please try for me."

He moves his head agreeing then says, "I will try for you."

"Good."

He looks to Beau then types. "Her smile is one I miss, and I'm happy she found you. Be the man she deserves."

Beau holds out his hand to Chase. "I will do everything in my power to do just that."

I'm crying again. "Don't give up or I will come back here and fight your skinny ass."

He smiles and says, "I know you will."

Wrapping my arms around him, I want him to know I care about him, that I can now move forward and I wish only the best for him. He struggles to pick his arms up high enough to hug me, so Beau moves in to help. I tell him I love him and place a kiss on his cheek. I can feel a swell of sadness in my chest as I turn to leave but he catches my fingers. I turn back to see him type.

"You are a beautiful soul, Amelia Reston."

"So are you. Always remember that."

*

Out in the hall before we can clear the doorway, Jenny moves past us to Chase. Beau and I watch as she leans down in front of him, touching his hand and they share a tender moment. We find his parents in the foyer waiting for us to say our goodbyes, and then we walk down the stony path to the car. I pull Beau close to me, needing to feel him all around me.

"Thank you for coming with me."

"I'm glad I was here. How do you feel?"

"Emotionally drained, but happy. I just hope it was enough to keep him fighting."

"Well, he seems to have the devotion of his aide."

"I saw that too. Everyone deserves the love of another. I feel we both had closure today, at least I hope he did."

"You gave him the okay to do just that. Now, where to?"

"How about ice cream. I saw a little country store on the way here with a giant ice cream cone displayed outside. Want to stop?"

"Good eye."

He kisses me then shuts the car door behind me walking to the driver's side. I hope coming here was enough for Chase to forgive himself. We've both been through so much, and now it's time to let it go.

CHAPTER 37

Beau

When I left home six months ago, I was single, writing songs, and missing something in my life. But now with my wife sitting next to me, I'm in love and looking forward to our future. We come with some baggage, but nothing is going to stop us.

The long driveway leading to my parent's house is surrounded by fields of peanuts ready for harvest. I've seen them for years but now they hold more meaning than before. This farm has been in our family for many years and hopefully many years to come.

Amelia puts the window down looking out at the fields, as Poppy hangs her head out taking in the scents new to her.

"Poppy is going to love this. I've seen peanuts growing while on vacation, but now that you have filled me in, I can't wait to help with the harvest someday."

"My dad will jump at that chance. Be prepared my mother will try and introduce you to each family member, relative or neighbor while you are here. She means well, but it can get to be a little much."

"She's a proud momma. This is going to be so much fun."

*

We pull up in front of my parent's house and of course they are all sitting on the porch. My sister's two kids are riding bikes around the loop of the driveway. I see my brother sitting with a few of his friends on the steps.

"We could keep driving to the cabin."

She touches my arm, giving me the look that gets her anything she wants from me.

"No way, I've been looking forward to this."

"I hope you feel that way in 24 hours." I park the car and see my brother heading towards us, then he opens the door for her.

"Welcome Amelia." He holds out his hand to help her out.

"Thank you, Jake."

"Wow, you are prettier than the pictures. Dude, she's too good for your ugly mug." He leans into hug her mouthing to me, "Oh my god." He backs away from her, looking at the over excited lab in the back seat.

"She's anxious to get out of the car. May I?"

"Please."

He opens the door of the SUV petting her first, then lets her out. She bounces around us then heads to the grass to relieve herself. She runs back to us as he reaches down to pet her again.

"She's cute."

I slap my brother on the back. "Much cuter than you."

"Good to see you big bro. How was the tour, full of hot girls wanting your body?"

I put my arm around Amelia's shoulder. "Only one hot girl wanted this body, so I married her."

"Jake." My mother comes over to us. "Stop taking so much time with them. Amelia has a lot more people to meet."

My mother is itching to get her arms around Amelia, another girl added to the family makes her very happy, especially since it meant I was now married. She hugs me, then kisses my cheek.

"Hey mom."

"It's good to see you, son, you look happy, but I should whip your butt for going off and getting married without us." She smiles at Amelia. "But all is forgiven. Amelia, it's so good to finally meet you in person." Her arms wrap my wife in a wonderful hug.

"It's good to finally see you too."

"My son does things a little differently, but he has a good heart. Your father will be here for lunch. Something came up at the barn. He sends his apologies for not being here. Now, let me introduce you to the rest of the family."

She guides Amelia over to the others, who come off the porch to meet her and welcome us home. Amelia fits into the family right away. She meets each member individually, and when it comes to my sister Meg's two kids, she shines, showing her unique ability to get them to listen to her every word.

A huge lunch is set up on the back deck with a load of Reston family favorites. They go all out and are even making homemade ice cream. As we pass the tables, Amelia bumps me when she points out the sliced watermelon.

"Best night of my life," she says.

I kiss her cheek. "I agree."

*

We go straight to eating, asking Amelia more questions. The best one by far is from my brother.

"What do you see in Beau, Amelia?"

My mother comes up next to me handing me a beer.

"Thank you, Mom."

He continues needing an answer. "I can see how you fell for her so fast, but what did you see in him, Amelia?"

My mother whispers next to me. "A light surrounds her,

and you have not stopped smiling. You really fell in love with her, didn't you?"

"I did. I know it's corny to say she completes me, but it's true."

"Nothing is wrong with that."

"Come on Amelia, was it his stardom or his fortune?"

I intervene. "Jake, really?"

"What?"

"Your brother is hot."

Jake makes a motion like he's throwing up. "That can't be it."

Amelia laughs at his actions. "He's kind and loves with his whole heart." The room gets quiet. "He's sweet, supportive, and passionate. He loves me exactly as I am, and I love him in the same way. Oh, and he's a great kisser." The room is no longer silent, there is laughter as we all look at Jake who is holding his stomach.

"Too much information. He's a goofy looking guy, no way."

She giggles. "You asked."

I slap him on the back of his head. "Enough, get out of here."

Mom sends him on his way with a slice of pie, enjoying the interaction between her boys. "The cabin is all ready for the two of you. I put some food in the fridge, and it's been cleaned. I will keep your brother and his friends away for tonight, but they will probably be over there first thing tomorrow. He misses hanging out with you, no matter what he says."

"I miss him too. Maybe next time he could come out on tour."

"I could use a distraction," says my sister.

"Meg, you are invited anytime you want."

"Thanks, I appreciate the standing offer."

Mom stands to leave. "Well he starts college in the fall, and you know how we feel about that. Besides he likes to play so much more than you did at that age, for sure."

"Enough talking about Jake. It's my turn to have some sister-in-law time before you take her away to the cabin. Amelia, would you like dessert?"

"Yes, definitely."

Meg walks Amelia over to the dessert table pointing out the best choices. They're talking, laughing, and looking over at me, and I only hope she's not embarrassing me with a story from my past.

I see my father and uncle come into the room and I go to greet them. My father hugs me as he always does and lets me know how much he's missed me. I point out Amelia to him and he smiles telling me he's happy for us both and can't wait to meet her. My uncle slaps me on my back and congratulates me. I can be gone for months, but when I step back into the family it's like I never left.

*

We pull up to the cabin and let Poppy out to run. The cabin is built next to a stream that runs through our property. It was one of my grandfather's favorite places to sit and listen to the quiet or pluck out a tune on his guitar. I knew I wanted to build back here, so renovating the old cabin was an obvious choice and it turned out better than I ever dreamed. I meet Amelia in front of the SUV.

"Can you hear it?"

She looks to me then listens. "What?"

"Quiet. No traffic, no phones ringing. and no cameras. It's peaceful."

Holding her backpack on one shoulder and placing her hand around my neck she rises on her toes to kiss me when we hear a loud crash.

"What was that?"

"Sounded like a tree. See, everything here is falling for you."

"Cheesy line but it works."

"Come on, I'll show you around." I scoop her up carrying her over to the porch then over the threshold, as Poppy runs in past us. "Wow, my mom outdid herself. The place looks good."

"Beau, its adorable."

"Now it's a home with you."

"Show me all of it."

*

The rest of the day and into the night is just for the two of us. We are almost asleep, when a phone vibrates loudly on the counter in the kitchen. She moves and I slip out of bed.

"Yours or mine, she sleepily asks."

"Mine. It's Jason." I answer it reluctantly. "Trying to sleep here."

"Well, this can't wait."

"Don't do that."

"What?"

"That usually means my personal time is being cut short or there's a big change coming."

"Beau, change is good, right?"

I make my way back to the bedroom lying next to her. "Spill it." Amelia sits up beside me with the sheet hooked under her arms. Even Poppy is awake now.

"Jason, it's better to rip off the bandage quickly."

"It seems the studio over-booked."

"How?"

"I don't know but they did. I'm thinking we try another studio in town, say Studio Six?"

"Not my first pick."

"I know, but it's either we try, or we put it off until January."

"Wait this album is part of my contract, shouldn't Spot On Records make this work out?"

"Well it's not totally their fault. I supposedly dropped the ball on confirming the studio when I was on vacation at the beach."

"You? Never. It must be something else. I saw you do business while we were at the beach house even though we were all on strict orders not to. Or were you preoccupied with a certain female companion who kept your mind fuzzy?"

"Love doesn't come as easy for everyone like it did for you and Amelia. Anna is fresh out of a relationship and not ready for another commitment. I will let you know about Studio Six once they get back to me. Look, if we have to wait, we will, I'm not going to complain about a little extra down time."

"Fine, maybe they've changed since the takeover. Will you be here for the party?"

"Wouldn't miss it, will you be out of bed when I arrive?"

"No promises." I hang up tossing the phone over onto the nightstand.

"What's the difference in studios?"

"A vibe and in this case, management working inefficiently." I reach up under the sheet as she jumps holding her breath trying not to giggle. "Now that we are awake…"

She curls into me touching my face and bringing her lips to mine but stopping a breath away. "How about chocolate cream pie?"

"I saw that in the fridge. Pie it is."

Out of our bed and into the kitchen, we cut slices of pie and head out onto the front porch to an amazing end to our first day.

CHAPTER 38

Beau

Jason's call really didn't bother me much last night, because Amelia helped me remember we were on break. Loving each other is worth any lost sleep, so we stayed in bed a little longer this morning.

Wade picked up Jordan at the airport today, then they dropped off her luggage at his house, taking a small tour of his place. Afterwards, they came to the cabin for brunch. After eating, we decided to take a hike. Wade and I went ahead of the girls giving them some time to talk...

"Jordan, stop. What does his house look like, and are the tattoos all over?" I turn my phone to her. "Lily wants to know."

"Text her back and tell her noneyabusiness!"

"I told her you will get back to her." I put my phone in my back pocket. "So, tell me about his house."

"It's small, masculine in décor. But the barn is amazing. It's basically his second home. Pool table, pinball machines and hunting gear are everywhere. The fridge is full of beer, and there is an incredible bar made from hand carved wood that he said Beau helped him make. He also has two motorcycles and a big ass pickup truck. Amelia, I really like him, he's my kind of fun wrapped up in all those muscles."

"I think he likes you too."

She blushes. "He's definitely growing on me."

*

Beau

Yesterday after the hike, we decide to float the river today before the cookout. We make phone calls and are scheduled to meet at nine this morning. There's a lot of laughter, raft flipping, and great friends to introduce Amelia to. My sister plans most of the dinner, but the burgers and hotdogs are my responsibility.

Amelia steps into the kitchen while I prepare the aluminum tray of hotdogs, putting the finishing touches on a braid in her wet hair from a shower. I notice she is wearing jean shorts and one of my old band shirts. Her hands come up under my shirt, and I straighten my back as she runs her nose across the fabric.

"This is torture."

"If that's how you feel." She begins to walk away.

I grab a towel wiping my hands, twisting to swallow her up in my arms covering her sweet mouth with mine while tasting mint toothpaste. She doesn't wiggle, she molds herself against me.

"I'm actually feeling a lot of things."

She wickedly smiles. "Um I can tell."

We hear a loud interruption from Jordan.

"Oh my god, you have a room to do all that in, so why don't you go, and I will cover for you. Where's the booze old man?"

"What the hell Jordan. Old man?" I look at Amelia who is stifling a laugh. "You do know Wade is older than me, right?"

"Yes, and I think older men are sexy, but you are close behind." She slinks down onto a stool. "So, what's happening, family party first, get freaky party later for the adults?"

I pick up the pan of dogs. "Come on ladies, grab that other pan, those utensils, and follow the old man to the grill. We have lots of hungry people coming."

"For an older guy he does have a nice ass," Jordan says.

My wife responds, "It's firm." They both giggle as I hold the door open for Jordan then for Amelia who teases me with another kiss.

"I guess I'm not hurt then. You really think my ass is firm?"

Wade steps up on the porch. "Yep it is."

"Not cool man, not cool."

*

My family and friends along with a few neighbors are all over the yard. My sister Meg texts me that one of her kids has thrown up, so she is going to be late. I send a message to Jake who goes to retrieve everything from her. He drops them off, sets up some tables, and then leaves to shower.

When he returns, he's with three friends, along with two girls I don't recognize. Amelia, Jordan and I are standing by the grill when they approach. The boys go to Amelia and Jordan and the girls stand next to me. They introduce themselves then ask permission to take a photo. I'm always happy to take pictures with people as long as they are cool, and they are, so my brother must have spoken to them before they arrived.

After the hotdogs and burgers are cooked, it is time to eat. Meg comes in with one of the kids, leaving her husband at home with little Lewis. I'm sorry he's sick, but I'm happy she didn't have to miss out on her own planned party.

The sun sets, lights are strung from tree to tree, and everyone is playing a game or just hanging out by the fire pits. I love coming home and being able to just relax amongst them. I'm knocked forward by someone who just hit me in the shoulder. I turn to find out who and why, when I see Wade. He's smiling and it's making me kind of uncomfortable.

"What the heck?"

He stumbles almost falling over the chair as I reach out for his arm to help him sit down. He takes in a deep breath and re-positions his ball cap on his head.

"How did you know?"

"What, that you might be drunk?"

"Come on Beau, you know."

"I don't know, so why don't you enlighten me."

"Women."

"You need to be more explicit with what you are asking."

He leans forward leaning his elbows on his knees. "They, I mean, she."

"She who?" I wanted to get him to say her name.

"She's soft, and curvy but fiercely strong. She's funny, career-driven, and smells of coconuts, sand, and sun if that is even a thing."

"What are you talking about?"

That's when his hat comes off his head and he thrusts it at me. "Jordan, you ass. How did you know you loved Amelia and that you wanted to spend the rest of your life with her? One woman forever?"

He's holding up a number one on his left hand. I look over at Amelia playing a game of horseshoes with my uncle. I could tell him every little thing about her that made me fall in love, but I think he just wants to know that what he's feeling is real.

"So, you're having feelings for Jordan?"

"Lots of feelings."

"It has to be more than a physical attraction. I know you talk to her a lot on the phone, you invited her here, and you get all high-school-crush around her. Are you interested in marriage?"

"No, no I'm not talking marriage, but I could be exclusive

with her. I feel she could handle my lifestyle, the times apart, and all the public stuff we do. I miss her when we go a few days without talking."

"There you go. It hits you like a kick to the chest, or a ball to the face how much you miss being with her, doesn't it?"

"This shouldn't hurt, right?"

"No, it's going to be a big deal in the best way possible. My advice to you is to go with this feeling and see where it takes you. We don't get guarantees in life but if we have an opportunity to experience love, then we need to pay attention because it could be the best part of our lives."

"You're right. I need to act on these feelings. Who knows, maybe she feels the same about me?"

"Correct. Now, let me get you some food and water."

*

Around 9:00 p.m., some of the families with kids leave, and by ten it's just the die-hard grown-ups ready to drink and as Jordan said, "get freaky" party. Music is such a big part of our lives that we never have a party without it, but it's not us playing tonight, it's all the music we grew up with as well as current songs that inspire some smooth and some very awkward dance moves from everyone. Beer games are set up in a couple of places and a rather loud game of horseshoes continues. After my conversation with Wade, I encourage him to drink some water, so his head stays in a good place.

*

Sometime around 2:30 in the morning Amelia and I come inside, leaving Jordan and Wade around the fire pit.

I'm in need of my wife, so we take to the couch in the cabin. With a little touch from her, my body reacts and a small grin forms on her lips. She's lying on top of me and our hands are all over, our mouths crash together heightening our desires.

She moves her hand slowly between us as a low growl escapes me. Her hips move and her fingers are in my hair holding me just where she wants me, when a loud rapping at the door stops us and she falls to my chest burying her head in my neck.

"Who can that be?" she groans.

"I'm going to hurt whoever is on the other side of the door." I kiss her rolling her to the left of me throwing her a blanket. I stand up pulling on my boxers as she covers up. I open the door to find Jordan.

"I need your assistance."

Amelia is off the sofa standing next to me holding onto the blanket.

"What's wrong, where's Wade?"

"He was trying to tell me something and he couldn't get it out. He kept saying how he liked the way I smelled of coconuts and sand, and that he likes that I'm a strong woman then he threw up outside of his truck, then rolled out before I could get around to help him down. He is a big guy and I can't get him up. I'm scared some little animal is going to feast on him if I don't get him inside. Can you help me Beau, maybe we could stay here tonight because if I get him home, how do I get him out of the truck?"

"Is he covered in puke, because that will be cause for an outside shower."

"I would do that if I could because it might wake him up. I feel he was struggling with his words and it made him sick."

Amelia reaches for her hand. "Come on in. I'll fix coffee."

"Thank you."

I go to leave when Jordan touches my arm.

"You might need some clothes."

I walk over to the sofa and find my shorts pulling them on,

and then I put on my shirt. She's eyeing my every move.

"What?"

Jordan steps aside for me to pass. "Everyone in your band is hot. Was that a requirement when they joined you?"

"Amelia."

I hear my wife giggle behind me. "Jordan stop, get over here and help me make some food."

Unwillingly back in my clothes, I head out to find Wade lying on the ground spread out fast asleep. I go back to get a bottle of water from the cooler letting it drip on his face and he comes up spitting, shaking his head.

"What happened?"

"I guess you tried to tell Jordan how you felt then threw up."

He wipes off his face.

"Damn, what does that mean?"

"You drank too much trying to get the courage to tell her how you feel." I hold out my hand. "Come on, Amelia is making coffee and you need a shower."

"Was she upset?"

"She couldn't get you up. You can make this right, but for now you smell. Let's go buddy."

He follows me to the outside shower, and I give him some clothes. When he is done showering and dressing, he makes it into the house and sits at the bar next to Jordan. I stand beside Amelia who has the blanket still wrapped around her like it is a dress. I kiss her shoulder as she leans into me. Wade half smiles at Jordan as she pours him coffee then slides a sandwich over to him. She nudges him, he smiles, and all is back to normal. I grab a bite of Amelia's sandwich.

"Now if you two don't mind, I'm taking my wife to bed."

They both in unison say thank you and not long after, we crawl into bed, we hear the other bedroom door shut.

"You are such a nice guy."

"I'm a man in love and I'm rooting for him. I want everyone to have the chance to feel like I do." Now where were we before the interruption?"

"We were making love on the sofa. Should we go out there?"

I pin her beneath me. "No, I think we are fine right here."

CHAPTER 39

Amelia

Beau spends the next morning fishing with his dad and brother while Jordan and I spend the morning riding four wheelers with his sister and her two friends. Poppy spends a lot of time with Beau's parents at their house with the grandkids. Lily and Sophia surprise us by coming down for a couple of days, giving me time with my friends before leaving for Nashville. I will miss having them so close but being with Beau in Nashville is where I want to be.

*

We leave three days later. We need to find a place to live while Beau is working in the recording studio. We look at houses, townhomes, and apartments. It takes us about five days to settle on a flat in the heart of Nashville. It is in an old building with lots of exposed beams, wood with an industrial feel, yet it has a warm feel. The owner is in Europe for the next two years for his job. So, finding this place is either luck, good timing, or it's meant to fall into our laps. Either way we take it. The owner had his personal belongings put into storage because if all went well, at the end of his two years he would not be coming back.

Before studio time, Beau and the boys meet and work out the kinks of the new music or introduce arrangements before laying down tracks. I spend my days buying furniture and shopping for linens and groceries. When the guys are at our home, they consume a lot of food, which gives me ample opportunities to cook. Poppy is home with my parents until we get settled.

In town, I am Amelia Reston, wife of a popular singer, and this opens many doors for me. When I am spotted by his fans, I am inevitably asked many times when we are going to start a family. I usually reply with a short, "When the time is right."

At the coffee shop down from our building this morning, I sit at a table in the corner where the barista now knows my name. I am listening to an interview that Beau gave yesterday. My phone buzzes and I look to see my mom on the screen.

"Good morning."

"Where are you today?"

"Coffee house right now."

"Is something wrong?"

"No, why?"

"Amelia tell me, what's weighing heavy on those shoulders? The last couple of times we've spoken, I've heard it."

"You hear what?"

"Apprehension."

"I'm just preoccupied."

"Come on, tell me."

"The question of when we are going to start a family keeps coming up, through interviews, people on the street, people at the library."

"I've noticed that too."

"I don't know what else to say. Why is it so interesting for everyone?"

"Because your husband is well known, a man of interest. You are newlyweds. It's a natural question, maybe not wanted, but natural. What's stopping you from finding a doctor?"

I pause as she hits it, figures it out. "I'm scared of my reality."

There's silence on the other end. "I know you are. But you and I both know not knowing is eating away at you. Sweetie, if you know for sure, then you can make plans."

"I know. That's what Beau said. I did find a couple of doctors who may be able to help."

"So, he's on board?"

"Yes. He's kind of letting me drive the next step. We aren't necessarily ready to start a family."

"Make the call. It's your first step."

"I'll think about it. Now, what's up with you?"

"Your dad and I want to come up this weekend and bring Poppy. I think she misses you."

"That works great, then she won't have to fly alone."

"Oh, and before I forget, I got a call from Chase's mom. She said she hadn't heard from you since you left and was wondering if you had opened the envelope?"

"I forgot I had it."

"Well when you do look over it, just let her know. I'm excited to see your new place. We can stay at a hotel nearby if you send me some options near you."

"That's silly. We have an extra bedroom; you and dad can stay with us. Let me know when your flight arrives, and I'll pick you up at the airport."

"I don't want to put you out."

"You won't, besides it will give us more time to spend together if you stay with us."

"Sounds good. I love you."

"I love you too, mom."

I can't believe I forgot to even open the envelope that was given to me by Chase's parents. I tuck my phone in my back pocket and grab the coffee, telling Lydia goodbye as I leave the coffee shop. My next stop is the studio to drop off the sheet music Beau left this morning. They had a cancellation, so they were setting up and getting ready for next week. Mom's right, I need to face this dark cloud hanging over me, over us. I'm still scared about the outcome, but I just need to do it.

*

Arriving at the studio, I'm met by Roger the security guy who has come to know me well, so he opens the door without me giving my ID. I make it down the hall to studio B which is where Beau is going over music with the band. Jason is standing outside the room meeting me first.

"Amelia, I didn't know you were coming by today."

"I have a folder for Beau that he texted me about earlier. Is this a good time?"

"Yes, of course."

He knocks on the glass and everyone turns to us. The guys wave to me as Beau puts down his guitar and comes out to greet me. He wastes no time kissing me and might I say in a "want you" kind of way. I hear whistling from the room. He waves them off, and we walk down the hall to an empty room where he backs me against the closed door and kisses me even more. I love how he can wake up every nerve in my body, having them all scream with joy.

"You missed me this much since leaving this morning."

"Yes, I've missed every sweet part of you." He trails his finger down my buttoned shirt releasing the first one. "See even the buttons of your shirt are on my side."

I reach up catching the shirt between my fingers.

"Not the place, Mister."

"Every place is a good place."

"Don't try and melt me with those sexy blue eyes, these

lips, or this country boy charm you have going on, I come bearing your requested folder."

He takes it from me. "Thank you."

"You are welcome." He lays the folder behind him on a table. "I do need to talk to you about something. Do you have a minute?"

"Of course." His hand covers the side of my neck and his lips tease my ear.

"I got a call earlier from my mother. They are coming into town this weekend and I hope it's okay with you, but I offered the spare room to them."

"What time will they be here," he whispers.

"She's going to call with details once the flight is booked. They are bringing Poppy."

He stops, tips up my chin. "Good, she needs to see her new home."

He unbuttons my blouse again. "Beau."

"Buttons are so easy to undo. I'm sorry but you are the reason I forgot the sheet music this morning."

"Me?"

"How soon you forget."

"Oh, you mean our kitchen sex this morning. I remember it well."

"I can't seem to forget it." He nuzzles my ear.

"But this is not a private place; there are lots of people around."

His head falls to my shoulder. "You smell so good."

"Are we still on for dinner tonight with Jason and Anna?"

"Yes, at seven. I will be home about five. Maybe you could wait to shower when I get home."

I squirm away from him, finding three buttons undone.

"How do you do that?" He pulls me back to him.

"I'm always thinking how to get you out of your clothes."

"I've got to let you get back to the others." I button my blouse before we leave the room. "I will be naked in the shower waiting for you at five."

"That's what you leave me to think about the rest of the day?"

"Yes."

He steps towards me as I place my body halfway out the door.

"Amelia, I need a kiss goodbye."

"Is that wise." Before I can respond he is already kissing me.

I'm giggling between kisses, not really wanting to stop our playfulness.

I give him one last kiss before stepping into the hall. "I'll be wet and waiting for you."

He looks past me clearing his throat. I turn and see two of the guys in the band along with Jason in the hall. I look back at Beau as my cheeks turn a deep crimson, or at least the heat that is coming off them makes it seem that way. They begin to clap, and he can't hold back his laughter. I excuse myself to get past them and head for the door. Outside the chill hits me, and now I'm smiling, no longer embarrassed, just loving my husband and how he reacts when he's around me. I decide to hit up Truly's Dress shop before heading home today for something special to wear on our double date, and maybe something sheer for when we get home.

*

The whole car ride over to the restaurant we are touching each other. His smile is contagious and helps me forget the heavy decision before us.

"You're in a good mood."

"You do this to me."

"Then I promise to always do it. Before I forget, do you remember the envelope Chase's parents gave me the day we were there?"

"I've not thought about it since that day. What was in it?"

"I didn't open it. Maybe when we get home we can."

"Now I'm curious."

"About the envelope or what I'm not wearing under this dress?"

He turns to me, his left eyebrow arches, and there are no words as his head falls against the seat.

CHAPTER 40

Beau

Amelia got an appointment two weeks after her parents' visit. She was lucky to get in due to a last-minute cancellation in the office. Dr. Shelton is an obstetrician here in Nashville specializing in high risk pregnancy. During the appointment, the doctor did an in-office exam and ordered more tests. She then requested the records from Amelia's surgery for a complete evaluation. Over the next few weeks we wondered about the results and Amelia received a call from her office asking if we could come in and go over everything. It was 4:00 on a Wednesday afternoon and I cancelled the last hour of our session in the recording studio to be with her.

Now we sit listening to the facts that Dr. Shelton has for us; unfortunately, all the official medical terminology came down to heart-crushing news. Amelia would be able to get pregnant, but carrying a baby to term was extremely questionable. She didn't say we couldn't try, but the pregnancy carried with it a risk to both Amelia and the baby.

She excuses herself giving us time to process the information. Left alone I turn my attention to my wife, who is still sitting in her chair looking down at her lap. My heart is ripping into pieces, as this can't be easy for her to finally hear.

"Amelia, do you have any questions for Dr. Shelton?"

She looks out towards the window and back at me. No tears, just a faint smile.

"I'm thinking she used the word *possible* five times, *maybe* three times but she never said *it's hopeless* one time." She turns in her chair to me. "I need to know from you, if I can't have our biological child are you still open to adoption or fostering?"

"I've always been open."

"We've been so lucky to find each other, to fall in love, and be able to experience this wonderful crazy life together. I just don't want you to be disappointed."

I take her hand, seeing the pain in her eyes. "I don't want you to ever think I need something or someone more than you. Our lives have just begun. I'm with you in our journey wherever it takes us."

With tears in her eyes, she stands and so do I. She buries her face on my chest. We stand for a few minutes and I hear her sniffle. She finally looks up at me.

"I was holding on to hope."

"I know." I hold her as tight as I can, as we both shed tears for what may never be. After some time passes, I look down wiping off her tear-stained cheek with my thumb. "One day at a time."

She tosses the tissue in the trash can then grabs her purse. "Let's go eat."

"Where too?"

"Southern Biscuit?"

"No more questions for Dr. Shelton?"

"No. I think we have what we need. The rest is up to us."

*

Back at the apartment after eating, we change our clothes, prepared to spend the rest of the day just chilling. I flip through the mail, seeing her past me twisting up her hair then pinning it on top of her head.

"Beau, want some water or tea?"

"Water, please." The night of our double date with Jason

and Anna, we never opened the envelope from Chase's parents, as we had other things on our minds. She walks back with two glasses of water tossing me a bag of sour gummies. I reach for the brown envelope. "We still have this mysterious envelope to open, don't we?"

She doesn't seem interested at first because thinking of Chase brings her back to today's results. Maybe this is not a good time. I place it on the table in front of us.

"It's weird--maybe doing this today, but I need to open it."

I hand it to her; she hands me the bag of gummies. She sits up straight, pulling her legs up under her. She begins to unwind the string then opens the envelope dumping out the contents on her lap. The first thing to fall out is a bracelet. Next is a few photos and typed papers. I pick up the bracelet eyeing the charms on it. The charms include an apple, a starfish, and some colored beads. There's a college charm, a slice of pizza, and a beer mug charm. The last charm is a baseball. She's reading the letter then flips the cover sheet over to reveal what looks like a check.

She hands the letter to me. "You need to read this."

I do as she asks, while she flips through the other papers.

"Is this real?"

"Seems like it."

I reach for the check. "Amelia, I don't understand."

She's now looking at the bracelet touching each charm. "Chase gave this to me our first Christmas. It started with a few charms, and then he would give me another one for different occasions we experienced together. I thought it was a sweet gesture. But that was him, he *was* thoughtful and loving. I know it's hard to think of him that way, but he was."

"How did he go from this nice guy to one who attacked you?"

"I don't know what happened, but my guess is he was depressed about losing his dream to play ball for a major league team. He bottled up so much of what he was feeling and he turned to drinking. When that didn't help, he turned to recreational drugs, which lead him to the hard stuff. It caused him to hallucinate, wreck his apartment, and when I showed up that day he didn't know me. In his mind I guess he saw me as someone who was going to harm him."

"Which is why he attacked you?"

"Yes."

"How did you forgive?"

"The guy who attacked me was not the Chase I once knew. The accident on the field broke his bones, but it damaged so much more of him inside. I think he quietly slipped away every day. If you don't accept what is happening and seek help, you drown in a deep sea of despair."

"You would've been there for him just like you came to me when I needed you during my biopsy."

"We all would have done anything we could to help him. But getting the person to admit there's a problem is hard. I dealt with my anger, my sadness and my fear with help from my family and friends, but I realized after forgiving him, that I could be happy with my life."

"I'm *so* grateful you had that support."

"Me too. When I was ready to let someone in, you were there. I was in the dark a few times during that first year, but I found my light. And now Chase wants me to have all this money."

"He wants you to start a center or a private school. Had you talked about it?"

"We joked around about setting up a community center someday to help kids after school with tutoring and be able to play sports without the financial burdens, but it slipped away from us after his accident."

"Now he's giving you the opportunity with a $100,000 gift to start your own business."

"I don't know. It doesn't seem right taking the money."

"I get that. When you told me about what had happened to you, I wanted to destroy the person who hurt you. I wanted him to feel the pain he caused you. I was angry, but I was relieved when you said he had died, and at that time I felt no guilt in feeling that way. When I realized that you needed to forgive to move on, I dropped my anger and followed your lead. When we went to see him and I saw how he was with you, I could tell he cared deeply for you and that he was truly sorry for what he did. Maybe this is his way of assuring your future is one you want."

"I guess we should speak to a lawyer." She sets down the paperwork along with the bracelet, laying her head in my lap. "I want you involved in whatever is done with the money. Can you handle one more thing on your plate?"

"I can for you."

CHAPTER 41

Amelia

We have our first Christmas together along with our families in Nashville. We celebrate our first year of marriage with a trip back to Folley Beach. Life moves fast, so we enjoy each as much as possible.

Beau recorded his album and was on tour from August to December, coming home to me on December 18th, where we stayed locked up in the loft enjoying each other, giving him time to come back to reality from all the touring. He will be on a short three-week international tour starting in January, and in March he will be in Texas attending the McHenry and Stanton Rodeo. The medical issues with his throat continue to rear their ugly head when he is pushing too hard. He regularly visits the doctor and even sees a vocal therapist.

With the help of Chase's donation, we began a new business adventure four months after learning what Chase had in mind. *Together Strong* is our new company that allows us to help many already-established community centers and give financial help to develop programs for children from five to eighteen years old. We set it up to be a place that will offer tutoring, a place to be active in sports of all kinds, and a place to learn about music. We give instruments, sports equipment, and educational supplies to enhance their opportunities. We develop a place to build up, support and encourage kids to accomplish their dreams, goals, or just getting a passing grade in school. We've been able to develop relationships within the communities we help and secure sponsorships to continue helping.

This business allows me the opportunity to live out my dream of working with children and allows us the opportunity to supply the tools they need to grow in a safe environment. Beau is the light of everyone's day when he visits, leading them in a round of songs or teaching a lesson or two.

Chase is not able to be here physically, but each gym is named "Chase Hall" just for him. He lives this dream, through videos and pictures that we send to him every month. His physical condition has not changed much, but his smile is bigger these days and there's a light in his eyes that we thought had been extinguished.

*

Beau and I are thankful every day to love and laugh as we do and have such supportive people around us. But nothing could have prepared us for the heartbreak that was about to happen to us.

*

I find out on a Thursday that I am pregnant, while Beau is about to leave for his international tour. I want to tell him as soon as I find out, so I head home to share the news. We are both shocked, scared, and happy all at the same time. It's been over a year since seeing Dr. Shelton and a few other specialists. We weren't trying to purposely get pregnant, but I guess it was meant to be. We knew what could happen so my appointments would be more frequent, and I entered the "high-risk pregnancy status". I was to join Beau on tour, but the pregnancy had grounded me, so we called continuously, and I promised to take it easy, which I did per doctor's orders. For the next two months, I progressed without complications. I welcomed the second trimester with a positive outlook that sided on caution.

Beau was to spend two weeks with me before heading to the rodeo in Texas. But today just before his plane was to take off from Italy to bring him home, I received the news that sucked the air out of my body leaving me numb. Dr. Shelton tried to explain what happened, but I knew. I had been warned but it didn't help the pain in my chest or the tears that followed.

I had started bleeding in the shower that morning. I drove myself to see the doctor, where I was told our baby was gone. I didn't want to worry Beau while he was flying, but I couldn't hide it from him when he called. All my careful measures didn't mean anything; losing the baby was inevitable. My uterus was not strong enough to carry a baby. I was told this many times, but when I had our baby growing in my belly, I got lost in the joy of having a child that was a part of Beau and myself, and I blocked everything else out. Dr. Shelton said we could run tests in a few weeks, but when I asked her to tell me the truth, she wasn't hopeful.

*

It was raining when I left her office, and it made me feel the sky was crying with me. This was overwhelming to me, it hurt beyond words. I called no one and went home to wait until Beau returned. I changed my clothes, washed my face, and crawled into bed hugging my husband's pillow as hard as I could. My body let me down. I cried myself to sleep out of exhaustion.

When I wake up, Beau is lying beside me on the bed asleep. I snuggle up against him, and I feel him shift to bring me closer to him. He kisses my head, apologizing for not being with me. The long flight home was not easy for him, knowing what had happened and not being here for me. His tears match mine. I kiss him over and over in hopes to comfort him, but our words of heartbreak pour out of us. The dream of having our own little baby was taken away leaving us both devastated.

The growl in my stomach wakes him up as we both get out of bed. I go to the bathroom and he heads to the kitchen. When I join him there, I pick up the medicine bottle, look at it, then set it down pouring a glass of water, but not taking it.

He picks up the bottle reading the label. "Why don't you take it?"

"It's to take the pain away that I'm experiencing from the miscarriage." I stop and choke back my tears. "But I want to feel everything. I may never be able to experience a pregnancy again. I'm mourning the loss of our baby through this pain." I turn to face him. "I'm sorry, I don't know what else to do."

Beau covers me with his body rocking us back and forth.

"You have nothing to be sorry about; you've done nothing wrong." He cups my face with his hands kissing me. "We will get through this, but I don't want you in pain. Will you please take the medicine?"

I look up at him and shake my head. "I can't. Please trust me."

He doesn't like it, but he accepts it.

*

The next morning Beau gets up first to fix breakfast. I make it into the shower, and I stand as the hot water runs over my body--each drop of water connected with each raw nerve. My hands fall to my belly and the tears begin again, and I crumble to the floor in blood mixed with water. When I don't come out of the shower as expected, Beau comes in, finding me huddled in the corner of the shower. He cuts off the water, picks me up, holding me against him. He sets me down to wrap a towel around me. He has tears in his eyes when he see's blood on the floor and the expression on his face is one I will never forget.

"It's normal, it will stop."

He shakes his head, kissing my forehead. "I can help clean up."

"It's fine. I will be out in a minute."

He holds my hand as long as he can before reaching the doorway. One more look back at me and he leaves. I exhale, trying to stop from crying as I go about cleaning up and comb my wet hair. I slip on clothes and head out to meet him for breakfast. He's at the sink with the water running, looking out the window when I reach him, but his hands are not in the sink. I touch his back with my hand bringing his thoughts back to what he is doing. He turns off the water. I pour coffee, he sets plates of food in front of us, and we eat in silence, a silence that he breaks.

*

He reaches over the island and takes my hand in his. "I said I would be here to support and love you through everything. I'm sorry I wasn't here when you needed me the most."

"You couldn't have prevented this and neither could I. We both knew it could happen."

"I knew there was a chance. I want you to know that I was happy and committed for however long we could carry the pregnancy. But knowing the pain you were in and not being here, hurt in a way I can't even explain. Amelia, I love you so much, and knowing something could happen to take you away from me has led me to a decision I need to talk to you about."

"What do mean?"

"I'm thinking we should take measures, so you won't be put in this situation again."

My stomach just sunk but I had to ask. "What measures?"

"A vasectomy."

"You can't. Please don't."

"It's a simple procedure."

"But one day you might want to have a child of your own."

"What? I would only want children with you."

"You didn't know I had this issue when we got married. I can't let you give up the dream of having your own child."

His hand reaches for my arm. "Amelia."

"No. I can't let you do it. Look we're upset, in time we will get through this, and then we will make the right decision at the right time."

"I don't want you to go through this again." He stands, walking to the sink.

"Beau, this pregnancy was a blessing. We got to experience a little bit of a miracle."

He turns to me. "You are the love of my life. Next time could be worse."

He moves past me heading into the living room. I walk after him.

"Can't we talk about it some more, before such drastic measures are taken?"

"I won't do it right now and I won't if you don't agree. I just need you to know how I feel. I don't want to gamble with your life."

"I would never do that."

He picks up my hand placing it to his lips. "We can talk this over later. I'm going to shower."

As he walks away, I process his words and grip my shirt like it is going to keep me from losing myself. I can't let him give up on one day having a child of his own. I need to find a way to make him understand.

CHAPTER 42

Beau

I run until I can't run any more, but the anger inside is the same. I can't have her risk her life to have a child, and if I don't have the procedure she could. I've watched her struggling this past week. She's lost in her thoughts, she's sad, and she's trying to mask it in hopes of making me feel better.

I hit the brick wall in front of me with both fists. Why does someone with such a warm, loving heart have to endure this kind of pain over and over? She doesn't deserve any of this. I fall onto the concrete, leaning my head against the same wall that has left my knuckles to bleed. Here is where I sit, as darkness takes away the light of day. I finally stand knowing what I need to do and begin to run back home. I leave for Texas in two days, I need to make this right.

When I get home, Amelia is setting out plates, four to be exact. Music is playing and I can smell her roasted chicken in the oven. She's dressed in blue jeans and a sweater. She's the most beautiful woman, the best part of me, and I need her to understand.

"What's all this," I ask?

"Jason and Anna are coming over for dinner. She called while you were out. I hope it's okay?"

"Is it?" I grab a grape off the tray.

She wipes her hand on a towel. "Sure. It will be nice."

That's what she's been doing. Trying to be brave, to smile,

and even have guest over letting me know she's fine, but when her eyes look at me, I can see she's not okay. I touch her arm so she will look at me and see me and hear the words I need to say.

"Amelia, I need to talk to you."

"What is it?"

As the words came out of her mouth, the doorbell rings.

"Can we talk later?"

She kisses me. "Why don't you grab a shower and I will let them inside."

We separate--her to the door and I to the shower, but not before glancing back at her. She takes in a deep breath while shaking her hands. This is not what she wants, she's doing it for me.

*

When I return, they are sitting around the bar talking. Jason sees me coming over and hands me a beer, leaving the two ladies to talk. He leans in.

"How is Amelia?"

"I'm not sure. She's trying to feel better for me when I need her to let everything out."

"What happened to your hands?"

"I hit a wall. I'm fine."

"Clearly you're not."

"She's not admitting how she's feeling because she's trying to cover up for me. I need her to get angry. I don't want to leave for Texas knowing she's bottling up all this emotion."

"Amelia is a strong woman."

"She is, but this can't be suppressed."

"What about you? Are you telling her everything?"

"I told her I want a vasectomy."

"That's pretty serious. Are you sure?"

"Yes. It's breaking my heart to see her so sad, to blame herself for not being able to give me a child. Hell Jason, I need her. She's the most important person in my life. I've come to accept that what the doctor said is the truth. This is nothing she did, and she doesn't deserve to hurt like this."

"Just give her time."

Amelia rounds the corner.

"Dinner is ready. Is everything alright?"

I smile knowing whatever I say is a lie, but for now I do.

"Yes, we were going over plans for Texas."

"Well come on before dinner gets cold."

*

The conversation over dinner was light with no mention of the miscarriage. As our friends leave, I go in search of Amelia finding her on the balcony with a glass of wine. This will be hard because I know it will upset her, but we need to get this out, and we need to both be on board.

I stand next to her as she picks up a glass of wine handing it to me.

"Drink?"

"Amelia."

"Please."

I turn up the glass drinking a healthy amount, then set it on the table behind me. She downs her glass, touching her finger to the corner of her mouth.

"I forgot how good it was."

"Do you want to go inside? Are you cold?"

"No. I'm enjoying the slight chill in the air." She reaches over putting her hand on the front of my shirt playing with a button, when she looks up at me with glassy, watery eyes. "I'm having a hard time with all of this."

I take her immediately into my arms feeling her warm breath all the way through my shirt. I kiss the top of her head.

"I know."

"I've been walking around here trying to be brave, but it's only caused me to be crazier. I've been going over everything in my head wondering if I could have changed something or been different in some way when my final thought always comes back to the same thing. I don't have control over any of this and it sucks." She wipes tears off her cheeks. "I don't want you to have a vasectomy, but I want to talk over options with Dr. Shelton to prevent me from becoming pregnant in the future. I've been on a roller coaster of emotions for the past few days, I will continue to be like that for a while, and I just need you to understand that."

"I do, but it hurts to see you like this."

"We need to get you out of here and onto Texas, but I also know that won't be easy for you."

"No, because I will be thinking of you."

"I know. I was pushing you away, and I apologize for doing that. You've always been here for me, and I need to realize this is happening to the both of us, not just me." She picks up my hands. "I saw your knuckles from your run earlier, and I realized what I was doing to you. This is new territory. I don't know how to maneuver through this dark water either. But I promise to tell you how I'm really feeling, and I won't mask my feelings with fake smiles. But you have to promise not to punch anything else." She kisses both my hands.

She provokes a chuckle out of me. "You have my word."

"Beau, we are a love story to be proud of. You are the miracle that renewed my heart, woke me up to love, and each day with you is my blessing. Every day I wake up to this handsome face, I smile. When you touch me with these amazingly talented hands, I melt. I never want you or I to hurt like we have this past week, but if something does happen, I will keep talking to you and I will always fight for us."

I cup her face with my hand and kiss her. "I will always put you first, I will talk to you, and I will always fight for us." She kisses me as our tears mix and our hearts begin the process of healing.

She wipes off her face. "What do you say we have a normal night of watching a movie in bed while finishing this bottle of wine. You in?"

"I'm in."

"Good."

I lean in kissing her. The anger and sadness start to melt away. I take in the feel of her in my arms, and I begin to lift the weight off my shoulders but more important, hers. Looking out over the city, I know someday we will share our love with another, but until that day, we have each other to hold, to love, and to be in this life, the one we create.

CHAPTER 43

Amelia

Over the past three years I've been through so many changes. I fell in love, got married, and started a business with my husband. We had a miscarriage and then six months later we decided on filing for adoption. Soon after that, we suffered a second even more devastating miscarriage, which left me in the hospital. Through all the tears, and long, sleepless nights that followed, we decided on a partial hysterectomy to prevent any future pregnancies. Each day I feel the loss, but each day I also grow stronger.

We eventually bought the loft in Nashville, and there are rare moments when we go back to North Carolina to find quiet from our hectic but wonderful life in the cabin. My parents now inhabit my house next to my grandparents, which is great especially now since Grandpa just had hip surgery. We've mended, moved forward, and are now looking forward with hopes of new adventures.

Poppy is the most adorable, easy-to-get-along-with traveler and has taken well to her new life as a jet setter. She spends time in the studio with Beau when I need to travel, and then when she's with me, she's right by my side sharing her unspoken love.

My friends are always visiting on long weekends giving us an opportunity to indulge in a rowdy girls night out. Lily and Zach had a baby boy about three months ago, and Sophia moved in with Tim, and they just got engaged. Jason and Anna are dating seriously, but neither are looking into marriage, at least not yet. I've become close to her and lucky to be able to consider her another sister. Jordan landed a job in New York where she and Wade have an apartment, but they also rent here in Nashville and have his house in North Carolina. A busy life but it suits them.

*

I fasten my earring and check out my appearance before we get ready to leave for the music awards show being held tonight in Nashville. Beau has been nominated for entertainer of the year. I catch a glimpse of him in front of the mirror adjusting his bow tie as I slip into my heels.

"You are looking mighty fine tonight; may I help you with that?"

"Yes, thank you." He steps away from the mirror.

"This is your night; I can feel it."

"However it ends, I'm a winner because I'm coming home with you."

Our attention goes to the knock at the door.

"Come in."

Jason steps inside. "Sorry to interrupt you two, but I've been sent by the rowdy crew in the kitchen to get your butts out of this room."

Beau takes another look. "Good job." He offers me his hand. "Ready?"

I don't move.

"Is everything okay?"

"Yes, um, Jason, we will be right out."

He slips out closing the door behind him.

"Amelia what is it?"

"Our life *is* good, isn't it?"

"Better than good." He tugs at my chin between his two fingers.

"How did we get this fortunate to find each other and love the way we do?"

"Fate, destiny, and all those magical words in the dictionary brought us together, but what's inside keeps us here."

"I'm so proud of you. You are a phenomenal song writer, singer and a beautiful person inside and out. This night is for you and for all of your hard work."

"I love that you believe in me so strongly. Writing about our life and loving you is easy. As for what's inside of me, you drive all of it."

My hand touches his face and we kiss. Before joining the others, I snap a picture of us.

"Are you posting?"

"No, this one is just for us."

Jordan is with Wade tonight as his plus one. Beau's parents are here as well to show their support. He's been nominated for the past two years and didn't win, but this year feels different. He will also be performing along with the other four nominees, which surely will fire up the crowd having all of them on stage at one time.

We enter the kitchen, and Jordan, with Wade's assistance, is holding a tray with glasses full of champagne.

"Get your beautiful asses over here! We've been waiting to toast the man who will be taking home country music's top award tonight," she says.

We all cheer for him, but he's not about the attention or the fuss that the night is bringing him. The songs he's been writing and singing have all come from deep within his heart, our life. He had to overcome a throat issue causing him to cancel two concerts this past year, but he is better than ever and deserves everything that tonight brings.

So, this *is* for him, his craft, the second love of his life, and we will treasure every moment, snapping a lot of pictures to remember it all. We will be attending a few parties after the show that will keep us up late, probably grabbing breakfast on the way home, then slipping into our bed and sleeping well into the next day.

After a round of drinks, everyone uses the bathroom and checks their look, except for Beau and I who only look at each other.

"You are absolutely stunning in my favorite color."

"Thank you."

His mom comes over dressed in a pretty black mid-length dress, looking amazing and she reaches up pulling his face to her and kissing his cheek. "Let me hit the bathroom. Don't leave me," she says.

We all laugh, as his father puts an arm around his son's shoulders.

"This is a big night. Are you nervous?"

"Maybe."

"Well you shouldn't be. You've earned your spot in this business and I'm proud of you. It must have something to do with your upbringing."

He slaps Beau on the shoulder then winks. It makes me giggle. Jason informs us the car is outside and it's time to leave. His mother comes running out from the bathroom following her husband out the door.

Beau takes my hand lifting it to his lips. "Let's do this."

CHAPTER 44

Amelia

The night of the awards show in Nashville was a magical evening for everyone. Beau's performance was solid, hot, and sparked a new lineup for years to come. Having all the entertainers who were up for entertainer of the year performing at the same time gave me chills, and I'm sure it was the same for many who were there. But what got to me the most was when his name was announced as Entertainer of the Year. It was fast and slow motion all at the same time, with lots of tears. He thanked the fans, his band, and his manager. He thanked the team that works hard to keep everything moving along and his label. He thanked his family. He then paused and looked to me. "Amelia, you are my best friend, my partner, and the love of my life. The road we travel is ours, thank you for loving me as deeply as I love you and for the support you always give for me to have this dream. I love you!" He signed off with a little gesture he always sends to me. I am thankful every day that I attended a concert, wore a bright red dress, and met a man who has truly brought back love to my life. He gives me hope for our future and my words, unlike his songs, will never touch others, but I know who holds them close.

*

Today is the first day of a much-needed vacation. We've been going strong since the awards show, with the responsibilities of tending to the already- established centers we have, leaving us little time to ourselves. We came back to Folley Beach because this is where we started our lives together and with the announcement I have for Beau, well let's just say this time I get to pop a very big question that will surprise him.

I hear him drop something above me, so I take off upstairs to see if he's alright. I climb the stairs two at a time, which I will thank my trainer later when I get back to the gym. I run down the hall to the master suite at the end of the house, but I don't see him. Before I know what's happening, he grabs me around my waist and in a very clever move drops us both onto the bed. I catch the breath he's knocked out of me and begin to giggle.

"What is wrong with you? I thought you were hurt."

"I'm lonely, does that count as hurt? Unpacking is a lonely task."

"No. Geez. My stomach feels weird now."

"Are you lovesick over me? I know what that's like."

I go to swat at him and he catches my wrist in his hand kissing each finger, with a look that is making me forget the many stairs I just ascended. He trails his kisses up my arm with precision.

"I thought you were hungry?"

"I am."

He moves, taking his kissing trail up my arm to my neck. The scruff on his face tickles me and I let out a snort. It fuels his pursuit of having me lose my mind one inch at a time. This man has a way with words and can master a beautiful song, but it's his way with me that leaves me helpless and craving more of him. While his fingers play over every curve of my body, I can't help but sigh.

"I love it when you do that."

"You react favorably to my touch."

My next move is swift allowing me to flip over on top of him and when my intentions become evident, our bodies collide in a beautiful dance of our souls finding their place, letting go and loving.

*

As the sun begins to go down, I'm famished as I'm sure he is too.

"I need food, you hungry?"

His fingers walk down my spine leaving me with a playful tap on my bare bottom.

"Ouch, I say." I scoot away from him standing just out of reach, pulling the sheet to wrap myself. He never flinches as I expose him. I see a spark in his eye and I back away from him ready to take off out the room and down the stairs. He lunges, falling onto the end of the bed as he reaches for me. I squeal running away down the stairs across the floor when he stops on the landing.

"You win this one."

I look up at him wearing nothing. "Yeah I do!"

He disappears only to come down wearing swim trunks and a t shirt. He slips an arm around me, kissing my shoulder as I look to my left catching a glimpse of him.

"The chase is over, you're mine."

"I'm all for that, now what about some food?"

"Cook or sandwich?"

"Sandwich."

"Beer?"

"Yes. Chips, pickles and ooh cake. Pull it all out."

"If we stay this busy all week, then we will need more food."

*

Halfway through my sandwich seems a good time to ask

277

my important question.

"Beau are you ready to be a daddy?"

He stops chewing. "What?"

"Are you..."

"Amelia, did Mrs. Stanley call you?"

"Yes."

"And?"

"I have something for you." I get off the stool going over to open a cabinet pulling out a bag. I come back to sit next to him. "Before you open this, I want you to know that us being together from the beginning to now has been the best time of my life." I can feel the tears swelling in my eyes.

"I feel the same, but why are you crying?"

"Open it."

He looks at me with concern, but does as I ask. He reaches in removing first some tissue paper, then pulls out a blue pair of baby western boots. So tiny they seem to be more ornamental then wearable. He knows what it means immediately.

"Does this mean..."

"We've been chosen."

"When?"

"Two days ago."

"Is it real this time?"

"Yes."

He sets the boots on the counter with the bag and pulls me up off the stool.

"We're going to be parents?"

"Yes."

We embrace, letting go of the emotions that have been

kept inside over the past few years. We've experienced phone calls like this before, but birth parents change their minds. This time there is a clear decision and papers have been drawn.

"What do we do now?"

"There is something else in the bag."

He looks back in the bag pulling out another pair of boots, pink this time.

"Amelia?"

"Twins. A boy and a girl. They are three weeks old, and ready to meet their new parents. So, I'm asking, are you ready to be a father?"

"Yes, I'm ready. Are you ready to be a mom?"

"I am. Twins, we are the parents of twins!"

He catches me up twirling me around in circles.

*

We spend the next couple of days at the beach house planning for our new little family, then go to Nashville to get ready for their arrival. We are heading to Georgia in two days to pick them up after meeting with lawyers and the adoption agency. We've been given the ultimate blessing, and we'll be forever grateful and humbled by the decision of their parents.

The office is warm with a sofa, two chairs, and toys in the corner. This is the room where we are to meet our babies for the first time. I'm going over the items in the diaper bag, checking over the list in my head, when I feel Beau's hands turn me to him and I say what he's thinking.

"I know, I'm obsessing."

He kisses my forehead. "Just a little, it's sweet."

The door opens, and that's when a line of people come in,

headed by Mrs. Stanley. We see two baby carriers immediately being held by two ladies who place them both onto the table in front of us.

"I'm leaving the two of you to get acquainted with your babies. I'm right outside if you have any questions. When you're ready just call me on that phone. They have bottles already prepared, as they will need to eat in about a half an hour."

I reach over hugging Mrs. Stanley. "Thank you. Thank you so much."

Beau reaches for her, hugging her and thanking her for everything. The door shuts as I feel his arms and his kiss on the top of my head, as we peer down for the first time at the two beautiful babies in front of us. We're crying, hugging each other, and just taking time to look at them both. We immediately begin to notice their slight changes.

"They are so small."

"I can't wait to get them out of their seats."

"Okay. Momma, I will follow your lead."

As we go about unhooking them, they stir stretching their arms, their legs, and making the sweetest cooing sounds. I take the little girl who is dressed in a white and pink striped sleeper. He takes the boy who is dressed in the same sleeper but with blue stripes. We are feeling every emotion while holding them in our arms.

We notice our little boy has a dirty diaper, so Beau is about to have his first lesson. With both babies now clean, we sit on the sofa side by side. We can't stop looking at them until they begin to fuss for their bottles. He's holding both babies and as the bottles warm, I take a few pictures. When the bottles are ready, we switch babies and begin to feed them.

"Amelia, what about their names. Do we still want to go with what we picked out now that we've seen them?

"I think so. What about you?"

"Mia Elizabeth, Owen Walker." He looks at them, then back at me "Our little miracles could not be more perfect." He leans over kissing me as our love just grew by two.

We sit side by side feeding our babies when he begins to sing. I listen to the words closely filling me with joy. It's not a full song yet but in a few days it will be. It's time to burp them and he follows my lead, surprising himself, when Mia burps easily. He cradles her back in his arms as she begins to fuss wanting the rest of her bottle as does Owen.

"That was a beautiful song. When did you start writing it?"

"The night you told me about the babies."

"Songs come so easy for you."

"Especially when I write about us."

"And now you have two children for even more inspiration."

He smiles.

"It's our life. The best song ever."

The End

ACKNOWLEDGEMENT

Thank you for reading Watermelon Red!

A big thank you to "Team Armstrong" for being a strong support in my writing journey. A group of family and friends who help in so many ways and are always there for me. I love you all!

Thanks to Philip Andrews Photography for the cover photo. You picked a venue, used my grandfather's guitar and created an awesome book cover.

Thank you to my new editor, Terri Shelton who made the editing process easy and informative. Good luck in your new editing business!

*tashelton64@gmail.com

Thank you to my family for not hiding my computer. You see me through the whole process and only you know what that means. I love you!

ABOUT THE AUTHOR

Leigh Armstrong lives in Virginia with her husband, David and has two children. She is a full-time daydreamer who enjoys reading, quiet moments at the river and the power of coffee. She published her first book, "My Heart" in 2018 and her second book, "Release My Heart" in 2019. Both are part of the Heart Series.

To find out more about Leigh go to:

Website: www.leigharmstrong2018.com

or

Email: leigharmstrong2018@yahoo.com

www.ingramcontent.com/pod-product-compliance
Lightning Source LLC
Chambersburg PA
CBHW061948170626
46813CB00006B/2579